ADMIRAL

ADMIRAL

SEAN DANKER

A ROC BOOK

ROC
Published by New American Library,
an imprint of Penguin Random House LLC
375 Hudson Street, New York, New York 10014

This book is an original publication of New American Library.

First Printing, May 2016

Copyright © Sean Danker-Smith, 2016
Penguin Random House supports copyright. Copyright fuels creativity, encourages diverse voices,
promotes free speech, and creates a vibrant culture. Thank you for buying an authorized
edition of this book and for complying with copyright laws by not reproducing, scanning, or
distributing any part of it in any form without permission. You are supporting writers and
allowing Penguin Random House to continue to publish books for every reader.

Roc and the Roc colophon are registered trademarks of Penguin Random House LLC.

For more information about Penguin Random House, visit penguin.com.

LIBRARY OF CONGRESS CATALOGING-IN-PUBLICATION DATA:

Danker, Sean.
Admiral/Sean Danker.
p. cm.
ISBN 978-0-451-47579-4 (hardback)
1. Space warfare—Fiction. I. Title.
PS3604.A537A46 2016
813'.6—dc23   2015032659

Printed in the United States of America
10 9 8 7 6 5 4 3 2 1

Designed by Kelly Lipovich

Penguin
Random
House

FOR EVERYONE WHO ONLY HEARS
FROM ME WHEN I NEED SOMETHING

ADMIRAL

1

THERE were voices.

"An admiral? Is this a joke?" one of the voices said.

"It's the seal. Look at this. I think someone's done something to it."

"Is he alive?"

"This isn't even *our ship*."

"He's breathing. I have him."

I was distracted from the pain racking my body by a pair of soft lips on mine, and a rush of welcome, secondhand oxygen. The kindness didn't last. A powerful fist smashed into my sternum.

The hand drew back for another blow, but I managed to grab the wrist and hold it. I didn't need to be hit again.

Coughing, I opened my eyes just to shut them again. There were three lights blinding me. I released the wrist, then slowly sat up and groaned. Someone backed away from me. The deck was cold, and the air didn't taste right.

I opened one eye and squinted up. Three people stood over me. Two young women, one young man. They wore only service-issue undergarments. Like me, they must have just come out of their sleepers.

I had no circulation in my limbs. My mouth was dry. The world was skipping frames, and my mind was stumbling to catch up. Sleepers were good at shutting down brain function; they weren't as good at bringing it back. I could feel my heart twitching in a way that I didn't particularly like, though the sleeper wasn't to blame for that.

I felt like a dead man. I'd had bad wake-ups before, but nothing like this. Apart from a few readouts, the sleeper bay was completely dark. No lights, no emergency lights. Tangled as my head was, I knew that couldn't be right.

The deck was metal, and not especially clean. I could feel an aggressive nonslip pattern of ridges under my palm. That was unexpected.

"What's happening?" I asked, rubbing at my eyes and trying to make myself focus. It was as if I had all the negative effects of ethanol poisoning, but none of its perks. Every part of my brain was struggling except my memory. "Where are we?"

The three exchanged looks.

"Undetermined, sir." That came from the shorter of the two females. The tall one watched me suspiciously, and the young man looked like he was trying to wake up from a bad dream. I knew exactly how he felt.

"Did you pull me?"

"You were showing warning lights. Something's wrong with this unit," the young man said, tapping the sleeper's plastic shield. "The power's gone, sir."

"Thank you." That was why these three had their hand-lights. My thoughts weren't so jumbled that I didn't know they'd just saved my life by getting me out of that sleeper.

I didn't know where we were, but it wasn't Payne Station. The paralysis was wearing off. I wanted to close my eyes and lie back down.

So I got to my feet, wobbling only a little. I reached up, touching my hair. It was short. I'd already known that; I was just checking.

The taller of the two women was eye to eye with me, and I'm nearly two meters. The look she was giving me wasn't particularly friendly.

I rubbed my face, finding stubble. I shook my head and considered the three young people, thinking fast.

I eyed the young man. "Are you a tech?"

He nodded. "Ensign Nils. Trainee."

"Trainee?"

"Graduate, sir."

I looked them over, trying to understand. "All of you?"

"Yes, sir," they replied as one.

Evagardian trainees. All graduates. I sort of waved my hand at them.

"And you're all going to the *Julian*."

"Yes, sir." Nice chorus.

"First assignment?"

"Yes, sir."

I pinched the bridge of my nose and groaned. They politely just stood there, staring at me. We were all shivering.

I pulled myself together and tried to look as though I was in control of my life. How had these three gotten onto a ship transporting me? I took a deep breath to keep my temper under control.

"Relax," I told the trainees, who were standing stiffly, all earnest propriety. Giving their military customs and courtesies their all, insofar as they could in their underwear. I waved at them again. "You're not in uniform." I frowned. "But I suppose you ought to be. Get dressed."

They shifted uncomfortably, and I realized that without power they couldn't access the lockers on their sleepers.

Nils cleared his throat. "Sir?"

I turned to him. He had a little muscle that he probably hadn't had before service training. He embodied every tech cliché, so he couldn't really be anything else. He was pale, and a little twitchy.

Then again, so was I.

"What?"

He panned his light over the ceiling, showing hard lines and rough gray metal. "Sir, this is a Commonwealth vessel. Ganraen."

"I doubt that." I rubbed at my sore joints, swearing internally.

"*Sir,*" the tall girl said, very firmly. "The engineering markings are all here." She used her own light to show me a faded plaque on the bulkhead. It was the emblem of the Ganraen Royal Trade Commission, and a map of the deck.

Well, it was pretty hard to argue with that.

"Yes, it's Ganraen *built*," I said, looking around. These graduates couldn't have been intended to revive on this vessel. How had this happened? It wasn't just the wake-up. It wasn't the state of my health, or my malfunctioning brain. Something was very wrong here.

The tall one didn't seem to like me much. I'd been conscious for only a minute; what could I have possibly done? The disapproving look on her face looked so at home that maybe it wasn't personal. She had that kind of face, the kind where you thought that maybe the fierce scowl was the default setting.

"What's your name?" I asked her.

"Lieutenant Deilani reports as ordered, Admiral."

"Admiral?" I blinked, taken aback. Making a point of looking bland, she panned her light past me. Indeed, my sleeper had all the right markings. There was an Imperial Admiral's crest, plain as day.

"I'll be damned," I said, gazing at it. "I've been promoted. Drinks for everyone. Especially me." It was time to change the subject, and I addressed Lieutenant Deilani. "What's your area?"

I was curious; I'd met a few young officers over the years, and kids with brand-new commissions usually didn't run around with chips on their shoulders like hers. It struck me as a little ungrateful.

"Bio, sir."

I pictured this young woman bossing people around a medbay and decided she'd be good at it.

The third trainee was standing at parade rest. Unlike the other two, who had standard service haircuts, her hair had not been cut recently. There was only one way someone in the Service could dodge the haircut, and that was to need that hair for ceremonial or culturally significant purposes. That meant this shorter girl probably came from a tiered bloodline, a family whose genes were considered valuable.

She was pretty. Not gorgeous, but she was natural. She hadn't augmented herself that I could see. She hadn't tweaked her complexion or done anything too obvious to her features.

She did have that aristocratic poise, though.

"Name?"

"Salmagard."

"What do you do, Lieutenant? If you don't mind saying?"

"Private, sir." She was staring at me with the same interest I was getting from Deilani, but with none of the animosity. Her voice was soft and musical.

I stared back at her, not sure I'd heard correctly. And I didn't like the way she was looking at me. It wasn't hostility on her face, but there was an intensity in her dark eyes that made me uncomfortable.

I could see the gears turning in her mind.

And the tall one—Deilani—now looked even more threatening. I forced myself to focus.

Salmagard was an enlisted aristocrat? Was that even allowed? I'd never heard of them doing that. Aristocrats were supposed to be a big part of the Imperial Service's officer corps; there was a long tradition of it. I'd never given it any thought, but if someone from one of these families couldn't pass officer aptitudes, didn't they usually just find another career?

I didn't know. And I didn't know the first thing about Private Salmagard, but I had a feeling she wasn't the type to fail anything she didn't want to fail.

This was a lot of strangeness to wake up to.

Maybe this was why Ensign Nils seemed so lost.

"Sorry," I said, smiling at her. "I wouldn't have guessed."

"I'm in negotiations, sir."

Maybe she was kidding. No, she didn't seem like the type, not at a time like this. Why not? Why *wouldn't* she be a negotiator? It looked like this was that kind of day.

Was it day?

I focused. The glare from the hand-lights was hurting my eyes. Salmagard's placid mask was perfect. She wasn't letting anything slip out, not a trace of individuality. Her eyes were still fixed on me.

I'd known Nils was a tech by looking at him. What did Salmagard look like?

Well, she looked a bit like a real negotiator. Like, a real, actual one. One that talked to people.

But I wasn't sure Evagard actually had those.

She wasn't kidding. And she recognized me. The other two didn't, but Salmagard did.

I kept my bearing. It wasn't as though this was the first time my life hadn't gone as planned.

"All right," I said, blinking.

I took Nils' light and studied the markings on the plaque. The graduates were correct. This was a Ganraen vessel refitted by the Evagardian Empire, and I was pretty sure it was Captain Tremma's freighter. And Tremma wouldn't leave his passengers to wake up alone in the dark without a word.

The deck under my bare toes told me something was off about the gravity, but we weren't in motion. If we were having a power failure, we were lucky to have gravity at all.

That was assuming this gravity was artificial. What if it wasn't? Were we in dock? Landed?

"Admiral?" Nils pressed, looking uncertain. I'd been lost in my thoughts. There was something wild in his eyes. These circumstances were well outside his comfort zone.

"Right," I said, waking up. They were looking to me for answers, or at least guidance. Admiral indeed. The sleeper bay was freezing cold; I needed to get these three dressed and out of here.

I opened my locker, which I'd never locked in the first place, and rummaged through my bag, coming up with a folding knife.

I flicked it open and knelt by the nearest sleeper, motioning Nils over. "Put your light on that. Right here." He did so. I ran my fingers lightly over the plastic, found the spot I was looking for, and gave it a sharp strike with the handle of the knife. The trainees were bewildered. They'd probably never even seen a metal knife outside a museum. They'd been trained with lighter and stronger synthetic blades. Or at least, one of them had. Maybe the lieutenant too—imperial officer courses were supposed to have a token close-combat component.

But Deilani didn't need a knife. She had those bony elbows. And that look she was giving me.

It wasn't working. I whacked the panel again. "Did they change it?" I rubbed my chin. The stubble was killing me. It had to go. "It's supposed to pop right off." Well, it wasn't *supposed* to—but I'd broken into lockers before. It wasn't a difficult task; I should've been able to do this in my sleep.

I was still misfiring, and the look Deilani was giving me wasn't getting any warmer.

This wasn't working. I sighed and got up, going to the bay door. Just in time, I remembered there was no power, and grabbed the handle instead of hitting the palm switch. The rubber grip was cool to the touch, but the hatch didn't budge. I adjusted my grip, planted my feet, and put my back into it. Nothing.

I blew out my breath and drew back, shaking my sore hands. It was obviously stuck.

"Well," I said. "This is awkward."

"Permit me, sir." Private Salmagard stepped past me, taking a firm grip on the handle. Surprised, I stepped aside. I'd been about to ask Nils for a hand.

Salmagard wrenched the hatch open, letting in a blast of icy cold. The air in the corridor wasn't much warmer than that in the bay, and it was also pitch-black.

Salmagard stepped aside, bowing her head.

I cleared my throat. "Thank you, Private." I listened. There was no sound.

I'd never experienced a completely silent ship before. The only systems running were auxiliaries with their own power supplies, like sleeper readouts. This lack of sound wasn't peaceful or calming; it was terrifying. Something was *catastrophically* wrong. When your ship is on emergency power, you're in trouble. When your ship hasn't got any power at all, if you're not dead, you will be soon.

I went back into the bay. "We're in trouble." I took my pistol from the locker, and both Deilani and Nils took a step back with wide eyes. It probably wasn't every day they saw an unsecured weapon on a spacecraft.

"That's not service issue," Nils said. He probably didn't mean to say it aloud.

"We need to hurry. There's no life support," I told him. "But if this is the ship I think it is, there's still plenty of air." I took aim. "Why would you lock your personals on a transfer to the *Julian*? Nobody's going to steal from imperial sleepers." I shot the lock, and Nils' locker sprang open. I freed the other two as well. The Empress could bill me. Everyone went to their lockers and got dressed.

Deilani wore an officer's white shipboard fatigues. That uniform couldn't be much fun to maintain, but she'd done a nice job with it. Salmagard's black negotiator's fatigues were every bit as impeccable as Deilani's whites. In contrast, Nils' tech uniform was rumpled, and his rank insignias were crooked, but even Evagardian techs aren't realistically expected to be in regs. Some things were the same no matter where you went.

They were all staring at me again, or rather at my clothes.

"What? You can't expect me to wear my dress whites when I'm traveling," I said, straightening my somewhat shabby jacket, as though that could hide some of the holes, stains, and scorches.

It had been a long time since I'd dressed this way. It felt good. Alien, but good.

"At least you don't have to salute me like this. Let's find out what's going on." I took the emergency hand-light off my sleeper, slung my pitiful bag of belongings over my shoulder, and went into the corridor, shining the light around.

I tried to focus. I was almost afraid to look at Private Salmagard. I wasn't misreading the way she was looking at me; I wasn't that lucky. She thought she knew who I was, but she still hadn't said anything. It wasn't enough to act calm—until I knew what was going on, I had to *be* calm.

I let out a long breath, looking down the narrow corridor. It had been a long time since I'd been aboard this ship.

These old Ganraen freighters were some of the ugliest ships in existence. Dark, cramped, all metal and sharp edges. Everything was gray, except for where things had rusted to brown. There were handholds all over in case of a gravity loss. I imagined trying to navigate these rusty, jagged corridors in zero-g, and shuddered at the thought. A ship like this would be a death trap without gravity. Would it kill these guys to add a little padding?

On the bright side, the ship would be even uglier with the lights on.

"What *is* it, sir?" Nils asked. "What is this ship?"

"Ganraen cargo freighter," I told him, still staring into the gloom. "Privateer class, maybe? I don't know."

"How did we get *on* it?" Deilani demanded.

"I could guess," I said. "But I don't think you'd like it."

Fresh graduates on their way to their first assignment expected to be flown around the galaxy in the Empire's latest ships, not whatever bucket happened to be going in the right direction. It didn't matter because they were asleep in any case, but I didn't want to spoil their illusions. On a ship this size there was a lot of air, but we still needed to get a move on.

"Captain Tremma should be on the bridge." I looked at Nils. "This is his ship. I think. You've studied Ganraen spacecraft, haven't you?"

"Yes, sir. Extensively." There was a note of pride there. Nils seemed like the type to know ships.

"This one's been refitted to meet Evagardian specs, but it's probably still more or less recognizable. Where do you think we are in relation to the bridge?"

He considered it, gazing down the unlit corridor. A moment passed.

"Sir, this is an old ship, and I don't recognize the layout. But big Ganraen ships always launch from the stern," he said, shrugging.

And sleepers were kept near escape craft so disoriented passengers wouldn't have to be shepherded far to reach safety. Nils thought we were on a lower deck near the stern, and that felt right.

"Sounds legit. We need to go up." The lifts were useless without power, but there were plenty of old-fashioned ladders.

We traversed the freighter, the trainees trailing me obediently.

Whatever their feelings on the plausibility of my impressive promotion, no one else was taking the lead. Deilani was struggling with that, but we were all confused, and we all wanted to know what was going on.

It was a long walk from one end of the ship to the other, made even longer because I didn't know where I was going. Our lights showed us nothing but Ganraen corridor after Ganraen corridor. They all looked alike, and they were all stiflingly tight. Loose grating rattled underfoot every time we crossed a maintenance hatch.

There were safety covers on the deck that weren't even secured with magnets.

Now I was *really* hoping the gravity would hold. This ship was a death trap. Maybe we were lucky it didn't have power.

I preferred Evagardian ship design. The Ganraens built utilitarian vessels, but even the newer ones came out looking grim, even sinister, and Tremma's freighter was not new. Panels were missing from bulkheads, exposing piping and circuitry. The ship was well maintained, but it wasn't always easy for Tremma to get his hands on Ganraen materials, even during peacetime.

If we looked in the engine room we'd find half of everything jury-rigged, or just broken down and neglected.

That was my guess about all of this—that we'd simply broken down. What I didn't understand was where Tremma was hiding. He should've turned up minutes after the sleepers spat out the trainees, power or no power. There was no positive reading for this situation.

As we clanked through the dark, empty corridors, my apprehension grew.

Once we found the arterial corridor that ran the vessel's full length, it was simple enough to follow it to the bridge. We had to pry open the hatch, and the graduates' surprise was obvious. The rest of the ship had led them to expect a Ganraen cockpit: a cramped space with three consoles for three Ganraen flight officers, but what they got was a minimalist Evagardian command bridge.

It was a spacious chamber with five consoles, and panoramic viewports, which were currently as dark as everything else. The floor and bulkheads were white and clean. With the way I was feeling, the padded chairs looked inviting. The bridge was modern and luxurious compared to the rest of the ship.

It was also deserted. My light fell on an old-fashioned cup on the floor, and a dark stain. I knelt to touch it. Dry.

I sank into the command chair.

I was thirsty. Hungry too. So were the others. I pointed at the control chair beside mine, realized how imperious I looked, and made the gesture a little less flamboyant. Trying to sound appropriately military, I issued my first order. "Ensign," I said to Nils. "Dismantle that so we can get at the power cell." I tossed him my knife and leaned back to think. An encouragingly short amount of time passed before I heard him get to work.

He was what, twenty? And Salmagard was about the same age. Deilani might be a year or two older; she would've had more training. This was a charming start to their careers.

"What could cause the gravity to feel this way?" I asked after a moment, not opening my eyes. I couldn't do this alone. I wasn't up to it. I needed the trainees to pull their weight.

"The gravity drive could still be spinning down from the power loss, sir." That was a good answer, but Nils was wrong. This felt different.

"It's not that," I said. "I wish it was. But we'd be able to feel it in this ship."

"Suppose we're adrift in the belt," Deilani said, running a hand over one of the consoles. "The interference could account for it . . . sir," she added, a little too deliberately. It wasn't petulance or haughtiness in her voice—it was open dislike. I still didn't know what I'd done to offend her. I understood that meeting such a young admiral struck her as odd, but didn't we have bigger problems?

"Not that, either." Her theory wasn't out of the question, but the odds were too slim. "The belt isn't even on the way," I mused. "But what is?"

"When were we transferred from the personnel carrier, sir?" That came from Salmagard. She had a lovely voice. There was no hint of accusation in her words. Her face was calm. No hidden meaning. It was just a question. She wasn't giving me a knowing look.

She knew, though. I could feel it.

"I'd like to know that too. I guess you came from Marragard?" I eyed their rank insignias.

Marragard was where imperial servicemen were gathered for graduation from the most prestigious academies, and only the best would be assigned to the *Julian*. "Then we must've picked you up on the Demenis side. So Tremma probably picked you up at Burton Station. That's only two hops to Payne Station. Safe route."

Deilani narrowed her eyes. "Why are we taking the long way?"

I realized that Salmagard wasn't playing dumb for me; she was doing it because Deilani was better off curious than burdened by the truth. I tried to rally, thinking of an answer for the lieutenant. I had nothing.

"I know why *I'm* taking it. Why *you're* taking it—that's not a bad question," I said. "I'm guessing your ride had a failure of some kind, and Tremma happened to be there at the right time. Someone decided to move you along to keep to schedule. Can't keep the *Julian* at Payne Station forever."

The *Julian* was the Evagardian Empire's brand-new flagship. Supposedly the greatest warship ever built. The Empress herself was said to be aboard her now, overseeing the second leg of her maiden voyage. After her next tour, the *Julian* would continue to be seen at major trade hubs and high-traffic stations, an unmistakable reminder of the Empress' absolute military superiority after the Empire's crushing victory over the Ganraen Commonwealth.

And these three had been assigned to her. That meant they were good; personnel selection for the pride of the armada had to be especially rigorous.

I was hoping to reach the *Julian* as well, just not for the same reasons. Salmagard was no longer discreetly watching me. The fact that she wasn't sharing her conclusions with Deilani at least hinted that she'd drawn some of the right ones. I was lucky that Salmagard was there. This was all very strange, and I wasn't at my best. I needed a friend.

The route Tremma had been taking . . . Well, we could be anywhere. Thinking about it made my head hurt worse.

"You're very young for an admiral, sir."

I looked up at Deilani. "I know," I told her.

"I've got it, Admiral." Nils sounded pleased with himself. His timing was good.

I got up and went over to him. "I'll take it from here. Get that panel off, uncover the ports."

Nils gave me a look that was half suspicion, half admiration. He'd guessed what I had in mind.

The energy cell was used to power the mechanisms that physically moved the chair when a vessel was under fire, adjusting as the ship shakes and rolls so the commander doesn't lose concentration. I tossed the cell to Nils, who knew exactly what to do. In minutes he had power running to the console.

I was hoping the computer would have something to say about the state of the ship. Not that I knew how to ask. "If you would," I said, motioning Nils into the chair.

Deilani was staring at my hand.

"What?"

"You have very courtly manners, Admiral." She sort of wiggled her hand. "Can you teach me to do that?"

Next time I'd just point.

"Nils," I prodded, turning away from her without a reply. The ensign looked uncertain, but game. There was no doubt he knew his way around ship systems better than I did. It was time to get answers.

The system was running in its most basic emergency mode, so Nils had to physically enter data with his fingers, which he was impressively good at.

"Something's wrong with it," he reported immediately. "Sir," he added hastily.

I was so different from the officers these three had been exposed to that they just couldn't see me as one. My lack of uniform didn't help, and neither did my sudden promotion to admiral. It probably didn't seem believable to them, but that crest on my sleeper was hard to argue with. Deilani wanted to argue; I had a feeling she just wasn't sure how to go about it. We were all off-balance.

But someone had to take charge, and my gut told me I was a better choice than Lieutenant Deilani, at least for now.

"The system's corrupted," Nils said.

"How?"

He shook his head. "I don't know, sir. I can't do anything with it."

"Is there damage to the ship?"

"I wouldn't know how to check with this," he said, a bit sheepishly. "Not without at least basic protocols running." He looked over his shoulder at me. "Sir, I want to try to get emergency power online."

"Won't do any good if the reactor's damaged," Deilani pointed out. She wasn't even looking at Nils. She was looking at me. She was *always* looking at me. It wasn't like I'd never been stared at before, but this was starting to wear me down.

"I don't think it is. I don't think there's any damage to the ship," Nils replied. "Anything that would knock out the power, *then* fail-safe the sleepers, would set off hit-confirm protocols—but the zero-g handles and oxygen masks in the corridors hadn't been deployed, and neither had the automatic sealant. There's no sign out there or in here that anything's hit us. Even just a small meteor would put us on breach alert, but there hasn't been anything."

I should have noticed that.

"You're right," I said, grateful to have the ensign there. "If you think you can get power, do it." I turned to Salmagard and Deilani. "There should be an executive escape craft near the bridge—find it and get a survival pack. We're all dehydrated, and I don't want to have to go banging on pipes yet."

I wasn't kidding myself; giving Deilani something to do

wouldn't make her happy, but I couldn't think with her here, trying to glare her way through my skull.

Salmagard looked pleased by the order, and Deilani appeared faintly annoyed. "Go on. Don't act like you're not thirsty too," I said, turning back to Nils. They took their lights and left the bridge to search. At least Deilani didn't argue.

"I'm not coming up with much, sir. I've never seen an Evagardian system so crippled."

"No pressure. But we might be dead if you don't figure it out."

He gave me a funny look. "One idea," he said. "This ship *has* been refitted and repurposed with our tech. There might be a power supply that I can tap to run provisional functions temporarily."

"How long is temporarily?"

"Depends on how much we use it, sir."

"Case by case? What source?"

"If I'm reading this correctly, there's a shuttle."

"Ah." I thumped my fist into my open palm. "I should've thought of that. But there should be more than one on a ship like this."

"There's only one that I can reroute here and now."

"Odd. Could we do it manually?"

Nils shook his head. "That would be a lot more complicated than swapping an energy pack," he said, eyeing the bundle of wires on the console beside him.

The shuttle's cells wouldn't be enough to move the ship, but they would get the computers running for a while, and maybe even air recycling.

"Sounds good," I said.

"Wait a minute, sir. If we use that power it's going to leave the shuttle useless."

He had a point—we didn't know where we were. The ship was crippled. The shuttle might be our only way off the freighter. If we were *near* something, escape craft would be enough, but if we weren't . . . I started to laugh.

"Go ahead and use the shuttle," I said, dropping back into the command chair. I slouched down, gazing at the ceiling. "We can't use it in any case. How would we get the bay doors open? How would we cycle the airlocks? We couldn't get to it. We definitely couldn't launch it."

Nils blanched, then did as I told him. Emergency lights came on. The ship was no longer black now, just dim. I let out my breath, staring at the light overhead. It wasn't much, but at least we weren't *completely* dead in the cosmos.

"I'm not going to run the lights on the whole ship," Nils was saying. "Only where the motion sensors are tripped."

"Fine. See if there's anyone else moving." Now I'd find out where Tremma was. And after that, where *we* were.

"Can't, sir. I'm locked out of security."

"Are you serious?" I didn't understand. I sat up in my chair, turning to look at him. "How did it get this way?" Nils just shook his head. "Well, turn on the viewport."

"That I can do." He fiddled with the console for only a moment before the large screens came to life. I got to my feet, watching the feeds light up. I stepped back, and the blood drained from the ensign's face. It would have been good to see a star formation, or Payne Station. Or another ship. A recognizable system, anything. But all I saw was shifting patterns of dark sickly green.

We weren't adrift. We were on a *planet*. That explained the gravity.

I swore quietly. Nils continued to stare, dumbstruck. And yet—this was not as bad as if we'd seen empty space, which was what I'd been fearing.

"What is it?" Nils squinted at the feeds.

"I don't know. Raise the screens," I said. Nils did so. We looked out through the transparent carbon shield at the green mist. It was lighter here than it had been on the screens.

"We're in atmosphere," Nils said, licking his lips.

"Yeah, but whose?"

2

I was on a dead ship on an unknown planet with three trainees freshly graduated into the Imperial Service.

I tried to look on the bright side.

We were somewhere. That was a relief. It was better than floating with no power in space. Wherever this planet was, it raised our chances of rescue from zero to more than zero.

Nils couldn't determine our location. He could get at only the most basic functions, and most of those only by improvised means. I was still impressed; he knew what he was doing, even with a broken system that was barely giving us ones and zeroes to work with.

We were coming to grips with how limited our options were when Deilani and Salmagard returned. I could tell that Salmagard hadn't shared her thoughts on me with Deilani, because the lieutenant was just as surly and suspicious as before.

They had located a survival kit, and even imperial field rations tasted good under the circumstances. It was surreal to be having a field ration picnic with imperial trainees on the bridge of a ship stranded on a planet that we had no means to identify.

As bizarre as our predicament was, at least we could all agree on one thing: we didn't know where this rock was, but we needed to get off of it. Even Deilani couldn't argue with that.

The question was, how would we do that? With the combiners off-line, the only food on the ship was in the survival packs. Fortunately, there were probably enough of those aboard to last a while, if it came to that. There was water too, which would be reachable if we could find some tools.

Air was the immediate problem. Nils had gotten the recyclers running, but he hadn't been able to localize them. Running life support for the entire freighter would deplete our shuttle's cells in no time at all, and that was all the power we had. Life support had to stay off, but we were still in a better place than we had been half an hour ago. My mind was starting to pull itself together, and clear thinking wasn't making our situation look any less serious.

The trainees were almost finished eating. They weren't panicking, but I had a feeling that was only because I wasn't panicking. Ships weren't made to exist, much less function, without their computers.

I *had* to find out how we'd ended up in this fix. My sleeper malfunctioning? Well, that was one thing. But Tremma's absence? That alarmed me. The ship seemingly intact, but the computer in digital tatters? I didn't have an explanation. I didn't even have a guess.

The three graduates weren't speaking. They didn't know one another. They had never met before; they just happened to be assigned to the same ship. This was even less comfortable for them than it was for me. Nils didn't even know how to deal with Lieu-tenant Deilani, much less an admiral. Even Salmagard's natural grace couldn't smooth it out for the three of them.

Deilani hadn't taken her eyes off me. I wasn't naive enough to think that I could ignore her forever, but I hoped she wouldn't become a serious problem, at least not until we'd gotten out of this mess.

Salmagard gazed at the swirling green mist outside. I watched her, trying to read her, but not getting anywhere.

She looked a little familiar, but I knew we'd never met.

She could be thinking anything, but I remembered the way she'd looked at me when I'd just come out of my sleeper. If she *had* recognized me, she was determined to keep quiet.

I felt queasy. I needed her to give me something.

Nils was grim, but not too grim. He knew how bad off we were, but he was playing it cool. Maybe he was too proud to look dejected in front of Salmagard. From what I'd heard about the Imperial Service academies, I was surprised they hadn't managed to stamp the impulse to impress a pretty girl out of him. Maybe the rumors were exaggerated.

Time to take charge. I was an admiral now.

"Admiral," Deilani said, still watching me.

"Yes, Lieutenant?"

"Which fleet do you command?"

"I don't command any," I replied. "It's an honorary title. Obvi-ously."

Her eyes narrowed. Deilani wasn't stupid. To have gotten into bio with a commission and overachieved to the point that she was assigned to the *Julian*, Deilani had to have drive and intelligence off the charts. It didn't take a genius to see that I didn't add up.

But I needed her to stop worrying about me, and focus on more pressing issues.

I cleared my throat. "If Captain Tremma's on this ship, he's either dead or locked up. And I don't think he's locked up. We need to find out what happened to him and his pilot officer."

"Isn't two a small crew for a ship this size?" Deilani continued to scrutinize me. She'd latched on. She wasn't going to let go until she got what she wanted. She must have been a terror in the classroom.

It was a good question, but it probably wasn't in my best interests to answer it. "It's a Ganraen ship," I pointed out instead.

"Right." Nils nodded. Deilani looked puzzled.

"Androids," he told her. "Or maybe just AI and automated systems. They use that stuff a lot more than we do. But none of it's functioning because the system's down."

Not exactly true, but it would do for now.

They were more or less finished eating. "They're expecting us at Payne Station. The *Julian* won't wait forever. Let's find Tremma and get out of here," I said, waving at the viewports, and the mist beyond. "I've got places to be. And this place gives me the creeps."

"Where do we look, sir?" Deilani arched an eyebrow at me.

I returned her look, praying for patience. It was a fair question. The ship was enormous. A big Ganraen freighter like this was shaped roughly like an oblong box. The sheer amount of space inside it was staggering. We didn't have the time or supplies to just look around and hope for the best. And my patience with Deilani wouldn't last that long.

"I'm still thinking about that, Lieutenant. Would you be able to pull a log off an airlock console?" I asked Nils.

"I think so, sir."

"Let's see if any of the personnel loaders have cycled," I sug-gested. If Tremma wasn't on the ship, I was curious to know what might've made him feel the need to leave.

"I may be able to do that from here once the system's reset, sir."

"What we really need is a map."

"I'll see about that too, sir."

"Nils, I'm glad you're here."

"Thank you, sir."

"Admiral," Deilani said, hands on hips.

"Yes, Lieutenant?"

"Which academy did you graduate from?"

I felt my temper begin to rise, and stifled it. She wasn't taking the hint.

Salmagard was taking care of the plastic wrappers from the field rations, and our empty water bottles, packing them back into the survival kit. She was listening to every word, but she didn't so much as look in my direction.

"Rothschild," I lied, giving Deilani a tired look.

"So did I, sir."

She was baiting me. Salmagard continued to ignore us. Nils didn't care; he just wanted to get through the day. Why couldn't I have gotten three of him?

I felt a sudden contraction behind my eyes.

"Oh, dear." I looked down to find my hands trembling.

There were three pairs of eyes on me.

"Are you all right, sir?" Nils asked, cocking his head.

"We're in trouble. Get on there," I said, pointing at the console. "Find me a map. Playtime's over."

"Yes, sir."

I got up and stepped away. If I dealt with this now, it was going to be pretty obvious. And slipping away would be just as bad. I had to wait. I took some shaky breaths.

"Admiral?"

"*Yes*, Lieutenant?"

"What's the trouble, sir?" She knew. She was a doctor, after all. And she had spent our entire time together staring at me. She'd probably noticed before I had. Maybe that was why she was so pissed off.

"We don't know where we are, and our ship isn't working," I replied, keeping my tone even. "Things are not ideal. And I'm not having a good wake-up," I added. That was true, at least.

She gave me a pitying look. "Do better," she said.

"All right," I said, putting up my hands. "All right."

Salmagard and Nils turned to look at me. Deilani folded her arms. Was that smugness?

I gave her a disgusted look, and reached into my bag.

"Let's keep the judgment to a minimum," I said, taking out a hypo and injecting myself.

Deilani turned to the others, jerking her chin at me.

"Our honorary admiral," she said.

"Hey, come on," I said. I was feeling better already. "Even admirals can have vices, right? I'm on vacation."

"What did you just take?" Deilani asked, cutting me off.

"That's kind of personal," I replied, glancing at Salmagard. She was completely expressionless.

Deilani twitched an eyebrow. "From the withdrawal, I'm going to say synthetic opiates."

"You cheated," I said. "Who told you?"

Deilani just looked at me. I sighed.

"All right, you got me. I'm dependent. You can report me when we get to Payne Station. I'm sure that'll be great. They'll probably demote me and garnish some wages or something."

She gave me another one of those pitying looks. "I don't know who you are," she said, "but you aren't getting off that easy."

"What? For this?" I held up my empty hypo.

"For impersonating an officer. You're going to prison."

"I wish," I said.

Deilani blinked, and Salmagard cut in.

"Sir, can we activate a beacon?" she asked.

It was a sensible suggestion, and a good rescue. We needed to get on task. "Worry about me later, Lieutenant. I'm the least of your problems."

I turned to Salmagard. "No. I don't think so." I shook my head. "Maybe we could if this was still a Ganraen ship, but it's full of Evagardian systems, and if the computer's down, there is no beacon. I would *love* to know what's wrong with the systems," I added to Nils.

"Yes, sir."

"Is it sabotage? Because if it looks like sabotage, then we're getting somewhere."

"I don't know, sir."

At first I hadn't been sure, but it couldn't be coincidence. Even a ship as old as this wouldn't just happen to fall apart at the same time my sleeper did. What had been done to my sleeper had also been done to this computer.

"Do you have a reason to suspect sabotage?" Deilani asked. She'd deflated a little, but she wouldn't let go. Not while there was still breath in her body. I respected that, but I wasn't at my best.

I spread my arms. "I think this is all pretty damn weird," I told her.

"But where are the androids?" Deilani pressed.

"Never deployed," I said. "Or we'd see them all over." There are no androids, kid. Ganraen ship, Evagardian crew. Evagardian systems. Androids didn't fit into that picture. I didn't have long before she worked that out.

"Admiral!" Nils said, looking up.

That sounded promising. I rubbed my wrist where I'd injected and turned my attention to the ensign.

"What is it?"

"The forward, starboard loader cycled once since the last reset," he reported. "I can't go back any farther."

I took that in. "I guess it's something. It's one more cycle than I'd expect. But just once? So he went outside, but he didn't come back in?"

"Yes, sir." He drummed his fingers on the panel, looking puzzled. "I don't get it, but it's right here. One cycle."

"All right. We have to assume that Tremma had some idea what this rock is— So why would he go outside?"

"A repair, sir?" Salmagard theorized.

I nodded. "That sounds right. We're broken down, after all. We should take a look. I hope he didn't run into trouble out there."

I looked at Deilani, who was considering the same notion. Dangerous indigenous life-forms were rare; only a few dozen had been discovered in known systems. Deilani would know at least a little about xenobiology, and she would know that this world was not one of those she had studied.

The gravity drive was shut down, but we were still on the floor. This was a planet, but not much of one. The gravity was too light. And you don't need life-forms to get you into trouble on an alien world. Anything could've happened to them out there.

Nils was the only one who looked alarmed. Salmagard was perfectly calm. Her face never seemed to change.

With our combined knowledge of spacecraft, Nils and I navigated the four of us in the direction of the airlock in question. There were a lot of corridors and a lot of ladders. We passed a long, dirty window overlooking one of the cargo bays. I glanced down at the massive stacks of crates inside. The white imperial containers were a stark contrast to the dark, grimy bay.

I wondered what Tremma was carrying. With the cease-fire in place, he should've been out of a job. Was that why he was ferrying graduates to their first assignment? Then what was in these crates? Leftovers?

Yet again, Deilani was monitoring me.

"Step it out," I said. "We don't have time for sightseeing."

"Can you teach me to walk like that?"

"Like what?" I asked, brushing past her.

"Like a model," she said, giving a little twitch of her hips.

"You don't have the figure," I told her. She rolled her eyes and kept walking. Maybe she'd give up if I kept refusing to bite.

Nils looked smug as we approached the airlock's pressure door. His navigation had been perfect, no easy task in a dark, foreign vessel. The airlock was sealed. That took me off guard; our side of it should have been open. I went to the small window in the blast door and peered into the cramped chamber. What I saw made me forget all about Deilani's persistent scrutiny.

"Suits," I said, looking at the rack by the doors. It was a Ganraen ship, but it had an Evagardian crew, so the suits were Evagardian as well. "EVs, I guess. Quick."

Instead of obeying, Deilani darted to the window to look for herself. It was amazing how fast her face turned as white as her uniform. She joined the rest of us without a word as we stripped down.

I'd only worn an imperial environment suit once before, but it went on easily enough. The EVs were skintight, the nanofabric adjusting to the wearer's body, and they were the purest white. They were also the most technologically advanced garments in the galaxy, bar none. I deployed my helmet, which emerged from my collar instantly. There was a hum, and the force shield that was my faceplate materialized, sealing me in. I keyed my suit's AI and checked that all my readouts were green.

The trainees slipped effortlessly into their suits. They'd obviously practiced this extensively; until recently there had been a war on, and they were bound for ship duty. They had to be ready to suit up quickly in a depressurization scenario.

To them, this technology was business as usual. Imperials take everything for granted.

I smashed the emergency carbon over the manual release with my elbow, and Nils yanked it down. The seal broke with a hiss, and a few centimeters of space appeared between the doors. Together, we pried them open. No power meant no decontamination, so we had to go in with our helmets activated.

I squeezed through and dropped to my knees beside the first

body. I couldn't tell which was Tremma; the upper half of this one was severely burned, and both bodies were in bulky tech suits intended to protect the wearers during heavy repairs and labor.

They hadn't protected these two well enough. The second corpse was badly burned too, his whole body.

When I met him briefly, years ago, Tremma had seemed to take pride in his ability to prepare for problems before they arose. He hadn't seen *this* coming.

He and his pilot officer were dead. Dead in the airlock, nothing but blackened remains.

Swallowing, I got back to my feet. I could see what had happened, even if I didn't understand the how or the why. I herded the trainees back into the ship, deactivating my helmet once the seal was engaged again.

This changed things. I had to think this through.

Something heavy struck me across the back. It would've been my head if I hadn't chosen that moment to move. I crashed to the ground, and Deilani's boot slammed me in the gut. Nils shouted something, probably an expletive. Salmagard slipped between me and the lieutenant. She didn't touch Deilani; she just blocked her with her body.

"Out of the way," the taller girl snapped. Salmagard said nothing, but held her ground.

"What are you *doing*?" Nils demanded, still frozen in place.

"There are two *dead men* in there, and *this* is not an admiral," Deilani said, making as though to move around Salmagard, who again managed to block her without touching her. I spat out a mouthful of blood. Good thing I'd deactivated my helmet, or that would've been all over my faceplate. "Listen to him talk—he's not even an officer. Listen to his *accent*. Where's his uniform? Look at him move. He's *not one of us*."

All very good points. I rolled over to probe my ribs. To have them cracked again so soon would be very upsetting. The deck was freezing, and the dim corridor blurred briefly. If I'd known this was coming, I'd have taken a larger dose when I injected a few minutes ago.

Strategically taking painkillers in advance. That was something a real admiral would do.

"LT, he was in an admiral's sleeper," Nils said, holding up his hands. "You *can't fake that*."

"Then what was wrong with it? Things don't go wrong with admirals' sleepers."

"Something in the seal. I *told* you."

"Which could have been caused if there was an unscheduled resuscitation," Deilani snapped. She had me there. "He's on chems. He probably screwed something up when he went back in. *He* killed them, and *we* saved him. He can't be an admiral. He's not even *Evagardian*."

"Am too," I said, wincing.

"Shut up. They were the only people on the ship. None of *us* did it, and that leaves him."

Deilani's reasoning was far from airtight, but it was understandable under the circumstances. Salmagard continued to protect me. She was well aware of the penalty for laying one's hands on an officer, which was why she could use only her person as a shield to protect me. She kept her hands clasped firmly behind her back.

Nils stared at me. He'd been suspicious too, but his suspicions hadn't been running in this direction. And now Deilani was looking at Private Salmagard as if she was an enemy combatant.

"Who," she bit out, her eyes burning, "in the Imperial Service does not travel with a uniform?"

"This man, clearly," Salmagard replied evenly. Her soft musical voice actually lessened my physical pain.

"Ow," I complained.

"Shut up!" Deilani snapped.

"You shut up," I shot back from the floor. Behind Salmagard.

Nils didn't know what to do. Salmagard obviously wasn't backing down, and if Deilani's blood pressure got any higher there would be a third corpse on this ship. I couldn't blame her for having a problem with me, but she needed to start thinking about the greater good.

"I don't know," Nils said. "He *kind* of talks like an officer."

"And you *kind of* talk like a man," Deilani shot back.

Nils opened his mouth to retort, remembered she outranked him, and shut it. "Sir?" he said to me questioningly.

"What?" I groaned, and lay back, closing my eyes. Deilani had startled me with that blow, and that had gotten my heart going. Now my chem-laden blood was rushing around a bit more enthusiastically than was optimal. I was light-headed.

There was also some pain in my ribs.

"Who are you really? I haven't been this confused since the Ganraens started the damn war."

"My name wouldn't mean anything to you," I told him.

"Then you're admitting you're not Evagardian," he said, looking stricken.

"I *am* Evagardian—"

"You're *not*. You talk like a Ganraen. Like a Ganraen from the capital," Deilani cut in, then fell silent, looking thoughtful. Yes, there was no Ganraen capital anymore, was there?

But I didn't like seeing her thoughtful. She'd drawn a couple wild conclusions, and I was worried about where her overly motivated mind was frolicking off to now.

"Nils!" I called, cutting her off. I was still flat on my back.

"Yes—er, sir?"

"Don't call him that," Deilani snarled.

These kids. "Guys, maybe this has escaped your attention, but we don't even know what planet we're on. We have a few days' worth of food, air, and water, and that's it. With no systems, we also have no beacon. You do get that, right?"

"Someone will notice that we came down," Nils said. "And that we didn't show at Payne Station. If we really are in trouble, we just have to wait."

"False." I held up a finger, enjoying the cool deck beneath me. It was calming. "Well, it's false if this planet is actually somewhere out of the way. And I'm thinking about what we saw outside. It didn't look familiar to me."

"Doesn't mean this body isn't in a developed system."

"No. But I'm telling you there's nothing like this on the route we were supposed to be taking."

"You think we're off course?"

"Impersonating a—" Deilani interrupted, but I cut her off again.

"I can prove I didn't burn those men, and I can prove that I belong in that sleeper."

"Tell us your *name*."

"I could tell you *anything*. It wouldn't have any meaning."

"So get out your holo. Show us some ID."

"About that," I said. Deilani made a disgusted noise and turned away.

Salmagard was looking down at me over her shoulder. That absolute neutrality. How proper of her. "Help me up, Private." I reached up to her. She pulled me to my feet, and I leaned heavily on her. I was still hurting.

I looked at Deilani. "If you want to arrest me, just hold on to that thought until we figure this out. And if that's going to happen, I'm going to need everybody. That includes me. Actually, the only one I haven't thought of a use for is a doctor."

I wasn't sure Deilani's face could get any redder, but it did. She lunged at me, and Salmagard pivoted to put herself between us. Awfully brave of her, I thought; Deilani was twenty centimeters taller than she was. Deilani drew up short, staring at me over Salmagard's head.

That look alone painted her as the one likeliest to be a murderer among us. But I didn't think she'd done it.

"He's got a point," Nils pointed out. "That's the whole crew in there, right?"

"How can it be? This ship is huge!" Deilani whirled on him.

"It is," I said. "Trust me."

"How can we?"

"You guys should never have been on this ship, but *that's* not on me." It was true, and it felt good to say it. It was all I had.

"What do you want to do?" Nils asked, looking past Deilani to me. The lieutenant's mouth became a tight line.

"Did you get a look at the bodies in there?" I asked.

Salmagard and Nils both looked away. I'd heard the Service academies were tough; they'd probably only seen things like that on screens before.

"I did," Salmagard said.

"Then you saw his arm."

"Yes."

"What are you *talking* about?" Deilani demanded.

I faced the lieutenant. "He burned himself. I think he burned the other man—damn it, let's say the one that was fully burned was Tremma. I think the pilot officer burned Tremma, then himself." I held up my left hand. "Using the tech suit's incinerator. It's just a guess from the way they were lying in there. Look for yourself."

"Why would they do that?"

"I have a feeling that's a question we're going to want to try to answer," I said. "Call it a hunch."

Deilani's eyes narrowed, but she didn't bite. "No. We're locking you down."

I held up my sidearm, which I'd been holding out of sight since the first blow fell. I wiggled it at them. "If I was your enemy, it's not like I couldn't have done something about it by now. I know you're not going to like this, Lieutenant, but I'm *not* your enemy. I need you three, and you need me." Well, I needed Nils and Salmagard. Deilani I could live without.

"You said you could prove it," Nils cut in. "Prove you didn't do it."

"I can. You can."

"What?"

"Pull the log off my sleeper. You can tell if it's been opened, and you can tell if the DNA sync is right. It's not part of the ship. It still has power."

Nils blinked. "That's a good idea."

"I'm just a passenger, guys. I'm on a long trip. My sleeper's been getting moved around a little bit." I made an inclusive gesture toward them. "Us traveling together? It's just some kind of mix-up. I've been aboard this ship once before, but that was a long time ago. I didn't expect to wake up here. I don't know what's going on. So can we move past this and get down to business?"

"I can check your log," Nils said.

"Thank you."

"What if you rigged it?" Deilani asked.

"If that was in my skill set, I wouldn't be here," I said honestly. Her look of loathing didn't change, but she believed me. That hatred wasn't all directed at me; some of it was for Salmagard, whom I was still clinging to. She was small, but she didn't have any difficulty supporting me.

It took longer for us to get back to the sleeper bay than it did for Nils to confirm my claims. I belonged in that admiral's sleeper. There was nothing Deilani could say to that.

"There's no name," Nils reported, looking up from his readout. "How can there be no name?"

"You just can't see it. You don't have credentials," I lied. "Of course it's going to protect my personal information. And it's not relevant. What matters is figuring out what killed Tremma and his PO. But I have no idea how to do that." I caught Deilani eyeing my sidearm. "Worried about this?" I pushed it into Salmagard's hands. "I don't need it." Instead of red, now Deilani was turning white again. She had remarkable circulation.

"What now, sir?" Nils asked, looking dazed.

I was still in pain, but I didn't know how long I could keep milking it. "Only one choice," I said, straightening up and letting Salmagard go. "The shuttle. It has its own systems; there's a chance they're still all right. If they are, we can find out where we are. Once we know that, we can make a play. There should be enough juice left to get us out of orbit. We'll just have to hope there's some power left after we open the bay doors. Right?" I looked at Nils, who nodded. "Questions?" Without waiting for any, I started to walk, hoping Deilani wouldn't make any more jokes about my gait. It wasn't as if it was my idea to walk this way, but I couldn't shake these habits overnight.

"There are two dead officers, sir. We'll need a report."

I looked over my shoulder at Lieutenant Deilani. "And I'll give one. I'm ranking officer, honorary or not, whether you buy it or not, so this is my watch. Don't worry about what you're going to say when we get out of here. That comes later. What did you think you would gain by putting your unit down a man under these circumstances?"

"I don't know, maybe a Rothschild Mark for apprehending a Ganraen spy," Deilani said, annoyed.

"You don't get the Mark for that kind of kid stuff," I said, and it was true. The Rothschild Mark was the highest imperial honor, and only about a dozen had been awarded over the last century or so.

"Kid stuff?" Nils raised an eyebrow.

I shrugged. "Spies aren't anything to get excited about."

"You know, another Rothschild Mark just got awarded, too," Nils said, perhaps hoping to ease the tension. "Didn't say to who or for what, though."

"They usually don't," Deilani said darkly. "You know though, don't you?" This she directed at Salmagard, who did not reply. Deilani was right. An aristocrat might have inside intel about something like that.

The Rothschild Mark wasn't exactly my favorite subject; I hoped they wouldn't linger on it.

"Don't get excited about awards from the Service," I told them.

"Why not?" Nils asked.

"Because when they give you that stuff," I told him, "you aren't the one they're patting on the back."

It was time to find the shuttle, and that meant locating the flight bay. I'd seen and dealt with some large vessels in my time, but I'd rarely had to navigate them without lifts or guide paths. I'd gotten too used to being part of an entourage. Navigating solo wasn't coming back to me easily.

Thankfully Nils had no difficulty getting us there, but we were both taken aback to find that the shuttle launch floor shared space with the main hold; there were only fixtures for a force screen to separate the shuttle from the cargo. You could have fit a full wing of the Ganraen royal residence in this chamber.

Stacks of white service-standard deep space transport containers dominated the space, laid out in an impeccable grid, six high, nearly reaching the thirty-meter ceiling. Each crate bore an imperial crest in black on its side. Not very subtle, but for this run the freighter hadn't been going anywhere it was likely to be boarded and searched. Clear Evagardian markings meant there was only a handful of cons Tremma could have been planning with this cargo.

I caught a glimpse of my face in the glossy white plastic of the nearest crate, and looked away, swallowing.

"What is all of this?" Deilani asked. "And why isn't it on an imperial transport?"

"It is."

"Why isn't it on a normal one?" she pressed.

I said nothing.

"The fighting's over," Nils said. "Maybe they're dispersing some of the surplus ordnance."

"These are not weapons containers," Salmagard observed softly, and I glanced back at her. She looked thoughtful. Her eyes flicked to me, but only for a moment.

So she didn't know everything. I wanted to educate her, but this wasn't the time. We made our way through the stacks of crates to the shuttle in front of the launch doors. It was an Evagardian craft, dragonfly-class. Neither cutting edge nor out-of-date, it was a fast shuttle mostly intended for ferrying officers and ambassadors from ship to station in style.

Obviously the freighter needed a shuttle, but this was an unusual choice. Tremma's ship would be expected to have something a little less flashy, and a little more utilitarian. The trainees probably wouldn't notice. No—Nils had. He was looking at the shuttle with obvious confusion.

"Why a dragonfly, though?" he asked. "It doesn't make sense, not in this ship."

"Come on," I said, startling him. "Let's get out of here."

"Nothing makes sense on this ship," Nils said, his eyes still on the shuttle. Damn it all, now he was thinking too; Deilani was enough to deal with. I jogged up the ramp and into the cabin, going straight to the cockpit.

"You're a pilot?" Deilani asked.

"No," I replied cheerily. "But how hard can it be?" She scowled at me. "Nils, take the chair." He sat down beside me.

"You're joking, right, sir?" It was starting to catch up with him. I hoped he'd keep his cool.

"Relax. I can fly it."

He looked relieved. I spotted Salmagard with her hand on the ramp control. "That might be premature," I told her.

Deilani leaned against the cockpit doorway, arms folded, looking expectant. I ignored her and began to power up the shuttle. The computer came online. I knew at once that something was wrong.

"What is it?" Nils asked, sensing my sudden tension.

"The system's stuttering," I replied, distracted. "Get a starscape while I check it out. I want to know where we are . . ." My subconscious shouted something at me, and I listened. I stopped in the act of reaching for my straps. "Run," I said.

"What?"

I grabbed Nils and dragged him out of the cockpit, pushing Deilani and Salmagard ahead of us. Fresh out of training, they knew how to go from stationary to full speed, even if they didn't understand why. We stumbled down the ramp, and I kept them in front of me, pushing on. I tried to put as many stacks of crates between us and the shuttle as I could.

The shuttle went up only seconds after we cleared the ramp. We were all deafened by the blast, which vaporized the nearest stacks, and broke many more free of their gravity restraints. I shoved Deilani out of the path of a falling crate, and kicked Nils' legs from beneath him to get his head down. Salmagard had the good sense to duck on her own. Containers were toppling all over, and the smell of burning plastic washed over the bay.

Coughing, I rolled over, visions of shattering carbon shield flashing through my mind. Screams, and the wailing of twisting, malforming metal. I felt a wave of nausea. That would've been a good time to lie back and go to sleep, but Salmagard was reaching down to help me to my feet. Grimacing, I took her hand and let her pull me up.

Deilani was on her hands and knees, groaning. It looked as if some debris had struck her, but it hadn't compromised her suit.

Nils was sprawled out; the fall to the floor had done him more harm than the explosion had, but it beat the alternative. Everyone was whole, but the bay wasn't.

Cracked and broken crates were everywhere. Pieces were still clattering to the deck, and I could see bits of the shuttle lodged in the bulkheads. It was hot, and the smell of melted polymer was strong in the air.

I leaned against the nearest stack, which felt warm through my suit, and slid down to sit. I could feel sharp pain in my back; I'd taken some shrapnel too. My EV chirped medical pings at me, like I needed it to tell me that I was bleeding.

My sleeper being tampered with was one thing. My sleeper and the ship. My sleeper, the ship, *and* the shuttle. And the ship's computer systems. I couldn't forget those.

Subtle.

"What just happened?" Nils choked out, getting to his feet. "The cells spiked. The levels just popped for no reason."

I wished he hadn't seen that. The power cells in the shuttle had been fixed to overload on start-up, probably helped along with . . . I wasn't going to think about it. There wasn't any money in it. I shook my head like that might help my ears stop ringing.

Salmagard appeared in front of me, which I took to mean Deilani was back on her feet and acting threatening. I figured I'd better say something before she did.

"I don't know about you guys," I said loudly enough that they'd all hear me over the buzzing in their ears. "But this is starting to feel a little like sabotage."

"And what the *hell* do you know about that?" Deilani's hands were opening and closing; those fingers wanted to be around my throat so badly that I truly sympathized. I pictured her shaking me by the neck the way she so obviously wanted to.

"Just save it," I said, drained.

"I won't take this from a chemical dependent," she spat. The emotion in her voice was telling. I was starting to get a feel for Deilani.

I looked at Salmagard, but once again she was making a point of ignoring me. She'd maintain her neutrality until Deilani physically assaulted me. I didn't blame her.

I watched her work her wrist experimentally.

"You *know* what's going on," Deilani pressed.

"Actually," I said, feeling detached. "I'm kind of baffled." It was true. At first I'd had some ideas, but now? This had gotten out of hand.

There must have been something about what I said, or how I said it, because Deilani backed down. Even she couldn't believe that I'd sabotage my own sleeper, the ship, *and* the only way off the ship. I hadn't done any of it. I really hadn't.

And the shuttle *had* been the only way. The escape craft wouldn't do us any good unless we could somehow get into orbit, and with no reactor and no ship's computer, that wasn't going to happen.

Crates and debris were still falling apart, and the sounds echoed through the vast bay.

Nils had staggered into the aisle to gaze back at the wreckage. Deilani put her hands against the crate opposite me and appeared to be getting herself under control.

Ten minutes ago I'd been impressed that these three weren't panicking. It wasn't that they were brave or well trained, though it was possible that they were both. They hadn't panicked because they were fresh out of training, and had no concept of exactly how large the galaxy was, and the true implications of being lost in it. Imperial training had no doubt confronted them with danger, but there had always been a safety net.

Now I was out of luck. I *knew* how bad it was.

Salmagard looked at me, troubled. *She* knew how serious this was even before things started blowing up. It wasn't surprise on her face. She was troubled because this was the confirmation of her suspicions. Maybe she'd been hoping to be wrong.

As for the shuttle, that had been the oldest trick in the book. Rig the power cells to overload. No real explosives, so it looks like an accident.

Much harder to do with newer shuttles.

"You're bleeding," Salmagard said.

"Medical's as good a place to go as any," I sighed. "Because we aren't going anywhere else."

3

TREMMA'S infirmary was outfitted to imperial specifications, with which Lieutenant Deilani was extremely familiar. Before she could learn to be a leader, she'd been forced to learn to be both scientist and doctor. Bio was a prestigious and demanding field, and the imperial academies were notoriously ruthless. It was the broad nature of her expertise and her lengthy training that allowed her to graduate as a second lieutenant, one rung up the ladder from most of the other freshly commissioned officers.

For all the good it was doing her.

The medical bay itself was a mixture of Ganraen and Evagardian stylings. New white fixtures stood out jarringly against the gray of the original Ganraen engineering. The room was cold, but at least the examination table was padded. I didn't care for the harsh lights, but my eyes were drawn to the lockers filled with chems and medicine.

Deilani didn't hide her lack of enthusiasm for treating me. She dabbed at me with soothing antiseptic before spraying on an icy bandage that applied a mild anesthetic. It wasn't a large cut, but it was over my eye, so we couldn't just let it bleed. I could feel my suit beginning to mend itself, repairing the tears where I'd been struck in the back by shrapnel.

"Give me your supply," she said, putting out her hand, and wearing the expression of someone only acting under the direst duress.

I decided to show a little trust in the hopes that maybe she'd send a little back my way. I handed over my hypos. She plugged one into a hand scanner, and her eyes narrowed. "This is high quality," she said, giving me another look. "Very pure." She frowned. "You'd almost have to be an admiral to afford this," she mused, giving me another funny look.

"It was a gift," I said. "You know how it is. Someone gives you something, it's ungrateful not to use it. I'm not into that stuff." I glanced at Salmagard. "Honest. I'm all about clean living. True story."

Deilani's curiosity had vanished, replaced by familiar contempt.

"I didn't know what it was," I went on. "I thought it was for my allergies. That's how they get you."

I'd given myself only half a dose earlier. It wouldn't hold me long. My eyes would start to look bloodshot. I'd probably be developing a little nervous tic soon. It would get worse fast, though.

It's true what they say: drugs and sleepers don't mix. My body chemistry was a disaster. We were in serious trouble and I needed to be at my best. I needed Deilani's help. It looked as though it was a good thing we had a doctor along after all.

She made a noise of frustration and closed her eyes. "We're going to have to shut this down here and now. A few more hits of this and you'll probably go into shock this soon after coming out of a sleeper."

"Sounds good."

She blinked at me. "That's it?"

"You think I use it for my health? No. Lieutenant, chem me off, by all means. The sooner, the better."

She looked me up and down.

"Yeah," she said. "All right."

She wanted me to have a miserable detox; what she didn't grasp was that I didn't care. My need for drugs had ended when the party did. I could handle any amount of suffering if it meant being free of my dependency. "Just don't kill me until you don't need me anymore."

"Then I'll give you a stim too."

"Now you're speaking my language."

Nils was still gaping at the shards of plastic that Deilani had pulled from my back. He looked impressed.

"I've had worse," I told him. My suit had almost finished repairing the tears.

"You look a little familiar. Sir," he added, squinting at me.

"Is it my lips? I've been told I have very common lips," I replied. He kept staring. I sighed.

"Do I?"

"Yes, sir."

"Stop treating him like an officer," Deilani groaned, but her heart wasn't in it. "Why was the shuttle sabotaged?"

"Ask Tremma," I told her. "I'm less worried about the why than the who at the moment."

"But what do we *do*?" Nils was close to panic. He was holding it together, but after that brush with death, we were all starting to feel it. Deilani didn't like me giving orders, but she was conspicuously quiet when it came to proposing solutions.

I straightened up a little, gently touching the cut over my eye. She'd done a nice job on it.

"We're out of options. You're good, but you're not good enough to get this whole ship moving, Nils. It's like you said. We'll have to wait for rescue."

"No power means no beacon," Deilani pointed out. "And if someone wanted us gone badly enough for this level of sabotage, then we probably are off course. We could be anywhere. Surely whoever sent us out here covered their tracks."

I was glad she was thinking clearly. "Probably," I admitted. "But there's something you're forgetting." I pointed at Salmagard. "She can't go missing forever. They'd come looking for you, but they might come looking for her even sooner. There *are* ways for them to find us. We're lucky. We're stationary. If we'd just been pointed out past the frontier and sent off still asleep, no one would ever find us. And I think that was our saboteur's plan. But that didn't happen, and that means we've got a chance."

"Provided we haven't been asleep for, say, a couple of years," Deilani said, massaging her temples.

Nils shook his head. "We haven't, ma'am. The sleeper records showed we were two weeks out from the courier. So that's longer than the trip was supposed to be, but it's not really a long time. Not long enough to send us too far." He was fidgeting. Nervous energy filled the room, hanging in the air like static electricity. "So we're already overdue."

"It's out of our hands now. We'll have to wait." I rubbed my chin, wondering if there was anything in Medical that I could use to shave. There were lasers that could remove body hair for surgery. I wondered where they were kept.

No. The stubble was good. It was helping me. It felt weird, but I was better off keeping it.

"Shuttle's gone," Nils said. "Emergency power won't last."

"We'll have to get creative," I said, focusing.

"Excuse me?"

"Lieutenant, you've just spent a substantial portion of your life training to become a leader." I looked at her expectantly. "Surely you know what to do."

It was the chemicals talking. Deilani just scowled at me. I went on. "We have to buy ourselves as much time as we can, and stay alive until they get here. That's it. That would be pretty simple if we didn't have two dead men in the airlock. They didn't kill *themselves*."

"Yes, they did," Deilani said. "We saw it was their own incinerators. But what made them do it? If it wasn't you. That wasn't one of them murdering the other, or a suicide thing."

"That's what I'd like to know. I wasn't going to worry about it as long as I thought we were just going to get out of here. Now that we're staying it's an issue again."

"Are we in danger? Apart from this?" Nils motioned at the ship in general.

"I don't know," I told him honestly. "I don't see how we could be. But they're dead, and ending up that way was not their goal—so something happened here. I can't explain it. We're missing something."

"How do we wait for rescue without life support?" Deilani was doing her best to stay on task, but she was afraid. I couldn't blame her. We could have died in that shuttle, and that wasn't something any of them would forget.

"Two ways." I got off the examination table and started to pace. Salmagard had been standing by the door with her hands behind her back and head bowed, but now she looked up to watch me. "First, the sleepers. We rig up some kind of power supply and just go back to sleep. The problem with that is that mine's no good, and even though your suspicions are *completely* unfounded, I'm sure you wouldn't be comfortable going under with me still up and about. And repairing my unit is probably beyond even the ensign's abilities. Likewise putting me in one of your sleepers would let the other two rest easy, but the third would be awake and alone on a dead ship on what looks to me like a dead planet. No power, no life support. Survivable, but not ideal."

I looked them over as they digested that.

"I think that at the end of the day, this is something we're better off facing together."

If I had three Salmagards, this would be easy. But Deilani wouldn't be willing to take her eyes off me, and there was enough doubt in Nils that neither would he. None of them were keen to get back in their sleepers—especially after seeing what had almost happened with mine. How could they trust anything when it seemed as if literally everything on this ship had been sabotaged? The sleepers were off the table.

"Then we're agreed," I said, sweeping my hand at the medbay. "This is our new home. We're lucky. We've got lots of resources on this tub. There's plenty of air and water—we just have to get at it, and use it intelligently. We have everything, or at least most of what we need. We're going to turn Medical into our own little tree house."

"Our what?" Deilani glared at me.

"Get some culture. Don't you know Old Earth history? I don't know how long the air's going to last. If we seal off a room like this, rig up a recycler and bleed in oxygen, we can last a while." Trainees or not, they understood the concept of an air pocket. "But we also need heat."

"EV suits will keep us warm," Deilani pointed out. Evagardians and their blind faith in Evagardian technology. I envied them.

"Until they run out of power, which will be sooner than you realize once the temperature equalizes. Which it will," I promised. "It'll get cold, and the suits will have to work harder to keep us warm. The EV charges won't last. We need to conserve them, and think about O_2 in case we have to leave the room once the air's gone out there. For water, for example. We can't go breaking open pipes in here. We'll have to bring in water by hand."

"We can just use a grav lift."

"We still have to open the door, and we'll lose air every time we do." I sat down on the examination table again, and they gathered around me.

I hoped my facade of confidence wasn't the only thing holding them together. It was a good thing I was used to being the center of attention.

"We were in deep space travel," I went on. "Most of the ship was sealed off and depressurized. There's not as much air as we think. We have to get to work. We don't have to rush. We don't need to panic, but we do need to get started. If we've overlooked something, the sooner we find out, the better. And things are far enough out of hand that I don't think we should be making irresponsible assumptions about how much time we've got."

"We're with you," Nils said. Deilani grimaced, but didn't protest. She probably had the highest test scores in the room, but Nils was the one making rational choices. He understood that we were all in this together.

"With four of us we can make this work." I pointed at Nils, making sure the gesture was all business. "You get the big job. Find a grav lift. Rip the recycler out of an escape craft, bring it here, get it running." Escape craft designed for use in open space weren't any good to us on the surface, except for whatever we might be able to scavenge from them.

"It's not going to be at full efficiency."

"Bring two if you have to. I'm not grading you. There aren't any points for Evagardian elegance here. There should be at least a dozen ECs on a ship this size. Do what you have to. And don't worry about being neat. Break what you have to break. They can bill me."

"Yes, sir." Nils took a deep breath and nodded.

"Private, I want you to collect survival packs. There'll be some by every airlock and loader, more by the ECs, and even more *in* the ECs. One's supposed to be enough for one person for a week—four of us, you do the math. If we end up with too much stuff in here, we can put some of it across the corridor so we won't have to go too far for it. Speaking of suit time, Lieutenant, find out if there's an EV charger. If there isn't, collect power packs and O_2 cartridges. I'll see about finding us a heat source."

"No."

"If it would help, you can think of these as orders."

"I don't acknowledge you as my superior, and I am not letting you have the run of this ship alone. *And*," she added, "you shouldn't move around until that booster thins."

Touching. Venomous distrust mingled with concern for my well-being. She was convinced I was a spy, and determined to hand me over alive. To her I was nothing but a big, juicy medal with her name on it.

Yet that didn't fully explain her animosity. She believed I was an enemy combatant, but she was treating it awfully personally.

Well, if this went well, we'd be stuck together for what could turn into a matter of weeks—so we'd have plenty of time to talk it over. I wasn't really looking forward to that. Maybe I could go into medical stasis or something.

For now, we had to build trust. It might reduce our productivity, but not as much as it would if things came to a head right here.

"All right," I said, trying to sound conciliatory. "Secure me. We'll do business over the com. How's that?"

She glowered at me for an uncomfortably long period of time. "All right."

"Less work for me," I said, as Nils and Salmagard trooped out.

"Get used to how this feels," Deilani said, strapping my wrist to the examination table. She engaged the patient safety catch. Even with one hand still loose, I wouldn't be able to get free unless I could grow another thumb.

"Give it a rest." I shook my head. "By order . . ."

I stopped myself. It was a sign of the depth of my exasperation that those words had come out. She was staring at me again.

"By order? By order of whom?"

"By order of the guy you need to be listening to," I told her sharply, and she flinched. "I'm good here," I said, tugging at the strap. It was tight. Seeing that, Deilani swallowed and backed out of the room.

I took a couple of deep breaths, then settled back and closed my eyes. If Deilani was determined to force me to slack off, who was I to argue? Besides, whatever she'd given me had sapped my energy, and not in a good way.

I did what I could over the com to help them find their way through the dark ship; or rather, I helped Nils. Salmagard was silent, and Deilani would run herself ragged before asking me for anything. At least they were all in shape.

"It's going to be ugly," Nils said of the recycler he was working to extract from an escape craft. "I don't have any tools. Do you know where I can find some?"

"Tremma's maintenance supply. But where that is, I don't know. Just break whatever you have to. Stuff on the inside of a Ganraen EC can't be all that sturdy. And if you can get that running in a timely fashion, you should see about a combiner."

"Really, sir?"

"Unless you want the last thing you ever eat to be field rations." The food produced by a molecular protein combiner was never anything to get excited about, but it was still a step up from field rations.

"You really think this is it, sir?" Nils sounded shaken. He still wasn't over the exploding shuttle. My hearing was still a little dull too.

Until a few weeks ago these trainees must have believed that they were going to war. The conflict with Ganrae hadn't been going one way or the other too decisively. Things had been leaning in the Empire's favor, but it hadn't been such a one-sided conflict that the Empire would be feeling invincible.

Maybe Nils had thought that nothing would happen to him on the *Julian*. That was reasonable, and the cease-fire had come abruptly with the destruction of the space station that served as the center of the Ganraen Commonwealth's government. He must've felt even safer knowing the fighting was over.

But now he had no choice but to think about his own mortality, a subject that his service training had probably glossed over.

"It's not outside the realm of possibility," I told him.

"Yes, sir."

Even in my suit, I could feel the temperature dropping. It wouldn't be long before our EV suits were the only things keeping us from freezing.

Salmagard returned, her grav cart stacked with survival packs. Enough to hold us for a while, even without a combiner. The meals in the packs came in numerous varieties, but the selection wasn't infinite. I did some quick mental math, and decided we'd be sick of all of them depressingly soon. Though when it came to rations like this, imperial ones were probably the best you could ask for.

I hoped Nils had the technical prowess to get a combiner running. We'd also need protein gel for it—and that would need to be kept at a certain temperature. Well, that would be easy. We could just leave it in the corridor and thaw it as needed. I couldn't even remember the last time I'd eaten food from a combiner. Ages ago.

I was too spoiled, and I needed to get over myself. I was going to be eating that sort of humble food three meals a day for the foreseeable future, and that was only if I lived through this.

Salmagard finished unloading her cart.

"Private," I said, and she went to parade rest. I looked down at my bound wrist. "You know I can't actually put you at ease."

"You're saying it would be wrong for me to follow your orders, sir?"

That surprised me. Her voice was perfectly even. I almost couldn't tell she was joking. She *was* joking, right? She had to be.

So she did have a sense of humor.

"You're sure?" I asked. "You might be better off on Deilani's good side. I don't have much to offer you."

"Yes, sir."

"Thank you." I cleared my throat. "Lieutenant?" I said into the com.

"Yes?" Deilani sounded a little out of breath. She was trying to compensate for not having a clue where she was going by running the whole way. Her pride couldn't be blamed on the Service. They hadn't taught her that. This was all her.

"Where are you?" I asked.

There was enough of a pause to indicate mild panic.

"You aren't lost, are you?" I stopped myself there. Only minutes ago I'd been praying that Deilani could let go of her personal feelings about me and focus on reality. Making fun of her at a time like this would be hypocritical. "Relax, Lieutenant. We're on a private channel. Where are you?"

She'd just taken a wrong turn on the way back to the airlock. I guided her back on track. I wouldn't have bothered her, but her cargo of O_2 and EV charges was a safety net that we needed to have as soon as possible.

Nils returned. He was right; the crippled recycler on his grav cart was not pretty. I didn't care, but it bothered him. He liked to take pride in his work, and his mental state was fragile at the moment.

"We're going to heat this room with a fuel cell," I announced. Salmagard's brows rose. Nils' jaw dropped.

"You'll bake us alive," he said. "We have no way to regulate it. Even with power, EVs can't balance those temperatures."

"Not once we lose the rest of our residual heat," I said. "It's going to be cold. And we'll put it in an isolation unit and quarantine it. That'll contain some of the heat." If we couldn't get usable power out of an energy source, why not at least benefit from the heat? There would be cells in the shuttle bay.

Nils didn't like it, but he didn't have a better idea. I sent Salmagard with him; it would take them both to get a cell onto a lift cart. They'd barely left when Deilani arrived. It was an enormous relief to see the supplies she brought. As the temperature dropped, these EV suits would be our last line of defense against the cold; we'd need to keep them charged. Freezing to death did not appeal to me.

"What now?" she asked, giving me a look. It was a new look. I wasn't sure what it meant, but it seemed encouraging.

I considered the question. Deilani didn't have the technical know-how to handle a protein combiner. That would have to be Nils. A lot of this would have to be Nils or myself. But I was tied to an examination table.

"I'm sure there'll be more urgent things than this, but for now why don't you see if you can find a viewer, some readers, and some archives? If we're stuck here for a while we'll need something to do. I'm serious."

Deilani left looking conflicted, and I was glad she didn't have a weapon. If we really did find ourselves waiting around for weeks on end, she'd be glad I'd asked her to do this.

I had some peace and quiet to figure out our next move. It would take time for Salmagard and Nils to extract a cell and get it back here without using lifts. The next item on the list would be water. We'd have to find some kind of containers, then think of the best way to access the water aboard the freighter. Not with the taps, of course—those were controlled by the computer. My inclination was to crack open a pipe, seal it, and just open it again when we needed more, but there was probably a more elegant way. Nils would know.

I sat up, instinctively touching the com control on my collar with my one free hand. Someone had just dropped off the shared feed. The change in the audio was subtle, almost undetectable, but in the quiet dimness of the empty medbay I couldn't miss it.

I shifted channels until I heard voices. No surprise: Nils and Deilani. Deilani's idea, no doubt.

". . . but *can* you do it?" Deilani was asking. She was trying to pressure him into something.

"I *could*. But I won't."

"You're refusing an order?"

"Ma'am, you don't have a chain of command, and even if you did, I would not be in it."

"Under these circumstances—" Deilani began, but Nils cut her off.

"Under these circumstances we do what we have to, and that means listening to whoever's got the best idea." I was proud of Nils, but I wished he'd shown this kind of backbone earlier.

So this was what they sounded like when I wasn't around. These trainees had been drilled to exude Evagardian presence. Restraint, professionalism, perfection. They were less guarded now. Deilani had plenty of bluster when we were face-to-face, but she was also trying to pull in the other trainees for support behind my back. Smart. Sort of.

"He's an enemy operative, and he's going to try something. He doesn't *want* an imperial rescue," Deilani was saying earnestly.

Actually, I hadn't thought that far ahead. It looked as though Deilani was worrying about my problems for me. That was sweet of her.

"But he's *getting* one, and he knows it because we've got a liner on the ship," Nils pointed out. He was right. If the Empire did find us, it was just as likely to be because of Salmagard's wonderful genes as me.

"Yes, and his only chance is if we aren't there to tell them who he really is." Deilani had thought this through.

"We don't *know* who he really is," Nils protested.

"*She* does."

It was time to step in. Deilani was going down a dangerous path, and she was putting Nils in a bad place, and from the sound of it she would soon be questioning Salmagard. Nils had no good options; disobey a man who *might* be an honorary admiral, or disobey a woman who was most certainly an imperial lieutenant.

This wasn't ideal. Why couldn't Deilani just mellow out? No, that wasn't a reasonable expectation. That was what made this so frustrating: her paranoia was legitimate. There was sabotage everywhere, and me on top of it. I knew how sketchy I must look to these three. Of course she was on edge. She was just following her training and trying to look out for her comrades, for the people she *knew* were her comrades.

She saw me as a threat, and she was trying to protect Nils and Salmagard. Maybe that meant she had the makings of a decent officer.

But she was going to get us all killed if she kept this up. Good intentions weren't enough.

"You two *did* see me hand off my weapon, didn't you?" I asked suddenly into the com.

The following silence was gratifying. I could picture their faces. Deilani rallied quickly.

"I daresay," she said tightly. "We could not expect a Ganraen agent to be *entirely* helpless, even unarmed."

And damn if that wasn't a damned reasonable thing to say. I sighed. I wanted to retort that surely a Ganraen operative couldn't possibly pose a threat to three imperials and their superior genes and training, but I decided against it.

"And just because you haven't done anything yet doesn't mean you won't later," she added. I groaned inwardly. She was being childish. If I fought her stubbornness with stubbornness, I wouldn't win.

"Admiral," Salmagard's soft, lustrous voice interrupted. I silently thanked the universe; without her, this ordeal would've been infinitely worse.

"What is it?" I heard Deilani hiss in frustration. She couldn't have seriously expected her little chat with Nils to stay private. If privacy was what she wanted, she should have encoded the channel. Did they teach that to young officers going into bio? Probably not.

"I have movement."

That took a second to sink in. "Where?"

"In the buffer ring."

That was at the reactor.

Never mind why anyone would be there—who could she have detected? "Nils, Deilani, where are you?"

"Bay Four."

"Bridge."

So it wasn't them. Why had Salmagard and Nils separated? No

time to think about it. I flicked out my knife and slashed the straps tying me to the examination table. I couldn't untie myself; it wasn't my fault Deilani had forgotten that I still had my knife. It wasn't my job to point that out to her. She was the officer, after all. Hadn't they taught her about attention to detail?

I turned on my EV suit's lights and left Medical.

"Are you tracking?" I asked over the com.

"No, sir. I've lost it."

"I'm on my way. Private, get back to Nils and hold up. I'm going to find Deilani. Keep scanning."

"Yes, sir."

"You're supposed to be secured!" Deilani said as I slid down a ladder to come face-to-face with her.

"A lot of things are supposed to happen, Lieutenant. You don't hear me whining. Don't act like you're not glad to see me. You know you don't know the way to engineering, and if there's somebody else on this ship, I don't want anyone moving around alone."

"Not friends of yours, then?"

"I don't have friends," I said.

She made an aggravated noise, but she followed me.

I didn't know what to think, so I didn't. I just ran, and with only minimal lights, that was difficult enough.

We found Nils and Salmagard outside the buffer. With the reactor shut down, the ring-shaped tank of mercury served no purpose. And without the reactor, the ship had no purpose. It was just a big metal box.

The core was in marginally better condition than the rest of the ship. There were signs that there had been maintenance recently, and some imperial materials on display. One panel on the gray wall was covered by a shiny smart-panel that glowed faintly. Seeing the Evagardian technology in this ship wasn't getting any less surreal.

"Where?" I asked Salmagard.

She pointed down at the maintenance trench beneath the ring. "It was brief—only a flicker." She sounded almost apologetic. "The readings are unusual. It's as though there's some kind of interference, Admiral."

She had a combat scanner clipped to her ear, and there was a tiny light on it, strobing almost unnoticeably. It was projecting its readings directly onto her eye. Evagardian technology.

Because she was a negotiator, that would be a standard piece of equipment for her. I wondered why she'd felt the need to put it on. Afraid of the dark? Jumping at shadows? Had she wanted reassurance that she really was alone?

"I've never heard of one of those giving a false positive."

I knelt at the edge of the trench and pointed my light down. For something to register on Salmagard's scanner, it had to have a certain amount of mass and it had to be alive, or at least move like it was.

Those things were hard to fool; I'd tried.

Salmagard wasn't tense, but she was ready. I could tell from her body language that she took the reading absolutely seriously. Because she was an aristocrat and as a trainee, it went without saying that she had never seen action before. As I looked at her face as she gazed into the trench, it seemed like she was ready for something to happen. Maybe even itching for it. Had they trained that into her, or was it just her style?

I had no reason not to believe her. She wasn't the twitchy type. I hadn't known her long, but I'd seen enough to know that much.

She was trusting me, so I would trust her, too.

4

"ADMIRAL?"

"Yes, Ensign?"

"What's happening?"

"I don't know." I got to my feet and pinched the bridge of my nose. "Are you *sure*?"

"Yes, sir." Salmagard didn't hesitate.

"What made you decide to scan?"

"No lights, sir."

Dead ship, probably a dead planet, and still looking over her shoulder. Salmagard took her job seriously.

There was someone else here. Someone who didn't want to make contact with us. That raised some interesting questions. I peered down into the maintenance trench.

Maybe now it was time to panic.

What had this mystery individual been doing with the reactor? What *could* he do with a cold reactor? Supposing this guy was our saboteur—or rather, *one* of our saboteurs—what more sabotage was there to do? You don't fix a ship so it'll get lost, then hitch a ride with it. Something else was going on.

I considered the layout of the reactor. Our new friend would need power, and a tech suit with clearance to open those inner hatches, so in theory he still had to be close.

"Lieutenant, go with the private. Ensign, with me. Take the right side, make plenty of noise. If there's someone here, I don't care if he's shy. I want to know who he is and what he's doing on this ship. Check all the way down to the coolant reservoir."

Deilani wouldn't want to be alone with me; she didn't like Salmagard, but she couldn't distrust her. And Nils was too crucial to our survival to be let out of my sight. "And stay on the main channel," I added, wagging my finger at the lieutenant.

Deilani gave me a defiant scowl, and Nils looked guilty.

We split up. The ensign and I climbed down into the trench. It was even colder, darker, and tighter than the ship's normal corridors. There were clear plastic shields over the panels, but they were old and filthy, making it difficult to see the machinery behind them. This wasn't the inferiority of Ganraen engineering; this was just neglect.

"Turn on your light," I told Nils. "We're not being subtle."

"Yes, sir."

"Keep your eyes open. If this guy noticed Salmagard and pulled out, he might not be friendly."

"Sir, how did we get a hostile aboard?" Nils asked, baffled.

"I am more confused than you are right now," I told him.

There was nothing to suggest we weren't alone. I saw no sign of a fifth living person on the ship. The freighter was old, and there was plenty of dirt and grime. Tremma's lax approach to maintenance was evident. Like the rest of the ship, panels were missing, and bulkheads were mismatched and shoddily welded. Wiring and pipes were exposed, sometimes hanging low from the ceiling.

Their training would have already exposed the three graduates to plenty of propaganda to strengthen their prejudices about galactic cultures, specifically those found in the Commonwealth. The state of this ship wasn't going to make them look on Ganraens any more kindly, but they had no context for what they were seeing.

Taking a Ganraen ship, making it half Evagardian, then trying to keep it running with a crew of two was a big job. This freighter received the best of care when it was in dry dock in a safe place, but that wasn't often. Just looking at this ship you'd almost think it had been built by an alien species.

But Ganraens were people, the same as everyone else. Though the war hadn't made it any easier for Evagardians to see them that way.

But they did build such ugly, uninviting ships.

"Hard to believe this thing even flies," the ensign muttered. He was spoiled. "When was the last time any of this was inspected?"

"Never," I guessed. The metal around us was pitted and corroded.

"Looks like it, sir. There are safety violations everywhere." Nils was appalled.

"Of course. These cores are twenty years old. The mercury in the ring hasn't been replaced in more than that. In fact, most of the work seals look like they came from Oasis."

"The station with all the pirates?"

"That's a broad generalization. And there aren't any pirates there anymore. Anyway, you don't even want to know about the guidance computers."

"How do you know all this?"

"I'm an admiral. I know everything."

Nils didn't push. "Who could be here? There were only our sleepers in the bay."

And a strange sight that had been: the sleek Evagardian sleepers in a cramped, rusty little room. No one deserved to wake up to that. I didn't think anyone's illusions survived the Imperial Service forever, but these graduates were having theirs battered a little early in their careers.

Still, it could've been worse.

"It's only a short jump series to Payne Station. It's not like a conscious passenger would lose a lot of time, even on a ship this slow. It wouldn't be strange at all if Tremma had added a third man to his team."

"Team? You mean 'crew,' sir."

I winced. That was a slip. Nils was giving me a look, but he didn't want to press.

"It wouldn't surprise me if he added another man, or even a couple of men. What I don't understand is why they would avoid us," I told him.

"Unless they had something to do with what happened in that airlock," Deilani said over the com.

"Why bother running, though? Where can they go? They can't leave the ship. Even if there's someone here who's up to no good, he's in the same fix we are. Rescue *will* come, they'll have scanners, and everyone will be accounted for. Avoiding us is pointless," I said.

"Is it? We still don't know where we are," Nils said. "This

planet could be anywhere. There could be a settlement a kilometer away for all we know."

"True," I admitted. "But I'm pretty well traveled, and I've never seen anything like what's outside this ship right now."

"It's a big galaxy," Deilani said. "Nobody could keep track of the climates of every world on record."

"Agreed. But it's not just the mist—it's the gravity. I've never felt this before. You aren't used to the difference because Evagardian worlds all use gravity cores to stay consistent with Old Earth force. But once you get out a bit, you'll get a feel for the differences. Trust me."

"Oh, we do," Deilani snarled.

I decided to change the subject. "You two have anything?"

"No signs, no readings," Salmagard reported. "Where are you?"

"We just cleared the trench on the second core."

I looked up at the high ceiling. There had once been catwalks overhead, but they hadn't survived the repurposing of the ship. One less thing to check. I pointed my light back into the trench. I'd have sworn something moved, but now there was nothing. My brain chemistry was playing tricks. I wished we had enough power for more lights.

"Sir?" Nils was looking at me intently. He was following me blindly, but was still keenly sensitive to my mood. As long as I acted like the situation was under control, he'd hold together.

"Which system are you from, Ensign?"

"Rothgard, sir."

"Which planet?"

"Bellegard."

"Nice," I said. Bellegard was known for white sandy beaches and pretty greenish waves. Of course, those picturesque islands were only one corner of that world, but it was the corner they always seemed keenest to show off.

I'd never been there.

"You'll have a good story for when you get back, about how you discovered a new planet. Maybe they'll name this rock after you." Well, it couldn't actually be a new planet if it had taken us only two weeks to get here. Why couldn't I *place* this place? I tapped my foot on the deck a couple of times, listening to the sound echo through the dead ship.

I had never felt this gravity before. I was sure of it.

If the navigational computers had been tampered with, and we'd boosted longer than we intended, we could theoretically be well into unregulated space. Not exactly unexplored space, but territory that was known only to the most daring surveyors. That wasn't a comforting thought.

"Watch your step, ma'am. There's something on the floor here," Salmagard said to Deilani.

"What is it?" I asked.

"Looks like a maintenance kit. Someone's been through here," she said, directing the words at me.

"Not necessarily—it could just be Tremma's style. He's not hung up on details," I told her.

"I noticed," Salmagard replied. There it was: that flash of disdain in her voice. I smiled. She could trade her class for the uniform, but she couldn't turn it off completely. What a fascinating girl. "We've cleared the third core. Moving into the cylinder. Visibility low," she added.

"There's dry ice under that mesh. Just keep your suit powered and dial up your filtration."

"Do we need to switch to O_2?" Deilani asked.

"It should be safe, but watch your monitor just in case. You picking anything up, Private?"

"Negative."

"Admiral?" The way Deilani said it made me wish she'd call me something else.

"What is it, Lieutenant?"

"The ladder here is heavily damaged. It doesn't look recent."

"Just make peace with the fact that this ship isn't up to code. Blame it on Ganraen engineering."

"This has nothing to do with engineering—this is some kind of combat damage."

I sighed. Couldn't these three take a hint and just *stop noticing things*? For their own sake as much as mine. How could I convince them that they were happier just getting on with their lives?

I didn't think I could.

"Why would there be a fight on a Ganraen freighter run by the Imperial Service, Admiral?" Deilani asked, and I could picture her fingers opening and closing again, practicing for my neck.

"No one said the Service ran this ship," I pointed out.

"So Captain Tremma was just the owner? Just a guy with a commercial freighter? You're saying the academies handed our sleepers to some freelance courier?"

She had a point. That would never happen.

"Er," I said.

"Go on, Admiral. Don't be shy."

"You're right. That doesn't seem very likely, does it?"

"Who did this?" I could hear her over the com, tapping on the metal.

"Not a clue," I replied, meaning it. I hadn't the faintest idea what had happened to the damn ladder. I could *guess*, but there was a high probability that with Tremma dead, no one would ever know. There was a pause.

"We'll have to find another way up, ma'am," Salmagard said to Deilani.

I still hadn't seen anything to suggest we weren't alone.

Something about this didn't feel right. Something about *all* of it didn't feel right. There was strangeness I could explain, even with the trainees' wild conspiracy theories, and then there was this. I'd have to be careful not to mention that to Deilani.

There was a sharp intake of breath over the com. "What is it?" I looked up at the paneled ceiling. Deilani and Salmagard had to be above us.

"Sir, there's a hatch up here to the outer corridor—we are completely depressurized on the other side."

"What?"

"There must be some kind of hull breach."

I swore, amazed. We hadn't even *suspected* a breach.

This was life without computers. We'd been completely oblivious.

"Better check it out," I said.

"Sir, there is some electronic interference."

It took a moment for Salmagard's words to sink in. "To your suit or your scanner?"

"Scanner, sir."

"But there's no *power*," I said. "What could interfere with a combat scanner? Apart from, like, military jammers?"

"I don't know, sir." Salmagard sounded calm. That was reassuring, though it wasn't a good sign that I was looking to the trainees for reassurance.

"Check it out. We're going to check the hatch here; if it's sealed, then we know our friend went your way."

"Into the depressurized zone?" Deilani asked, baffled.

"No other option. The ducts were all intact, but if he's got a tech suit and some tools he could be anywhere. Even if there was power, do you think any of the safety locks work down here?"

"Fair enough."

"Step it up," I told the ensign, and we hurried forward. We had to be sure we were clear on our end, even if the odds of finding anything were slim.

"Hard to see in this," Deilani grumbled over the com, though she sounded more curious than annoyed.

"In what?"

"This mist."

"Can you get a composition on it?" That could potentially tell us where we were.

"With a med scanner?" The contempt in her voice was thick.

"Just asking."

Deilani gasped. "Oh, Empress," she breathed.

I straightened up, focusing on the com. I'd heard her angry, but I'd never heard her like this.

"What is it?"

"Uh—substantial structural damage. The hull is . . . very breached."

"How bad?"

"It looks like something just ripped us open." She sounded as if she didn't believe what she was seeing. She wasn't thinking; she was completely absorbed in what she was seeing, and I heard a hint of her accent creep through.

Maybe that was why Deilani didn't like Salmagard; she was from Cohengard. She'd done a nice job hiding it, but now that I knew where she grew up, it was easy to understand where she was coming from.

Salmagard came from a privileged background. Deilani came from the one city in the entire Empire where people were seriously disadvantaged. I should've picked up on it sooner, but she'd been doing a passable Marragardian accent earlier. "There's something here—not rock. Tremendously dense material. Not much of it, though. Admiral, we'll need to decon. In fact, I'm not sure about this door," Deilani went on.

"Don't worry about it. I'm sure the computers were still up when we were hit. If there was a contamination hazard, that section would have sealed."

"I'm releasing precautionary nanomachines anyway."

"Why? Because it's green out there? Didn't you already do that, back at the airlock?"

"This isn't a debate."

I let her overrule me. The voice of caution was sometimes tiresome, but usually correct.

It took longer than I liked to leave engineering and join Deilani and Salmagard.

They were only faint outlines in the green mist that had filled the curved space that housed the radiation shield. The shield itself was shattered, of course—that was much easier to do than to tear open the side of an armored freighter. And this freighter was armored. Unfortunately, that was now evident to the trainees, and they were free to wonder why a boat like this needed armor.

"How?" I said stupidly, gazing at the damage. *"How?"*

"Weapons fire?" Deilani suggested.

I shook my head. "No."

"Meteor?" Nils wondered aloud.

"Impossible," I said.

"Why?"

"The repulsors would've stopped it."

"This tub has repulsors?" He sounded disbelieving.

"Why not?" Deilani said, and I looked over at her blurry form. "It's got military armor."

"What? Why?" Nils was bewildered.

"Look for yourself."

Irked, I joined them at the tear in the bulkhead. Outside was nothing but swirling green mist. We couldn't see anything at all. No landscape whatsoever. We were about halfway up the ship, which meant it was quite a long way to the ground. I pulled Deilani back from the edge. "Show me what you found."

She did. The stuff was black and heavy. It seemed like rock, but it was definitely new to me. It wasn't as though I'd visited every developed planet in the galaxy, and I was no geologist—but this stuff was strange.

"I don't suppose you're good with geology," I said.

"I don't suppose you'd like to explain that armor." I couldn't see her face, but her voice told the whole story.

"I don't suppose you'd like to lighten up."

"A disguised freighter with armor? And you want to tell us you're not a spy?"

"Hey," I said. "This isn't *my* ship. And I don't think this happened in zero-g."

"It didn't."

"Then it can't be the reason we landed. Is there a lot of this?"

"A couple of kilograms' worth. That's the biggest piece I saw; I can't see much. It's mostly like gravel."

"Uniform?" I asked curiously.

"No, not at all. It's a mineral, or something like one. These are broken pieces—see the smoother side?" She seemed impressed. When she was busy accusing me of espionage every five minutes, it was easy to forget that she was a scientist. I'd have to trust her on this one.

"I do now." So Deilani and I could get along; we just had to be totally preoccupied. "How'd it get in here?"

"Your guess is as good as mine. Maybe better."

"It's not," I assured her. Salmagard was standing by the tear in the bulkhead, gazing out. "What is it?" I asked. She couldn't possibly see much out there.

"My readings, Admiral. I think the interference is coming from outside."

"Just don't fall." I'd worry about readings and interference later. "You want to take a closer look at this?" I asked Deilani.

"Might as well; the nanomachines are already live."

"Fair enough. What could have done this to the ship?"

"Are you actually asking me?"

"Why shouldn't I? *I* don't know."

"You don't even want to know what all of this looks like to me," Deilani said. She'd gone through suspicion and into disgust, then come out on the other side. Maybe now she'd understand that this was as bizarre to me as it was to her, and calm down a little.

"Admiral?"

"Go ahead, Private."

"Sir, these anomalous readings could account for what I picked up earlier."

"How sure are you?"

"In light of the plausibility of it . . ." She trailed off, sounding embarrassed.

Bad readings were strange, but they were a lot more believable than some kind of phantom stowaway. I hoped she was right.

"Are you picking up movement out there too?"

"Yes. But there's also something interfering with the sensors. I'm trying different optics to penetrate this mist. It's not normal mist, sir."

"Clearly. If it was, it wouldn't be able to exist in no atmosphere." I stepped up to the tear and looked up. The mist above was paler than the mist below. "Is anything working, Private?" I asked.

"No, sir. My scanner could be malfunctioning."

I'd always envied those imperial combat scanners. It was like having an entire support team attached to your head, a support team I could've used once or twice. It wasn't doing us any good here, though.

What were the odds that Salmagard would have a defective one?

"So there was never anyone to begin with?" Nils asked.

"Who would it have been?" I shrugged. "And we've got bigger problems. This tear might go all the way down the hull. I don't think it's likely, but we could be bleeding air without realizing it. We need to start collecting O_2 tanks, and we need to find a water supply and stockpile some just in case."

The plan hadn't changed; we'd just gotten distracted. We had to stay focused on the essentials.

"I can collect O_2 reserves," Salmagard volunteered. I wondered what her family back on Earth would think of their little princess doing this kind of manual labor.

"Nils, go back to Medical. Take a look around and figure out whatever we're going to need power for—then you need to find power sources."

"Like what?"

"A latrine isn't much good without power, and we'd better keep one med table juiced, just in case. Think about hygiene, convenience. Comfort. We have to try to get ready for the long haul. Use your imagination. Ask Deilani if you have to. Just make it work, and stock it up. Private, give the lieutenant my weapon so she won't feel uncomfortable being alone with me."

Salmagard produced my sidearm and held it out to Deilani, who hesitated for only a moment before taking it. I couldn't read the trainees with their helmets deployed.

"What about us?" Deilani asked, watching them go.

"We're going to break into Tremma's quarters. I need a terminal that hasn't been affected by whatever put the ship out of commission."

"The captain's personal reader," she said.

"Right. I don't want to set up in Medical until we know more about what happened here. We might just be digging our own graves. Follow me."

"Cheery."

"You have a better idea?"

"No, I agree. Let's do it if we can."

We left engineering. I was tired of climbing ladders.

"How are you going to access his secure terminal?" Deilani asked.

"We'll think of something."

"And you're trying to convince me you're not some kind of criminal."

"I haven't been trying to convince you of anything," I told her. "Except maybe that it's not in your best interests to fixate on me when we might be in serious trouble. You want to know my secret?"

"Please," she said dryly.

"Fine. I don't like to tell people this because sometimes it makes them insecure," I told her. "But I'm a pretty great guy. Like, to the point that it's disruptive to the people around me."

"Oh, Empress. Just shut up."

"No, really," I said, shrugging. "That's why they made me an admiral. Because I'm such a catch." I looked back at her. "You can tell, can't you?"

"And I've got first-tier genes." She wanted to hit me.

"You might, for all I know." She didn't. Genes could gain value through deeds and accomplishments, but that value could also be lost. In Cohengard, it had been.

"I don't. I've been tested." There was a clatter, and Deilani let out a little cry, stumbling. I made a grab for her, but I was too slow. It wasn't a serious fall; she caught herself with her hands easily enough. I pointed my light at the deck. Her foot had gone straight through a corroded grate.

"This bloody *ship*," she swore, whacking the grating with her fist. It rattled loudly.

"I know." I put my hand out. She stared at it, then gave me an incredulous look.

"Are you helping me up or inviting me to dance?" she asked.

That stung a little. I adjusted my posture and folded my arms.

"Which do you prefer?" I asked. She groaned and pushed past me.

Tremma's quarters were easy to find; Evagardian ship layouts are elegant and efficient, and they don't vary much. This was a Ganraen ship, but in some ways it had been rearranged for the convenience of its imperial crew.

"At least we don't have to worry about security." I was looking on the bright side; having no power had its perks. On the other hand, having no power also meant there was nothing to physically move the door aside but us, and this one was less cooperative than the last few we'd encountered.

I put my hands on the metal and pushed with all my strength. "Shoot the seal," I told Deilani.

"What?"

"Hurry up. Just compromise it a little bit—that's all we need. Then we can open it."

"I don't believe this. The ship's falling apart and you want to break it even more." She positioned my pistol, activated her helmet, and looked away. We both flinched at the shot, though we couldn't possibly feel the sparks through our suits. I felt the seal break, and heaved on the handle. The heavy Ganraen door didn't slide easily in its track, and I needed Deilani's help to move it enough for us to get inside.

"Are you even up to physical standards?" she asked, annoyed.

"Whose standards?"

"You're not even trying anymore."

"It should be proof I'm not a bad guy," I said. "A bad guy would be in better shape. Go easy on me; I'm detoxing."

Tremma's cabin held no surprises for us. It wasn't as ugly as the rest of the ship, but he spent most of his time in a sleeper. There were a few mementos, touches of home—and Tremma's home appeared to be the Tressgard system, though I couldn't determine which planet from just these trinkets.

There was a commemorative statuette from a recent event at the Baykara Games at New Brittia, suggesting that Tremma had been in Free Trade space not long ago.

So, he was into that gladiatorial stuff. How un-Evagardian of him. The Empress frowned on death for entertainment, and it was illegal in Evagardian space.

Maybe he'd been there for work. I didn't know.

There was only one place in the Empire where imperials could legally kill one another in front of an audience, and that was very different from the Baykara blood-sport-for-profit model. That was at Valadilene, in the Vanguard and Acolyte selection programs, where the very best of imperial youths in the Service actually competed for the chance to give up their lives in pursuit of high positions in Evagard's most elite units.

Between the two, the Baykaras' barbaric killing for entertainment business offended me less.

I went to Tremma's desk and got to work on his console.

"How are you going to access it? An officer's codes can't be . . . How did you do that?" Deilani asked, narrowing her eyes.

"He left it unsecured."

She didn't back down.

"Is this why we split up? So they wouldn't see you do this?" She was looking at me like I'd done something wrong.

"See what? You're imagining things. Take a look at this."

"What is it?" Deilani gave up and joined me.

"It's our cargo manifest—look, we're on it. See? I'm an admiral on here, too. I just have good codes, that's all."

"Still no name. We'll see how smug you are when you're in prison," Deilani muttered, scowling. "You won't need a name there, either. Just a number."

I snorted.

"What are you doing?"

"I was wondering if there was something on this ship that might help explain some of this," I told her.

"What *are* we carrying?"

"All kinds of stuff . . . but look, with this we can confirm it. Four passengers in sleepers, two crew, inactive but on call—so they were probably in their sleepers until something woke them up."

"What, though?"

"Can't tell from just this. Wait a minute—there's an entry in the log. They accessed one of the cargo containers. Let's see what it is."

"'Marragardian marble,'" Deilani read over my shoulder. "What the hell would they want with— Oh. Oh, Founder. Why didn't I see it earlier?"

Armored ship. Imperial containers. Shady business everywhere. Obviously there wasn't anything as benign as marble in those crates in the hold. Deilani just hadn't thought it through; she'd been too busy thinking about me.

"Good question." I didn't even try not to sound smug. She swatted me. "I'm your superior, damn it."

"You're a pirate, or a stowaway, or a thief, or a spy—you are *not* an Evagardian officer."

"And you are not at all my type."

"A real officer, of course, could not lay a finger on an enlisted woman," she added.

"Rules are made to be broken," I pointed out. "And rules about fraternization aren't really rules. They're more like guidelines."

"Spoken like someone who knows nothing about the Service."

"It's the drugs. I never believed it about liners like the private. I do now. Say what you want about the gentry, they have their charms."

"It's weird," Deilani said, narrowing her eyes.

"What is?"

"You. You don't come off that way."

"What way?"

She gazed at me levelly. "Like someone who'd be acting like this."

I took her meaning. "How rude," I said. "Just because I don't conform to your narrow view of conventional masculinity, I'm still a red-blooded Evagardian admiral."

She snorted. "Even if you were, she's a negotiator."

"By choice, I'm sure. What if I told you that only added to her charm?"

"It's definitely the drugs. I want to shoot you so bad right now."

"If I was a spy, bringing me in dead would still get you a little career boost. But if I'm not, you'll be executed."

"You think you have some card to play."

I sighed. "Lieutenant," I said. "You are going to make some commander a very fine executive officer someday. But not today. So it looks like that marble crate that Tremma accessed wasn't vaporized by the shuttle—it's on the other side of the bay. Want to go see what's really in it?"

5

THE crate was standing open.

"By the Founder," Deilani breathed as we approached it. We could clearly see what was inside.

I was at a loss for words. I'd suspected this, but it still took my breath away.

We were standing in the vast cargo bay, surrounded by tall stacks of white crates. My head was spinning, and what I was seeing didn't help.

"This much juice could put a hole in the hull the size of a . . ."

"That's not marble, Admiral!"

"I can see that, Lieutenant!"

It was interesting to see Deilani flustered about something other than me.

The crates contained military ordnance: one of Evagard's more potent explosives, 14-14. It was packed into man-size charges, probably intended for leveling buildings, or putting holes in space stations. As I looked closer, I saw they were intended for ship-to-ship missiles. There was enough 14-14 here to decommission a dreadnaught.

Normally you would see weapons like this behind a lot of security. Guards, systems, heavy doors. There hadn't been anything keeping this crate shut but a palm lock.

I licked my lips. "Ensign, how we doing?"

"I think I can rig a recycler, sir," Nils replied over the com.

"Private?"

"I've broken into an O_2 reserve on the fourth deck, Admiral. I'm going to start moving them to Medical. I've also found some pressure jugs that we can use for water."

"You're the best. Carry on."

Deilani was looking at me, but I wasn't sure what she expected me to say. I cleared my throat. "So, Lieutenant—what did Captain Tremma want with this, ah, marble? Why would he want to take explosives outside? What is there here to blow up?"

"I was hoping you could tell me, Admiral."

We gazed at each other.

"I don't even have a guess." I was being truthful, and she could tell.

"Is that what all of this is? Weapons?" She turned around to look out at the bay, at the stacks of crates.

"I prefer not to comment."

She gave me a flat look. "It's a little late for you to play innocent."

"It's not my ship." I shrugged. "But yeah, probably. There was just a war on, after all. But that's not our problem right now."

We looked around the container. "The airlock cycles only once, and they die burning. It doesn't make sense," Deilani said.

"Why were they going outside in the first place? Well—now that we know about that damage, that's probably why. There may be more damage we don't know about. Something they had to address."

"With 14-14?"

"That's where it catches, isn't it?" I rubbed at the stubble on my chin, as if that could help me make peace with it.

"You really don't know what this is about?" The look she gave me was almost pleading.

"You're just now getting that?"

"I guess so." She looked down at her gloved hands, perhaps wishing she could bite her nails. She was scared. So was I.

"Private, anything on the scanner?"

"No, Admiral."

"I don't think there will be. We've confirmed there were only supposed to be six people aboard, and the computers weren't *always* down—particularly the security—so you can ease up if you like. I think we're dealing with faulty equipment."

"Yes, Admiral."

"Nils?"

"Sir?"

"You think it's possible the bay loaders might be on a different log than the personnel airlocks?"

A slight pause. "It wouldn't surprise me, sir. This ship has been extensively repurposed at enormous cost. If someone was going to cut corners, it would be with nonessential systems."

"I was thinking the same thing." I folded my arms and looked at Deilani. "Suppose Tremma and his PO weren't leaving."

She frowned, considering it. "What? You think they were coming back in?"

I shrugged. "It's possible. Look." I pointed at an empty rack inside the crate. "There's a charge missing. They opened this cargo; they must have done something with it."

"You think they blew the ship open?" Her eyes widened.

"No—no, I'm sure they didn't. That damage wasn't caused by explosives."

Deilani grimaced. "So they took it somewhere."

"They must've."

"But what did they want to do with it?"

"I don't know, but I'm dying to find out. Private, Ensign—take whatever you're lining up to Medical, then get down here to the cargo bay. We're taking a walk."

"Belay that," Deilani cut in. For a moment I thought I had another fight on my hands. "We can't open the hangar doors or cycle the airlocks without power. That hull breach is the only way out. We'll have to meet up there," she said.

I let out a covert sigh of relief. "She's right. Shall we?"

"Let's go."

We left the cargo bay, but it was a long walk. I looked at the containers that were intact and still stacked after the blast and swallowed hard. If that crate of explosive charges had been a little closer to the shuttle, we'd all be part of a small, but very smooth glass crater right now.

The wreckage of the shuttle was ugly. I'd seen an overloaded spacecraft go up before. It never really looked like an accident, but with no explosives used, you could never be sure. We'd been lucky. Deilani had to ease up a little now; she knew I couldn't possibly be responsible for all of it.

Salmagard was waiting for us on the observation deck in engineering, gazing down through the viewport at the dark, lifeless reactor. She had her arms folded across her abdomen, not exactly hugging herself, but it was a quiet reminder that the ship wasn't getting any warmer.

Nils showed up about five minutes later. I filled them both in.

We needed to have a look for ourselves. Getting out of the ship and onto the planet's surface wouldn't be easy. We'd have to climb down the side of the freighter, then make our way a considerable distance to the aft lander, where we'd see what we could find out. What had Tremma done with those explosives? The only way to find out would be to pick up his trail.

The deck shuddered. It was subtle, but I felt a distinct vibration in the metal underfoot.

"Did anyone feel that just now?" I asked, looking down. I felt a twinge of queasiness, and swallowed.

"Feel what?" Deilani asked.

"That shake."

"Yes, Admiral. There was a tremor."

"Thank you, Private."

Deilani muffled a snort.

"Add seismic activity to our list of circumstances beyond our control," I said, ignoring her. It had been only a mild tremor, but it was still enough to stir my memory.

We engaged our helmets and dragged the door open. The cling currents in our gloves were intended to hold us to bulkheads in zero-g, but they'd work well enough for this. I swung out onto the side of the freighter, mindful of the limited visibility. I kept one hand on the metal, raising and lowering the current through my glove to give me a controlled slide down. I'd have gone faster, but I couldn't see anything. The green mist was thick, and there could be anything below. Whatever was down there, I didn't want to hit it too fast.

Travel the galaxy enough, and you see some strange weather. But this mist, this cloying green mist was wrong. There was something off about it.

The dark ground came up out of nowhere, and I slowed my descent as the hull abruptly ended. There were still five meters to the ground. I jumped to the landing strut, and slid down that.

When I touched down it was immediately clear that I was standing on the same stuff Deilani had found in the tear in the hull. It looked black under my suit light. The green mist swirled in a way that made it difficult not to see movement everywhere.

The silent surface of the planet was decidedly eerie. At first the isolation offered by our predicament had been calming, even a comfort to me. Not anymore.

We were all a long way from home.

I backed away from the side of the ship as the mist swirled around me. The green tendrils seemed to creep over my body, and irrationally I wanted to brush them away.

Beyond the mist above, the sky was dark. There were large, hard points of light among the stars, but they did little to illuminate the planet's black surface. We had at least a couple of suns on our hands, but depending on what time of day this was, it seemed as though they weren't very motivated.

I could see the graduates' lights in the mist as they climbed down the side of the freighter. Salmagard was the first to reach the bottom. She landed with grace that was amplified by her form-fitting white EV suit, and the way the mist seemed to soften everything. Deilani touched down next, then Nils. What Deilani lacked in experience, she made up for in determination. Unlike the lieutenant, Nils had nothing to prove, and he did not hurry down.

Salmagard had probably trained extensively for this kind of unconventional maneuvering; for Nils and Deilani that training would've been more cursory. Both the ensign's and the lieutenant's EV suits were marred by smudges from the hull, but Salmagard's was still pristine.

"Is the channel good?"

"Minor interference," Nils reported. "We can just boost it a little. It's not bad."

"We should've brought surface gear," Deilani said, looking up from the black ground. She knelt, running her gloved palm over the peculiar mineral. "It's irresponsible to just walk around out here like this. This stuff could eat through an EV for all we know. There's no sampling, no workup on this. What if this is acidic, or it reacts to synthetics?"

"Then we're in trouble. But we're not here to survey the place. Visibility's about three, maybe four meters. Watch your feet. Private, are you getting anything?"

"No, Admiral."

"Good. Keep it that way."

"Yes, Admiral."

Because of the limited visibility, it was difficult to see just how massive the freighter was, or even its true shape. I knew it was just a very long box, but being unable to see its form in the mist made it seem bigger. The vessel was half a kilometer long, far from the largest ship out there—but still substantial enough to look impressive. It loomed over us like a mountain.

Not all Ganraen ships were this uninviting. The ones I was used to certainly weren't, though the Commonwealth had a long way to go if it wanted to catch up to Evagard.

I led the trainees underneath the landers, making for the main airlocks. The outside of the ship was no more attractive than the inside. When it was new, the freighter had probably been a light gray. That had been a long time ago. Now it was covered in burns and corrosion, its uneven surfaces reduced to a mottled brown and black.

If there were clues about Tremma's sojourn on the surface, this was where we'd find them. Overhead, the bottom of the freighter looked badly neglected. Where the battered and blackened metal wasn't openly burned, it was chipped, dented, and pitted. This ship had not had an easy life.

I could see the trainees looking up at the plasma burns, and other indications that Tremma's old tub had taken more eventful trails than the average cargo freighter. Deilani had already seen the weapons being stored in containers that were, by Salmagard's own word, not intended for ordnance. The damage was done. Not that it mattered. Captain Tremma was dead.

I doubted the old freighter would ever leave this world.

I occasionally lost sight of the trainees in the mist; it was particularly dark beneath the ship.

"Wait a minute," Deilani said. I looked around but didn't see her.

"What is it?"

"Mineral formation. Have a look."

I spotted someone's light and followed it. The formation was nothing more than a thick spike of rock about a meter high. A short distance away was another, this one half as tall.

"You're right," I said. "That is unusual." It stood to reason that Deilani would find this interesting, but I didn't. We needed to find out what Tremma'd been up to with those explosives so we could get back inside, back to conserving our suit energy and oxygen. We didn't have time to be explorers.

"It's brittle," she added.

"Don't break other people's planets."

"Shut up."

I'd have thought of a retort, but I'd almost fallen over an abandoned grav cart. "Guys, on me."

Deilani hurried over and put her gloved hand on the cart's handle. "They left this out here?"

"They must have used it to move the 14-14." I pointed. "That way." The cart had left a clear trail in the thin shale covering the ground. We followed it until we hit a wall of crumbled stone scattered beneath the lip of the freighter's lower buffers, and even piled up against the hull—farther than we could see through the mist. It was as though there'd been an avalanche of the stuff.

Deilani was at a loss. So was I.

The trail led on, skirting a steep hill. I wanted to climb the hill, but the mist was all but opaque. The climb would be a foolish risk; a perforated suit at this point would put a real damper on things.

Instead we followed the trail around the hill. The black ground was cracked beneath our feet, and it sometimes felt unstable to me, though no one else seemed bothered.

The trail curved away from the hillside, and it was all we would have to find our way back to the ship. We could home in on one another, but not on the freighter itself.

We found another formation, this one far larger. Like the first two we'd seen, it was round at its base. The diameter had to be nearly ten meters. The green mist was too heavy to see exactly how tall it was. Based on the proportions of the ones we'd seen earlier, I guessed it was about fifty meters high.

These weren't spikes—they were spires.

We marveled at it. Only the base of the spire was visible, but it was easy enough to imagine what it might look like if we could see it clearly. Something nagged at me. It seemed more like a structure than a formation, but there were no tool marks. Deilani seemed certain it was natural.

"Movement," Salmagard reported, peering at the smooth surface.

"Where?"

"There's something wrong with the reading, sir. It says it's coming from the stone."

I was reluctant to argue with Evagardian technology, but there was also Evagardian judgment to consider.

We moved on, finding the blast site shortly after. Going by the damage that had been done with only a single cylinder of 14-14, we were *very* lucky that crate hadn't been closer to the shuttle.

We climbed a gentle rise to reach the crater, where visibility was better. It was hard to tell in the mist, but the blast zone was probably at least a hundred meters in diameter.

That wasn't what we were looking at. We were looking back toward the hill we'd followed all the way from the freighter.

It wasn't a hill. Well, it was—but it hadn't started out as one.

It was a spire like the ones we'd seen before, only larger, and lying on its side, shattered.

It had once stood where this crater was. I thought about the distance we'd walked, the additional wreckage, and how much of the spire could be piled on top of the freighter. This thing could have been over a kilometer high. Not very tall compared to modern structures, but for such a slender mineral formation . . . and Tremma had *blasted* it. He'd knocked it over.

I started putting things together.

"I know where we are," I said, surprising myself. All three of them turned to me. They were just dark shapes in the green mist, but I could see the glow of all three faceplates looking in my direction. "We're in unregulated space on the Evagardian side of Demenis. We're past Payne Station. I think this system's actually closer to Oasis. It's a class two with one decent-sized body, and we're on it. At least, I think it was class two. I don't remember."

"I've never heard of anything like this," Deilani said, sounding dubious.

"You wouldn't have. I don't even remember what it's called. The Empire hasn't got any interest in it. The surveys didn't come back very attractive. The planet was a rock. It interfered with scanner readings . . . It was more trouble than it was worth. Which is why it sounded so strange when the Commonwealth sent a colony ship here. I only remember because they mentioned these spires in the survey, but they just called them vertical formations or something. But this is definitely what they were talking about."

I let my breath out, a little impressed with myself. It felt good to know. I looked around at the planet's surface with new eyes. We were close to Demenis. And it fit—a slight deviation from our course to Payne Station could very possibly bring us out here.

It was coming together.

"How would you know about a Commonwealth survey?" Deilani asked.

"Word gets around," I said, waving a hand. "Frontier exploration isn't a secret, Lieutenant. Though there isn't much of it out here. Well, maybe there'll be more now that Oasis is gone."

"There's a Ganraen colony here?" Nils asked.

"There was supposed to be." I spoke as I began to make my way down the side of the crater; we still hadn't seen the true breadth of the damage.

"Why colonize a ball like this?" Nils asked, looking at the black ground and green mist. "What can you do with this? And so far out? There's no trade here. No jump routes."

"The war was still on." I shrugged.

"Desperation?"

"Or foresight . . . Oh," I said as I crested the top, mindful of my footing. I took in the true size of the base of what had once been a spire. My previous estimates had been too conservative. It was larger than any man-made structure on Old Earth. There were jagged openings in the floor of the crater, each several meters across.

"Did the 14-14 make those cavities?" Deilani asked.

"They were already here," I replied. The blast had made the crater, but it hadn't created these breaks in the ground. We were looking down into—into what? Pits? An underground cavern, now opened by the blast? I went to the nearest one and started climbing down.

"Where are you going?" Deilani asked, reaching out to stop me.

"Tremma must have had a reason to want to destroy this. I want to know what it was."

"If you go down there, we'll lose you on tracker."

"Then you'll have to come too."

"I don't suppose this colony of yours would like to let us call home?" Nils asked, moving past Deilani to climb down beside me. "Because that could solve all our problems."

"They could be all the way on the other side of the rock," Deilani said.

"They're not," I said. "That would be the dark side; I don't think they'd land their colony there. They're on this side, though that could still be a long way off. I don't remember how big this thing's supposed to be."

"The gravity's a little weak," Deilani said, picking her way down. "But this mineral is extraordinarily dense. I'd say it's got three times the mass of Marragardium."

"So it's probably not very big," Nils said.

"Maybe no larger than the Old Earth Luna."

"Or we could be way off," I interrupted. "But it's something to think about. My optics are acting up."

"Mine too."

"I'm switching off," Nils said, disgusted.

"Private, what's your scanner say?"

"It's picking up chemical heat and movement, Admiral."

That didn't seem likely; the reading had to be faulty—but now we knew why. It was the planet, not the equipment. "Lights on. Just looking at it, you wouldn't expect this stuff to be so porous."

"Agreed. This is highly unusual, and it's making me uncomfortable. We'd better use safety wires if we're going in there," Deilani said.

"Line to each other. If we all run one to the surface we'll get tangled."

Deilani watched me struggle with the suit's interface.

"First time?" she asked dryly.

I cleared my throat. "No, I just opened the wrong menu. It's been a while."

"Right."

Deilani held up her wrist to me, and I pressed mine to it, linking us with a silver wire. The lieutenant connected to Nils, who connected to Salmagard. The lines would play out to their limit—about a hundred meters each—or stop at a command. It would take several tons of force, or a plasma cutter to sever them.

Salmagard found a solid bit of rubble from the blast, and tied onto it.

"What are we trying to find down here?" Nils asked.

"I don't know, but I'm curious about exactly what our ship is sitting on. Aren't you?"

"You don't think the ground might be unstable, do you?" There was a definite note of panic in Nils' voice.

"That's exactly what I think. And this blast didn't help." I remembered that tremor we'd felt earlier, and my mouth went dry.

"Are you all right?" Salmagard asked me. She was close, looking through my faceplate.

"Don't worry about me," I told her.

We began to climb into the pit. It was tricky going; though dense, the rock did not seem especially strong. It sometimes came away in our hands, or gave beneath our feet. I kept thinking about how much the freighter weighed, sitting on this stuff.

The walls of the pit were the same black of the ground above, and it seemed to absorb our lights. We were five or six meters down when Deilani called our attention to the wall of the—cavern? Yes, that was what it was. We were in what I was thinking of as a main shaft, which was more or less vertical—but dozens, even hundreds, of small vents, some as little as half a meter across, pocked the sides, revealing that this rock was every bit as porous as I'd feared. Was the entire planet made of this dense, brittle mineral? Just the upper layer?

With what this place did to scanners, who could say?

We examined the mineral formation Deilani was indicating. Only a little was visible: it was a cloudy, vaguely greenish sort of crystal. It was the first thing we'd seen that wasn't black rock.

"Think there's a big vein of it? Maybe it's valuable," Nils said.

"If it is, it belongs to the Ganraen colonials. If they're really here." Deilani touched the edge of the crystal with her finger, and it crumbled away as fine dust. "Just as sturdy as the rest. Pretty, though."

"I don't see much going on down here; I don't know what I expected. Let's see how deep this shaft goes and pull out. Do any of you see any reason someone might want to blow all this up?"

"I got nothing, Admiral. It's just a cave." Nils put his hand on the wall. "Kind of a scary one, if I'm being honest. I don't like small spaces."

"Neither do I. Private?"

"No, Admiral."

Salmagard took a light stick from her pouch and synced it to her suit's AI. I watched her toss it over the ledge, into the dark. The light was bright, but it was quickly gone.

"Twenty meters."

"The mist's thinner down here. It's thickest on the surface," Deilani observed.

"Fifty meters. Impact," Salmagard said.

"That's it?"

"No, sir. It's just bounced off something. Sixty."

"Admiral," Nils said, and I turned to him. He was staying well back from the ledge, looking up at the opening far above. I could hear his discomfort in his voice. This strange honeycomb of black gave me the creeps. Watching our lights play over the smooth walls, I saw more of the crystals.

"Yeah?"

"If there *is* a Ganraen colony here . . ."

"One hundred meters. Three impacts. What was that?"

"What?" I glanced back at Salmagard, who had cocked her head.

"I thought I saw something, but it's nothing, sir." She sounded sheepish.

I knew what she meant. The dark was oppressive. Black walls, moving lights. It was like the mist on the surface; it always looked as if there was something moving.

I turned back to Nils.

"The colonists might not know we're here if these scanner issues are planet wide," he continued.

"From what I remember, they are. They wrote this place off. Long list of reasons this wasn't a good place to settle."

"If they don't know, then they're not going to show up here unless we give them a reason to."

"One hundred twenty-five meters," Salmagard said.

"One second, Ensign." I turned to Salmagard. "Is that it, Private?"

"Yes, Admiral. Full stop, but according to the short-range

sonics there is at least another hundred-meter vertical. The shaft appears to widen farther down."

I let out a low whistle. "That is a long way." I edged back a little. "What were you saying, Ensign?"

"Sir, we could try to contact the Ganraens. Or at the very least get their attention."

"With whom we were at war two weeks ago," Deilani said. "If their flagship hadn't crashed into their capitol dome, we still would be. Actually, we still are. Their surrender was only provisional. It's a cease-fire, not a peace treaty. It's not over until the Empress' peace talks."

I opened my mouth to change the subject, but Nils beat me to it.

"Lieutenant, these colonists may not even *know* about the cease-fire," he pointed out, panning his light toward the surface. "But we have the law on our side. We're not combatants under these circumstances."

"What if they don't see it that way?" Deilani asked.

"Their genes might not be as refined as Salmagard's," I said, "but they're still just people. We're *all* a long way from home out here. They'll help us. At the very least they'll be reasonable. And regardless of what they know about the war, if we play it right, I think they'll welcome us with open arms. How do you want to get their attention, Nils?"

"The com array, sir."

"The *com* array," I burst out. "Son of a *bitch.*"

"What?"

"I think that's what this is about. Look—we didn't land here by choice. Something happened that made the ship land, probably system failure. Something went wrong, and the computer woke up Tremma. The only reason he could've had to set us down would be that he thought we weren't safe flying—he must've been confused when he woke up to find us so far past our destination. He put down here. This spire"—I gestured—"must have seemed like a threat to our security scanner—if the rest of this planet is anything to go by, it wasn't very stable. The landing made it worse, and the scanners picked up on the danger. Tremma didn't want it falling on his ship. Definitely not on his com array—not with no shields, and him not knowing if he could even lift off this rock."

"So they came out here to knock it down?"

"Our scanners don't understand this stuff." I touched the wall. "Whatever he used to calculate the charge placement was wrong; he did what he was trying to prevent. The spire dropped right across our back, and you can bet that's where we picked up that damage. The upper decks are probably breached too. I wonder how much of this is piled up on the hull."

"But it didn't get the com array."

"Probably not—so I guess they succeeded. Sort of."

"They were probably treating it like, well, normal rock."

"Yeah." I took a deep breath. It felt good to have at least a measure of understanding of our circumstances. We knew where we were, and I was getting a feel for what had happened.

Now we were making progress.

"The scanners were acting up—okay, I'll buy it. But it still doesn't explain what killed them," Deilani said.

"Fire killed them."

"Shut up, Nils. You're right, Lieutenant. And on that note, we've followed in their footsteps exactly. I wonder if we're not walking the same path that got them into trouble. Lieutenant, my weapon." I held out my hand. She hesitated, then ejected the magazine and handed it over. I tossed the sidearm into the pit. That was one less accident waiting to happen. Tremma's incinerator unit had obviously been a liability, so a firearm was as well. We were better off without it.

"Admiral, I'm reading movement below."

"It's time to give the scanner a rest. Bad readings have wasted too much of our time already. Let's get out of here." I started the climb back up. The suit's cling charge didn't have much grip on the black rock, but there was no shortage of handholds. I was out of shape, but not so far gone that this feeble gravity could keep me down. The trick was not letting our wires get snagged. Easy on the way down, devilishly challenging on the way up.

At least the EVs were suited to this; the nanofabric was strong enough not to tear, and because the suits conformed perfectly to our bodies, there was nothing to snag on sharp outcroppings.

My soft lifestyle of late hadn't done me any favors. We'd barely started, and I was already out of breath.

There was another tremor, and this time there was nothing subtle about it. The rock shuddered. One of my handholds came loose, and I barely kept hold. Deilani held grimly on, and Nils swore loudly. There was a crunch as something behind us gave, maybe the ledge we'd been standing on just a minute ago.

The shaking stopped. My helmet clearly picked up the crashing of everything knocked loose by the tremor.

My skin had gotten hot, and I'd begun to sweat. I kept my jaw tight, watching little shards of the mineral tumble down the slope, into the dark.

"Stay calm," I said, trying to follow my own advice. "Just keep moving."

Coming down here hadn't been very bright. Nothing we were

learning was making our predicament seem any less perilous. I had to do better.

It took several minutes to reach the surface. The others clambered out after me, and wasted no time putting a few meters between themselves and the pit.

So the spire had been sitting on this deep cavity. Interesting.

I took a few deep breaths, checked my oxygen levels, and began to climb out of the crater. I'd had enough of it out here. I wanted to get back to the ship, but we wouldn't be going inside just yet.

"Let's get back," I told the trainees. "We need to visually confirm that the array is still intact. If it is, that might give us a play."

"With the colonists?" Deilani asked, staggering after me.

"Nils is right. They're our best chance."

"What happened to waiting for rescue?" Nils was out of breath.

"The situation's changed. Even if the Empire can track us here, which is by no means certain, it could take longer than I thought for them to get to us. Our chances are better with the colony."

"Our chances of being executed," Deilani said.

6

IT was easy to slide down the side of a ship. A lot of things were easy when gravity was on your side. The same could be said of time.

The climb back up the side of the freighter was arduous, but none of the trainees complained.

The length of the ship took even longer to traverse on the outside. Luckily, the damage from the fallen spire wasn't as bad as I'd feared. The material was dense and heavy, but its fragility prevented it from causing any serious harm to the armored freighter. Apart from the giant tear down the side of the hull, there was no other obvious damage. The com array was still intact. From the top of the ship I could see in the distance the hazy outlines of spires that were even more gargantuan than the one Tremma had knocked down. There were dozens of them. Without the mist it might have looked like a forest where every tree was as tall and elegant as the Protectorate Tower on Old Earth. The view made me think of cathedrals and basilicas, Old Earth temples to ancient belief systems.

It was an awesome sight beneath the ocean of stars and dim suns, even veiled by the mist. But this planet would never be more than a curiosity, unless this strangely dense mineral turned out to be good for something. It was too inhospitable.

Now that Evagard had annexed the Demenis system, that might give it some value in a trade, or transportation context—but I didn't see it working out. I'd only been here a couple hours and I already wanted off. I had a feeling most people would feel the same way.

Nils was still examining the array. Salmagard was nearby, admiring the view as well. Deilani paced restlessly, checking her O_2 counter.

"Are you low?"

"No," she snapped. She was.

"Ensign?"

"I think we can do it, Admiral. We can get a ping off easily—that's no problem. I'm not sure we can get a real signal going, though," Nils said.

"Why not?"

"The power supply. There's plenty of stuff we can try to use, but something strong and *stable* enough to carry—that I don't know about."

"If we can locate the colonists, we can try to contact them directly. There has to be something we can broadcast with on this thing—we just have to find it. Can we go inside now?"

"Yes, sir. I know what I need to look for."

It took a full ten minutes to get back to the other end of the freighter, climb down the side, and make our way in through the tear. I would never take airlocks and lifts for granted again.

Nils set off to find what he needed to jury-rig the array, and I told Deilani to help him. Salmagard went back to stockpiling supplies, and I went back to thinking about details.

Like Nils said, sending a ping was easy. But if it found something, we'd only know if we had a way to pick it up when it bounced back, and something that could display that result. The com relay itself was part of the ship's systems, so it couldn't be trusted.

We'd have to use Tremma's personal reader. My first order of business was to retrieve it from his cabin and take it to our headquarters at Medical. Because we'd been outside, Deilani had released more decontamination nanomachines. They did their jobs well, but they also made my throat scratchy.

It still felt good to have my helmet deactivated.

The air in the freighter still tasted fresh by spacecraft standards. It had been through recyclers a thousand times, but it beat the alternative. Having literally scaled the side, walked across the top and along the length of this freighter, I knew how big it was, and vaguely how much breathable air was in it. That was encouraging, but even if things went well, there was a good chance we'd need all we could get.

Nils was going to have to be the one to use Tremma's reader to interpret the results of our ping. I set out to find him, though trekking through the freighter alone was starting to get to me.

The dim, empty corridors were no longer sinister. Now they were downright malevolent. My desire to get off this ship was growing by the minute. Without Nils to navigate, I had to slow down and be sure I was going the right way.

It wasn't as if I didn't know how to find my way around, but larger commercial vessels with power tended to give you plenty of help. Tremma's freighter gave me nothing but identical passage after identical passage. Captain Tremma's untimely death was at the front of my mind.

The back of my neck tingled, and I was getting sore from looking over my shoulder.

We still didn't have an explanation for what had happened in that airlock. A simple accident wasn't enough. Sabotage to the tech suits? I was having trouble picturing it. And why? There was simply no plausible explanation.

I found Nils with the com array and handed off the console to him. My limited technical skills would have to be put to work finding ways to extend the lives of our EV suits.

Using a ping to determine the Ganraen colony's location was simple. They might detect the ping and get interested, but we couldn't count on that. We'd have to do something less ambiguous, like sending an SOS. Building a beacon from scratch would be a big job, but Nils thought he was up to it. He needed this, something to occupy his mind so he wouldn't have to spend too much time alone with his nerves.

Salmagard was in Medical, struggling under the weight of a twenty-gallon cylinder of distilled water. She had it balanced across her shoulders, but was bent with the weight. I helped her set it down.

"Is this what good genes do? They make you think you're an ant?"

"A what?"

"Uh—an ant. An Old Earth organism able to lift more than its own weight. A lot of people regard them as our evolutionary superiors."

"Oh, yes." She *was* Earth-born, after all.

"Carrying water, probably not what your family had in mind for you. Your bloodline's pretty high tier, right?"

She shook her head. "No, sir."

I raised an eyebrow. "Really?"

"No, Admiral."

"But you look just like the Duchess. Don't tell me I'm imagining it."

Salmagard's resemblance to the paintings and images of the Grand Duchess was so profound that I'd just assumed she was carrying her genes, and so had Deilani and Nils. I knew there were supposed to be a couple extremely privileged bloodlines whose purpose was to make sure that the Duchess' DNA stayed alive.

She reddened slightly. "The resemblance is deliberate."

It took me a moment to catch her meaning. "You modified your appearance?"

"*I* didn't. It's part of an initiative to integrate my caste with the Service."

"But the gentry's been in the Service for ages. Aristocrats make up half the officer corps."

"To integrate us outside that role," Salmagard said.

"Ah. Well, that's been a long time coming, but to design the way the candidates look?" It was typically Evagardian; they were making a big show about setting the precedent of enlisted aristocrats. Harmless for the most part, and pleasingly progressive—but not terribly convenient for the people like Salmagard who ended up as showpieces styled after historical figures.

She looked uncomfortable. "*I* was not consulted." She touched her face—which I now realized was not hers at all. It didn't just look like the face of the great woman, it *was* the face of the Grand Duchess. "We all have the faces of Heroes of the Unification." She was referring to the power struggle on Old Earth during the twenty-first century. Its outcome—influenced by the young woman whose face Private Salmagard now wore—had decided mankind's path for the centuries that followed.

Evagard never stopped honoring its heroes. Hell, the new flagship was called the *Julian*. Half the planets and systems in the Empire were named after these people.

"The modification is purely aesthetic. We're otherwise ourselves," she added.

"What tier are you?"

"Ninth."

"And from Old Earth." So she was at the lower end of the gentry spectrum; the highest I'd ever seen had been a fifth tier—and I'd barely gotten a glimpse of her. Her family had to be wealthy.

"We just call it Earth," Salmagard said mildly.

I snorted. "You would."

Ninth. That was still light-years above the vast majority of imperials.

"So whose genes have you got? Not the Duchess'?"

"The Guardian's." Salmagard said it with a note of pride.

"I didn't know she had a line."

"She doesn't, but her DNA has been part of the core since before the Unification. She was bred for the Heir." So she was outwardly identical to the Grand Duchess, but genetically she was the normal product of her ancestry, which had at one point been touched by the genes of one of the great heroes. And now she was in the Imperial Service, in negotiations.

"There's no telling where you'll end up, is there?" I ran my hand through my hair. "I bet you wish you'd gone a different way. Not that I can talk."

"No, Admiral. My family is long overdue to be represented in service of the Empress."

"Is that why your parents wanted this?"

She nodded. "My family was rewarded."

"Were you tenth tier before your parents accepted this honor on your behalf?"

She nodded. "Yes, Admiral."

"Then they owe you a lot. But they must still have convinced you to serve somehow. And negotiations, of all things?"

"Because of my genes, it was thought I might be predisposed."

That made sense. The Guardian had been the greatest warrior in the history of the human species. Or at least, that was how imperial history liked to put it. The legends were probably exaggerated. "Even so, why would you choose this over Earth?"

Salmagard folded her hands behind her back and smiled. It was a small smile. Controlled—she had been brought up and then trained not to express herself, but apparently this so amused her that even she couldn't help but show it.

"What is it?" I asked, seeing the way she was looking at me.

She hesitated, obviously debating internally.

"Forget propriety," I told her. "I'm curious. Tell me what's on your mind."

She met my eyes. "You keep doing that," she said. "It's noticeable."

I looked down at my hand, realizing what she meant. I was so used to brushing my hair out of my eyes that it had become a reflex. Now that my hair was short, there was no need. But every time I moved my head a certain way, there was my hand with nothing to do. It was just muscle memory. My head also felt curiously light.

I'd get used to it eventually.

I sighed. "You're right. I need to be careful." I returned her gaze. "Do you think I should shave?"

"I couldn't possibly comment, sir." At least there was a hint of a smile there, if only for a moment.

"This is how I looked before," I said. "More or less. What do you think?"

"It's more to my liking, sir. What do you mean 'before'?"

"Before all this." I gestured at myself. "Is it all right for you to have a preference?"

"Do you know anything about being the first daughter of an Earth family?"

Suddenly a tremor rocked the ship. The medbay tilted around us. I wasn't ready for it, but Salmagard caught me before I could fall, and we struck the bulkhead, struggling to stay upright. Salmagard's water jug slammed into the metal with a bang, rebounding across the room.

After the initial jerk, there was a slow lean as the deck shifted arduously underfoot. The jug started to roll back. Equipment was everywhere, and we watched it slide slowly across the deck. I could feel a subtle vibration.

I kept my eyes open. I knew what I'd see if I closed them.

The ship came to a stop with us listing at about a thirty-degree angle. I let out my breath. I was still clinging to Salmagard, and she was looking at me questioningly.

"In case there was another one," I said defensively, and let her go. If I'd had half her poise, Deilani never would have doubted I was an officer. Admiral still would've been a tough sell, but it would've been a start.

But poise had never really been my thing. Something to work on if I lived long enough.

Walking, and even just staying on our feet, was difficult. The deck was now a hill. EV boots gave excellent purchase, but it still felt like a hard climb.

None of that was important; I'd heard Deilani's cry over the com when the tremor started.

"Nils?" I asked into the com. He was closer to Deilani than we were; if she was in trouble, he needed to take notice.

"Busy, Admiral."

It sounded like he had.

I was already in the corridor, running as fast as the dark, slanted floor would allow. The ensign's voice sounded strained. "Hold on," he ground out. "I've got you."

"Are you okay?"

"We need you," he gasped.

I ran faster. The bulkhead that opened to the planet's surface was now angled noticeably downward, making it more difficult to get out. I put more charge into my gloves, making my way up the side of the freighter as fast as I could. Salmagard was right behind me, but I was too focused on speed to worry about her.

I clambered over the top and took off at a sprint made awkward by the magnetism in my boots, and the planet's unfamiliar gravity. It was foolish to run through the mist, but I ignored that; the ensign didn't sound good. I could see distant spires around us, stars above, and the metal underfoot seemed to stretch on forever. I was gasping for breath, and so was Nils.

The array was still there, but now it was leaning dangerously.

"Where are you?" I looked all around, but there was nothing to see but green.

"Over here, down *here*," Nils hissed. I immediately realized what must have happened. I whirled and slid down the now-sloped deck. There was the ensign, clutching Tremma's reader to his chest with one arm and using the other to hold on to Deilani.

The lieutenant dangled over . . . absolutely nothing.

All the mist in the galaxy couldn't hide that black void. The ground had fallen away completely. There was nothing down there but mist and the dark. I stared for a moment, stunned, then Salmagard was there, and I joined her. Together, we lifted Nils over the lip of the hull, and he brought Deilani with him. We dragged them a couple meters back, away from the edge.

The lieutenant was shaking. I didn't blame her. Looking down, you'd think you could fall straight to the center of the planet. I clapped Nils on the shoulder. He'd done well. I hadn't pegged him for the heroic type.

I could picture what had happened: the starboard side of the freighter had simply dropped, flinging them from the array. Nils even had the presence of mind to hold on to the reader. Did that mean he had something?

I let him collect himself. Salmagard was hovering over Deilani, who was still on her hands and knees. She'd put full charge in both her gloves, pressed flat to the hull. I hoped we wouldn't have to pry her off, though I couldn't blame her.

I eyed the lip of the freighter. I was stalling. I didn't want to look down there again.

Leaving Nils on the deck, I got up and went gingerly to the

edge to see how bad it was. The hole really was as deep and black as it looked at first glance. Was the whole planet like this? That wasn't important. What mattered was that the ground *under the ship* was like this. A large amount of surface down there appeared to have just fallen away, and more green mist was emerging from it.

Salmagard joined me.

"Admiral?" It was subtle, but even she couldn't hide how shaken she was.

It was difficult to see, but we were poised on the rim of the chasm. It wouldn't take much for the freighter to just slide in. Seismic activity much less enthusiastic than what we'd just experienced could be the end of us.

Air and water had become the least of our problems.

"I suppose the gear went over the side?" I said.

"Yes, sir." Nils was still sprawled on his back, massaging his shoulder and breathing hard. "But I got the ping off."

"And?"

"There's something out there."

I closed my eyes and let out my breath. Holding out indefinitely for rescue had seemed reasonable when the planet had been behaving itself. Now we needed to do better. "Can you place it?"

"Maybe. Roughly."

"Good." I kept breathing. One breath at a time. "That's good, Nils. Because we can't stay here."

7

IT took some effort to coax Deilani off the hull, a task made even more difficult by the angle of the freighter. Nils had to physically guide her back inside the ship. The lieutenant wasn't the type to rattle easily, but hanging over that abyss had gotten to her. Maybe she had a thing about heights. Her movements were stiff, her face locked in a glassy stare very different from the one she usually had for me.

By the time we reached Medical she'd begun to pull herself together.

I tilted an examination table, locked it in position, and sat down. The angle of the ship was disorienting.

Nils was experimentally working his shoulder, and Deilani had begun to pace, which was a good sign. She absently drummed the fingers of her left hand on her thigh. I'd seen her do that before. It was a calming ritual for her. I hoped it was working.

Salmagard was by the door, hands behind her back, head bowed. That was the only indication that she was feeling fear, not something someone with her background probably had much experience with.

It was good to have the helmet off, but I still felt sick. I didn't know if it was the state of my health, or the perilous nature of our situation. Maybe it was just a guilty conscience. Plenty of that to go around.

"Nils, tell me what you got."

"The ping was received, so there's definitely a com array out there somewhere. That's all I can say for sure. There wasn't *time*. Everything else went over the side."

"Can you track it?"

"I don't know. Maybe."

"You better do it, because this boat could go anytime, and it looked like a long way down. Come on, people. Focus. If we don't do something, we really are finished."

"*Do* what?" Deilani snapped. "The ship is dead. The *planet* is dead."

"Not completely," Nils shot back. He had the console in his lap now. "But, Admiral, there's no navigational information for this planet, nothing for me to link the ping to." He gestured. "There's no map, and no way to orient ourselves. All I can do is set an arbitrary north and say the ping was received by something *that way*." He waved his arm and gave me a helpless look.

"How far?"

He stared at me in disbelief, realized I wasn't kidding, and looked down at his screen. He chewed his lip. "I might actually be able to calculate that."

"I'd get on it."

"This is insane," Deilani said.

"You'd rather stay here?"

"What's the alternative?"

"If this thing goes, that fall isn't survivable. We could strap in, find a way to preserve ourselves, *maybe*—but not the equipment and supplies we'll need. What if the ship ended up upside down? What if we're buried?"

"The fleet could get us out," Deilani said, rubbing at her temples.

"Exhume us, more like. Lieutenant, think about it. Just think about what would happen if there was another quake, and this ship fell into that chasm."

"Then let's secure it."

"To what? One of the spires? There's nothing on this planet solid enough to anchor a ship this size. Even the ground can't support us. If we *were* going to try to ride it out here, we'd have preparations to make and no guarantee of time. It could happen any second."

"All right! Let's hear *your* plan." She was still off balance from what had just happened. I couldn't blame her for being frayed. Just looking down at the chasm had been enough to make me feel ill.

"Nils?" I said. The ensign was gazing at the screen, looking dazed. "Nils!"

"I've run it four times," he said.

"What? What have you got?"

"Whatever picked up the signal is . . . a ways off."

"How far?"

"Ninety . . . ninety-eight hundred kilometers. Give or take." He continued to gaze at the screen. "Give or take," he repeated. "I don't know how big the planet is, so I just have to guess when I'm trying to compensate for curvature."

That quieted everyone down. I had pictured us strolling across the surface of the planet, trailing a caravan of gravity carts laden with oxygen.

But that was a little farther than walking distance.

"Right," Deilani said, squaring herself. "We get ready to ride this out. We'll need electromagnetic binders to secure our equipment and supplies, and a way to protect ourselves."

She was right. It was the very definition of a long shot, but it was the only shot. The air and the water were in the freighter, so the freighter was where we had to stay. It would certainly be a shift in lifestyle for me, but it wouldn't be the first time.

"Then we just strap in and wait to fall?" Nils asked.

"No," Deilani said. "We instigate it ourselves. The tremors only started after the shuttle blew; that means the shock conductors work fine, even without power. We set off our own charge. Maybe we can even place it so we go down facing the right way. We can't just take our chances—we have to try to get ahead of this."

That was a thought. This was all madness, of course—the odds of any of it working were exceedingly slim, but it was something like a plan. My plan, to hold out until rescue, sounded sensible and conservative in comparison, but it was still a reach. I had to keep an open mind.

Our lack of power would make us difficult to find, and without knowing how misdirected the imperials were in regard to our location, it could be a long time before we were found. And being found by imperials wasn't necessarily the best outcome. In fact, I wasn't really sure if it was preferable to just punching out here on this spiky rock.

I groaned. This—*this*—was what I had waiting for me? I'd come a long way to be stuck in a fix like this. I'd gotten so close; it didn't seem fair. The ship was huge; there had to be something we could use, something to give us an advantage. We probably had enough illegal weapons on the ship for a small war, but there was no one here to fight.

Still, it gave me an idea.

"Guys," I said. "We're forgetting something."

"What?" They all looked at me hopefully; it wasn't lost on Nils and Salmagard that Deilani's plan was thin at best. Even Deilani didn't like it, but she'd been trained to take charge, and that was what she was trying to do.

"We've forgotten that we're sitting in a freighter full of ordnance."

"Weapons?" Nils looked puzzled.

Deilani shut him up with a look and turned to me. "How can that help us?"

"Some of those containers were pretty big. There might be something we can use. Nils, call up the manifest."

"Uh—yes, Admiral. But I'm not reading any weapons here. These are imperial trade commodities, and according to the log, it's all meant for Free Trade space. It looks like after Payne Station the next stop was the Bazaar."

"That's just for show. There might be some Evagardian goods on this ship, but not what's listed there. The real manifest is there— it's just encrypted or hidden or something. I know you can get at it. Don't," I said, cutting him off. "Don't waste your breath.

Nobody gets as good as you are from school, even an imperial school. And besides, you're a maintenance tech, not a systems tech. You're too good to be all legit."

He gazed at me, face pale. "Reformed," he said after a moment.

"Nobody's judging you." I jerked a thumb at Deilani. "Except her. But you get used to it."

Nils took a deep breath and looked back at the screen. "I don't have any tools for this. The best I can do is . . . tricking it. It's risky. This is the only reader we've got."

"We could be dead in five minutes, Ensign. Throw the damn dice."

"Yes, Admiral. Just let me think." He was sweating.

Salmagard bowed her head again. Deilani had gone back to pacing.

"Don't take too long." I had a feeling the decisions we made here and now were going to be significant with regard to our collective futures. It was a lot of pressure, knowing that it might be possible for us to get through this, but only if we did everything right, and in time.

I was used to that kind of pressure. They weren't.

Salmagard was still and calm, but now her eyes were fixed on Nils. Even the Empire couldn't breed out nerves.

"I'll be damned," Nils said. "I seriously didn't expect that to work. This guy needs to update his systems." Just as I'd had a glimpse of the real Salmagard before, now I saw the real Nils. He spoke mildly, but there was triumph in his eyes. It was easy to picture him in his life before the Service, sitting in sustenance housing somewhere, wreaking havoc deep in the nets.

"Tremma's old-fashioned, obviously. Or he was, at any rate. Have you got it?"

"Looks that way. But these are mostly weapons from Commonwealth systems. A lot of Isakan stuff."

"Why don't you let me?" I asked, holding out my hand. He gave me a look, then glanced at Deilani, who had gone stony. He gave me the console, and I looked at the manifest.

Small arms, missiles, explosives, weapon systems to be mounted on every type of ship. Armor. Lots of armor. Indeed, only a little of it was imperial.

There was a crawler, but it was short range. It would never take us ten thousand kilometers . . . Gravity shields, EMP shields, EMP warheads . . . Like 14-14, some of this stuff wasn't meant to be transported without proper military procedure. The implications of Tremma's cargo would probably be lost on Nils. The graduates didn't have the context or the perspective to make sense of this, but I had a pretty good idea about the sorts of false-flag operations that Tremma had probably been up to before the cease-fire. I stayed on task. Deilani was hovering at my shoulder, and I leaned to let her see as well. The input of an officer couldn't hurt.

"Oh," I said.

"What?" Nils looked up sharply.

I pointed at the readout. "There's a personnel carrier. It's a flyer."

"What kind?"

"It says Avenger. Do you know it?"

"That's a Luna series."

"That's pretty much one of ours. It shouldn't be too different from imperial carriers," I said, thinking quickly.

"But it's still a flyer; we need a pilot," Nils pointed out.

"I can fly it," I said absently. "As long as it's ready to go. But it probably will be. Guys, if we have a chance, this is it."

"Will its propulsion even work on this surface?" Deilani asked, but she wasn't being contrary. There was hope in her voice.

"It's got a gravity drive. Why wouldn't it? This can work."

"Just because it's here doesn't mean it's ready to fly," Nils said. "It could be in pieces."

He still didn't quite grasp the realities of this freighter. This equipment was useless if it wasn't ready for action. That was all right. "It won't be," I told him. "We'll need to fuel it and get it online, but it'll be ready to go. The weapons systems won't be installed, but that won't keep us out of the air."

"What do we do?"

"Start by finding it. It shouldn't be hard. There can't be many containers down there big enough to hold it. Let's go." I was already on my feet and moving; without a second to spare, everything we did from this point forward had to be at top speed.

The dark, narrow Ganraen corridors felt tighter and more stifling now. With the clock ticking, they seemed longer as we raced down to the main cargo bay. There was always another panel hanging from the ceiling, or loose grate to trip on. I was sick of climbing ladders, and everything had been knocked askew when the ship tilted.

The crate for the flyer was the size of a building, and it had survived the blast from the shuttle. I had no idea how to open it, but there was a human-sized hatch in the side, which we were able to unseal.

Inside, our hand-lights showed us the personnel carrier. Just the sight of it gave me a spark of hope. It wasn't some featherweight combat craft—it was an air shuttle. It would have some range. Not much, but maybe enough. Ten thousand kilometers? I wasn't sure—but its effective range would be doubled because we weren't coming back. It was a chance, which was more than we had waiting for us if we stayed here.

The loading ramp at the rear of the flyer was already down, and the interior passenger area was lit with soft blue emergency lights. It was spacious, even comfortable. There was combat seating, impact padding, and carbon viewports. It smelled new. Luna engineering was an enormous step up from most of what you'd find in the Commonwealth. Compared to Tremma's freighter, the Avenger's interior was like a palace. I made my way to the cockpit to check the systems.

Sure enough, there were no fuel cells, but we could take care of that with the leftovers from the deceased shuttle. The computer didn't need anything but pilot officer codes, which I could provide from Tremma, or failing that, probably override. I'd never flown something like this, but I could wing it.

"We're in business," I said.

"What's the plan?" Deilani asked.

I thought about it. "We're at the wrong end of the bay. We need to get this thing over there in the open, where it can face the doors."

"There's no way to clear the shuttle wreckage from the launch zone."

"We don't need a launch zone. It doesn't matter what the thrusters do to what's behind us—we aren't coming back. We need the arm loader. You'll need a good power source for that, Nils."

He held up the reader. "It'll be sloppy, but I can do it. There are a lot of energy cells in these crates. There'll be something big enough to get the cargo system running."

"Are you up to operating it? It can't be as easy as the AI makes it look."

The cargo system was little more than an arm that ran on a series of rails on the ceiling, with claws that would latch onto crates and move them around. It was meant to be run by a computer.

"Only one way to find out, Admiral." Nils had that wild look again. I wasn't sure I liked that.

"Get on it. Go." I pointed meaningfully. Off he went, back through the passenger space and down the ramp.

I looked at Deilani and Salmagard. "We've got work to do too. Lieutenant, use this computer to find our range. Find out if it'll get us there."

"And if it won't?"

"You're an officer," I said. "Act like it."

She gave me a funny look, then sat down and keyed up the systems.

"My orders, Admiral?" Salmagard asked as we descended the ramp.

I panned my light around the inside of the Avenger's container. There was nothing here but the flyer itself, and two large crates that didn't look like what we needed. "Fuel cells," I said. "We can't go anywhere without fuel. We'll use the shuttle's reserves—they should still be around. Find a grav cart and meet me at the launch zone. We should be able to move a cell between the two of us."

Salmagard jogged off down the row of containers while I headed for the nearest bay wall before remembering that no power meant I couldn't use a console to locate the reserve cells for the freighter's shuttle. I'd have to find them the old-fashioned way, but they couldn't be far.

Deilani's voice came over the com. "This FPC isn't intended for long-range operations. It's a stealth model, meant for ground insertion, launched from a mobile platform. It won't take us far."

"Take a look at the fuel economy supposing we disable the stealth functions."

"That would buy us some flight time, I suppose . . ." A brief pause. "We'll need to keep the recyclers online, won't we?"

"Too early to say."

"I can disable weapons systems?"

"Of course. It doesn't even have weapons mounted."

The channel shifted; Deilani had just made the conversation private. "Admiral, you do realize that if we *do* this, we'll be walking right into the hands of the Ganraens."

"We've been over this. They're colonists, not soldiers. With a little luck, they'll treat us like the wayfarers we are."

"But hadn't we better have some kind of plan? They might be your people, but do they know that? You should be as worried as we are."

The propaganda had really gotten to her. She really thought these people might go straight to hostilities, when in truth the Ganraen colonists would just be curious and puzzled. They'd be wary. They might even detain us. They wouldn't hurt us, but Deilani could see them only as the enemy.

The graduates had been in training during the war. They had been heavily exposed to the Evagardian wartime views of the Commonwealth, which were less than flattering. The Empire liked to paint the Commonwealth as mad and corrupt, which, to be fair, was partially true. They also liked to point out that the royals would hire private military to fight their war for them, which Evagardians considered impolite.

None of that meant that these colonists were rabid animals that would murder us the moment we showed our faces.

"We couldn't fight an entire colony even if we wanted to," I said. "We've got a cease-fire. They're people just like you. Instead of an Empress, they have their Royals. Their ships are ugly and they aren't as excited about their DNA as imperials, but they're just as civilized as you or me. It'll be fine. Now, how far can that thing take us?"

"Normal operational range is about twenty-five hundred kilometers," Deilani sighed. "So make that five thousand."

"That's not much." But it made sense—this flyer was supposed to deploy from a strategic carrier.

"If we cut the stealth systems, that will give us more. If we fly at the most energy-efficient speed, we can get even more," Deilani told me. "But there's no atmosphere, so when we're out, we're out. There's no glide, no controlled descent. We have to land it before we go dry."

"The AI will force us to. It won't let us just drop out of the sky. So with everything you can do to max our range, how much does that buy?"

"I think—if you can fly this thing—if we went about it the right way, we'll still be five or six hundred short. And that would be a forced landing."

"Damn it, that's *almost* there."

"It's still a long way," she reminded me. "Maybe it doesn't sound like much, but it would take more than a week on foot."

"Yeah, but it's not *so far* that we can't try to figure something out."

"Even in this gravity, making that kind of hike isn't realistic. We don't even know the terrain," she scoffed. I couldn't blame her for putting up this resistance. On top of being a long shot, a trek like that wasn't likely to be much fun.

"We have the stamina," I said, hoping it was true.

"Maybe. But not the oxygen," Deilani countered.

Now I was the one pacing. "Are you sure? There is a *lot* of air on this ship—more than enough to get us there. What if we could find a way to take some with us?"

Deilani groaned over the com. "I *know*, but the problem is the EV suits. There might be a way to fill EV cartridges, but that's a specialized process—it's just like EV suit maintenance. It's got to be done by techs who know what they're doing and have specialized equipment. EV maintenance isn't its own career field because it's so easy, Admiral. It's not something we can do ourselves. If we try to jury-rig something, it's going to be extremely inefficient, and we'll lose as much air as we get to breathe. We can't carry enough *and* get it from standard tanks into these suits."

So our fancy EV suits were the problem.

"What if we used grav carts? Or changed into tech suits?"

"Tech suits would slow us down too much. They're for working, not walking. And grav carts can't handle anything but smooth terrain."

"Damn. Good point."

"It was a good idea," she said, surprising me. Was Deilani trying to comfort me?

"If carts are no good, then just work the numbers on what we can carry on our backs."

"I can't do that without knowing our transfer rate from O_2 tanks."

"Estimate. Be pessimistic if you have to."

"Even being optimistic, this plan will not work. It *won't*. So what do we do now?"

"Stay positive, Lieutenant. I'll figure something out."

8

PROMISING to think of something was easier than doing it. I could talk big all I wanted, but that wouldn't make six hundred kilometers any more manageable.

Salmagard found me sitting against the bulkhead by the lockers containing the reserve cells.

"Admiral?" She was standing over me with a gravity cart. I still couldn't read her. She was trusting me, and giving me more credit than I deserved. But under the circumstances, she didn't really have a choice.

"Right," I said, and got up, swallowing my nausea. This was pointless, but I couldn't tell her that. I couldn't tell Nils, either. They were working like people with hope.

I was boxed in, and I felt stifled. I was sweating despite my EV suit's efforts to cool me down. My mouth was dry. "Let's get started on these," I said. "We have to break them open."

It took both of us and a metal bar to lever open the lockup that housed the fuel cells. The cells themselves were hot to the touch, and even heavier than expected. The cart dipped noticeably under the weight.

We pushed the cell back to the Avenger and managed to install it, though it left us with burning muscles and aching backs. Salmagard didn't complain, so I didn't either.

There were three more to go. Before we could leave the container, Nils' voice was on the com.

"Hey—hey, where is everyone?"

"We're at the flyer," I replied.

"You're in the crate?"

"Yeah."

"Grab onto something."

"Wait—wait, don't—not with us *in here*," I hissed, but the container gave a jerk, and Salmagard and I were staggering for balance. I grabbed her and held on to one of the Avenger's landing struts as we swung wildly.

"Can't wait," Nils was saying. "Cell's draining right in front of me. I'm literally watching the readout go down. Got to do this now."

Nils put us down gently enough that there were no fatalities, but there was still plenty of pain.

"Okay," he said, sounding breathless, but invigorated. "That was pretty easy."

I wondered where he was. The robotic arm used to move the containers wasn't meant to be operated by hand—and if it was, then it would be with a feed. No power, no feeds. That meant Nils had to be somewhere from which he could see the entire bay. Somewhere high up. "Everybody needs to stay inside the flyer," he said.

Salmagard and I staggered up the ramp and grabbed handholds.

"I'm going to crack the box."

It was good that he'd thought to do that; I'd forgotten that to use the Avenger we'd first have to get it out of the container. There was a loud hiss, and the four walls fell away. The roof of the container remained suspended above, attached to the arm. The crane Nils was controlling moved it aside and dropped it with a resounding boom.

The freighter lurched. Metal groaned.

"Easy!" I shouted.

"Sorry," Nils said, though it came out as a squeak.

I hurried down the ramp to take stock of things. He'd moved us nearly to the end of the bay. We were now in the open, and the Avenger was facing the main doors. They weren't meant for launching vehicles, but they would do. The Ganraen Royal emblem stamped on the doors was massive, but faded with age.

He'd also moved us closer to the reserve cells. That would be useful if this plan wasn't already dead in the water. We simply didn't have the range we needed to reach the colony. I rubbed at my eyes.

I had to come clean with them. I'd tried. I had *tried* to help these three. This was just the hand we'd been dealt, and it was my fault. I couldn't make it right, but I could at least tell them the truth.

I stopped myself there, and turned to look back at the Avenger. Salmagard was descending the ramp with Deilani just behind her. I looked at the aircraft. The wings, the thrusters, the roof. Not especially broad, but broad enough?

"We're not done," I said, turning to Deilani.

"What?"

"We can do it. We can cover that distance. There's a way." I turned away and keyed the com. "Nils," I said. "There was a crawler on the manifest. Find it and crack it open while the arm still has juice."

"Crawler? But why?"

"Do it!"

"Yes, Admiral!" I motioned to the girls and started to run.

Above, the arm swung ahead of us, lowering to open a sizable— but not *too* sizable—crate. The walls thudded down, and Nils set down the roof instead of dropping it.

Inside was a terrain crawler. It was an Evagardian model, wearing a white-and-gray military pattern. Third Fleet markings. Surface ops. There were six wheels and seating for five. There was a mounting for a large weapon of some sort, and the fuel cells were strapped to the side.

We wouldn't even have to look for them.

"Nils, I want you to pick this up with the arm, and put it on top of the flyer."

"Excuse me?"

"You heard me, Ensign. The flyer can't take us all the way. We'll need a boost for those last few kilometers."

"On *top* of the personnel carrier?"

"People have been strapping things to the top of vehicles for centuries," I said.

"To *aircraft*?"

"It's a little unconventional, but it's a combat aircraft—it can handle it. And the gravity's light."

"It'll cost us fuel economy."

"Maybe it'll make up for it. It's no heavier than the weapons would be. It just brings us up to normal weight."

"It's an assault crawler. It's not meant for distance. Will it take us far enough on just those cells?" Deilani asked me.

That got us questioning looks from the ensign and Salmagard; they hadn't heard our conversation from earlier. They didn't know exactly how far we had to go.

"I don't know. We'll find out."

"We'll *find out*?"

"Hey," Nils cut in. "This thing is no good—I mean, it is—but it can't climb a mountain, and it can't get us across, say, a big trench. It can't swim."

"No oceans," I said. I was pretty sure I remembered that from the survey. "At least, I don't think there are. As for the rest—well, the crawler has a jumper, and in this gravity, that'll give us at least a little play if we need it."

"We're still gambling," Deilani said.

"We're gambling every second we stay here," I told her. "The ship could fall anytime. Do you want to die out there giving it a shot, or do you want to die down there waiting for help that might not come?"

"We don't even know if there are any people out there." Deilani was doing her best not to panic, but fear was bubbling to the surface. I didn't blame her, but we didn't have time.

"There's *something* out there," I said.

"All it did was pick up the signal—it could just be a probe. We don't have anything but your word to go on. You say there's a colony out there, but what if it's something else?"

"Like what?" I asked, genuinely curious.

"Like a military base."

"Then you'll fit right in."

"It's not a probe," Nils cut in. "A probe wouldn't have registered. Whatever's out there has a real com array. That still works," he added, as though impressed that Ganraen technology could even do that much. "And if there was a Commonwealth base here, we'd know about it. We all know how the front line stands—or how it stood before the cease-fire."

"We're close to Demenis," Deilani countered. "There could be bad people out there. Maybe your people," she said to me.

"So I'm a pirate now? Come on, Lieutenant. Enough."

"All right." Deilani put up her hands. "I'm sorry, all right?" She meant it. At first she'd felt obliged to contradict me, and now to play devil's advocate. But the time for arguing had come and gone a while ago.

"I'm all for trying to do this right," I told her plainly. "But we need to be together on this one. If this plan is worse than staying here, it can't be by much." I shrugged. "That's all I got. Are you coming or not?"

She nodded, eyes distant. "I'm with you."

Nils needed to hear that; his relief was audible over the com.

"Ensign, make it happen—put the crawler on the flyer. We'll lock it in with binders. We'll have to bring plenty of them, because we're going to put as many O_2 tanks as we can on that thing before we go. Lieutenant—everything we stockpiled in Medical—bring it up here and get it aboard. Private, we've got three more cells. Everybody go."

I had to be forgetting things, but I wasn't going to stop and worry about it. There wasn't time to think of everything; it was time for action.

Now that the plan was merely ambiguous instead of downright hopeless, the chore of moving the cells didn't seem so bad. Salmagard must have picked up on my dejection before, because she seemed energized.

Deilani gamely ran off to start hauling things up.

Salmagard and I had to pause as the crawler went by overhead; I trusted Nils, but I still didn't want to stand under it. He got it positioned on the roof . . . mostly straight. Straight enough; the Avenger's flying wouldn't be seriously affected.

As we were muscling the second cell into its slot, making the connections and sealing the shield over it, Nils clambered up with an armful of magnetic binders to fasten the crawler on.

"I want you to check the systems and make sure it's ready to go," I called up to him. "We aren't going to have time to mess with it out there."

"It is. Why *is* all this stuff ready to go, Admiral?"

"Use your imagination," I groaned, rubbing at my shoulder. Two more cells to go.

The deck moved beneath our feet. It was only a mild tremor, barely noticeable at all—but all three of us fell silent and kept absolutely still, as though our own weight and motion were enough to influence the entire freighter. Seconds passed.

We all started to breathe again, but the morale boost that had come with finalizing our plan was gone. We were no longer wondering if the freighter would be swallowed by the planet. It would be. The question was when.

It didn't take Nils long to finish, and after getting him to help us with the third cell, I sent him to work with Deilani. The flyer looked odd with the crawler sitting on it, but this was about staying alive, not staying dignified.

The next problem was deciding how much time we could devote to scrounging supplies. We didn't need very many survival packs; food and water weren't the problem. Out there we'd run out of air long before we got hungry, but we'd take some regardless.

The freighter was full of O_2 tanks. There was oxygen for use with every type of suit, for maintenance vehicles to be used on the hull, for emergencies, even for engineering functions.

But how much could we take with us once we left the flyer? We could pack plenty of it into the hold, but only so much could go on the crawler.

I tried to give the breathable-air problem the consideration it deserved. The obvious thing to do was take as much as possible; if we had to leave some behind after we landed, so be it—but could we justify the time?

The terrain shuddered and the freighter settled again.

The answer was no. We could not justify the time. None of us were kidding ourselves now, not about anything.

I moved into the cockpit, checking the systems. The padded seat and soft blue lights might have been soothing under different circumstances, but my mind was racing. The shuttle's reserve cells were feeding just fine; the Avenger had power, a welcome luxury. I plugged in the results of Nils' ping, which gave us a destination. I downloaded it to my EV suit's AI as well. We'd have to find our way even after the flyer was out of power.

As I familiarized myself with the controls, the trainees loaded O_2 tanks and other supplies.

I unclouded the front viewer and had a look at the bay from the perspective of the Avenger. I gazed at the bay doors for several long moments, before realizing why I was so hung up on them.

"Oh, no."

They didn't hear me. That was fine. I wasn't talking to them. I wasn't talking to anyone.

I shouldn't have been surprised that Deilani was watching me closely enough that she noticed the shift in my mood. She made her way to the cockpit and put her hand on my shoulder.

"What is it?"

"The bay doors. How are we going to get them open?"

"Well, they're just doors . . ." She looked past me. Yes, just twenty-meter-high doors that were something like two meters thick. One couldn't really pry them open with a bit of metal. And there was, of course, no power.

"Oh," she said, sounding faint. She sank into the copilot's seat, her eyes locked on the doors, just like mine. "What do we do?"

"I have no idea."

It was one thing to plug what amounted to a large battery into something like the arm on the ceiling. You couldn't do that with these doors. They were not going to open. That simply wasn't going to happen.

But did that mean we were trapped? Maybe not. Maybe this was a setback, not a deal breaker.

We just had to find a way out that didn't involve opening the doors. I looked toward the takeoff pad. Those doors wouldn't open either; it wasn't any different over there. Same problem.

Was there some other way out, some silly idea that would never occur to anyone? No. There were two pairs of bay doors. They were both sealed. Particularly well sealed, because in normal flight, opening them would depressurize the single largest space on the ship.

I sat back and closed my eyes. This was my life.

Deilani's expression was numb. None of this truly awful fortune seemed to surprise her much. Salmagard was dealing with it gracefully, and Nils was holding it together only because he thought he could count on me. Probably because I liked and appreciated him; he didn't seem like someone who was accustomed to being liked and appreciated.

I was glad I could do something for him before we all died here.

I listened to Salmagard and Nils working industriously behind us. I didn't feel up to it. I didn't want to tell them that I'd failed them like this. If we all ended up dead on a long shot, that was one thing, but a blunder like this . . . this stung.

Good thing I'd thrown away my sidearm, because I wanted to shoot myself.

I thought about what I'd done the last time I'd been presented with an unsolvable problem. I'd agonized. I'd given it my all and genuinely tried to be smart.

I'd tried to find a graceful way. An elegant way. A gentle way. It hadn't worked out.

In the end I'd been forced to take the direct approach. I'd needed results, and there hadn't been time to worry about the details.

This was no different. I couldn't be hung up on details.

"What do you think a ship like this costs?" I asked Deilani.

She looked over at me, puzzled, then cocked her head to one side. "You mean the ship, or *this* ship, with all the modifications?"

I smiled. "Either."

"In Evagardian Julians?"

"In whatever you like."

"A lot."

"Add it to my bill." I took a deep breath and got to my feet. "Though I don't have any money to pay it. Ensign," I said.

"Yes, Admiral?"

"Is there enough energy left in that cell to move the arm one more time?"

He looked dubious. "Just one more time? Maybe, I guess. Sir."

"You remember that crate of 14-14?"

"Yes, sir."

"Pick it up and put it in front of the bay doors."

They all caught on at the same moment. Salmagard's eyes widened, and she turned pale. That was the real measure of the absurdity of my plan. Only a truly mad notion would penetrate her calm that way.

Deilani squeaked something I didn't catch. Nils' jaw dropped, and he mouthed seven words at me that he didn't mean to mouth, but I understood perfectly.

"I know—I know!" I said, overruling them. "And I'm open to suggestions, but I bet you haven't got any. We'll dedicate the flyer's shields forward and give them full power. That might get us through it. You never know."

"Not that!" Deilani reached for me, as though to grab my neck and shake me, but caught herself. "The blast! It'll send us over for sure!"

"As soon as we blast the doors, we burn out. Right there, right then. We aren't going to wait around."

"What if it doesn't work?"

"Then it'll be a short flight."

Her mouth moved, but no sound came out. We didn't have time for this.

"It can work; 14-14 can get through armor, so it can definitely get through those doors."

"What if the—the *hole* isn't big enough?"

"You saw what one canister of that stuff did out there." I recalled the crater, and the size of the spire that Tremma's explosion had toppled. 14-14 had an impressive yield. No one could argue with that.

"That was just to bring down something that wasn't stable to begin with," Deilani argued.

"Yeah, but we've got way more. We've got all of it. The whole crate."

"You'll blow up half the planet."

"No one'll miss it." I shrugged. "I mean, I won't. But I'm not the sentimental type."

"Your colonists might," Nils said, dazed.

"We'll worry about them later. However it goes, it'll go down fast enough that it's not going to matter," I told Deilani frankly. "We'll either be in the open or the afterlife, and either way we won't know what hit us."

Nils let out a bark of laughter. Not a good sign, but at this point I didn't blame him. I was feeling a little twitchy myself, but that was probably the withdrawal.

"Wow," he said. "Wow. My parents were so proud when I made aptitudes."

"And they'll be proud that you had the initiative to do what it took to get out of this," I said. "Move the crate. You two, come with me."

"Where are we going?"

"We have to rig up a way to detonate the 14-14."

"How?"

"Those charges aren't meant to be set off by people without codes. We need something that can get through all that protective shielding and destabilize the 14-14. There should be surgical lasers in Medical."

"But you can't move the big ones, and the handhelds don't have enough power," Deilani said, hurrying after me.

"Not without a little encouragement."

Deilani looked blank. "What?"

"Let *me* worry about making it work. We just need a decent power pack from something in Medical, and as many surgical lasers as we can get."

"There'll be three," she stated flatly.

"How do you know?"

"It's a Class C Medical with a Class C kit. It's the bare minimum. Why have more on a ship with only two people on it?" she snapped.

I'd take her word for it. This was her job.

Kind of a brutal job, I decided. You couldn't expect a new officer to be half scientist, half doctor, and half leader. But Deilani was giving it her best, and probably wishing she'd just gone into something a little humbler instead.

The ground rumbled and the floor lurched. I kept moving. If I kept letting the past rear up and slow me down, we'd never get anything done. I was completely focused on what lay ahead.

There were two kinds of people in the universe: the people working for a better future, and the rest of us. Time wasn't on anyone's side, and neither was regret. If I let a little PTSD and some bad memories slow me down now, what good was I?

We ran.

Medical looked strangely empty without all the stuff we'd been stockpiling there; it was all in the back of the flyer now. It was also a mess, thanks to all those tremors and lurches.

Medical kits and equipment were everywhere. We'd have to look for the things we needed.

We started to search, but stopped almost immediately. I straightened, and so did Deilani. She looked at me, puzzled. "Did you hear that?"

"Yeah," I said, turning. "Did you feel anything?"

"It wasn't the ship," she said, hefting the medical lasers in her hand.

The three of us looked toward the counter, now cluttered with all of the equipment that had fallen out of the unsecured cabinets.

A canister of plastic bandage rustled, then fell to the deck and rolled.

Something on the counter was moving.

9

"DID you see that?"

"I saw it," Deilani said, not sounding happy. I knew how she felt. All three of our lights were pointed at the counter. The rustling continued. I craned my neck for a view, but the source of the sounds was obscured. "Did your Captain Tremma have a pet?"

"If he had, it would've been in his quarters. And I don't think he did. Wouldn't really fit my picture of him," I told her.

"What else could it be?"

"It can't *be* anything. It's impossible for there to be something alive on this ship that isn't us," I said firmly. "That's why I'm trying not to panic."

"Maybe it's a maintenance bot—a little one."

I picked up a metal basin. "I'm going to regret this," I said, approaching the counter.

"Admiral!" Her concerned voice was a bit more shrill than her usual barking tone.

"*Something* happened to Tremma and his officer," I said, not taking my eyes off the counter. "And once this ship goes, nobody's ever going to find out what. I'm curious. Aren't you?"

The thing on the counter suddenly changed directions, and I slammed the basin down, scattering medical supplies. Deilani gasped.

"Did you get it?"

"I think so," I replied, feeling something bump against the metal.

"Did you see it?"

"No," I said, concentrating on holding the basin in place. I could both hear and feel the thing inside scrabbling around on the smooth metal. My skin crawled. I looked at Salmagard. She was from Old Earth. "You think it's a—a rat?" That was an Earth mammal about the right size. But this didn't sound like something soft and furry.

She shook her head.

"How is this *possible*?" Deilani stepped forward, then backed away again.

"It's not," I told her. "This little guy is motivated." It was scrambling around in there nonstop, making quite a bit of noise on the metal. "Maybe he's a local."

"You said there wasn't any indigenous life," Deilani accused. Her eyes were wide, and she'd backed up all the way to the wall.

"Did I say that? All I know is the original survey didn't find any, but by the way this planet interferes with sensors, I'm not surprised. And I don't want to sound like I looked closely at those findings. I just heard a few things, that's all. I'm not an expert."

"But we were out there. How could this place support life?"

"There are a lot of different kinds of life," I replied, eyeing the basin. I took my hand away, and the metal bowl immediately began to move along the counter. I quickly anchored it again. "And there are less hospitable planets than this one."

"I don't believe it."

"Neither do I," I said honestly. There had to be an explanation for this. A malfunctioning piece of equipment? No, a burst O_2 cartridge would rocket around for a moment, but it wouldn't sound like this. A surgical claw wouldn't be this frenetic, either. Whatever this was, it was alive. The only explanation was that it belonged on this ship, brought along by one of the crew. Uncommon, but not unheard of.

I was at a loss.

"What do we do?" Deilani asked. We didn't have time for this.

"Let's dump it in something clear so we can see it. If it's a hamster I'm going to be mad."

"It's not, sir." Salmagard looked very confident. And she would be, I supposed. Maybe she'd even had a real hamster growing up. My family certainly hadn't been able to afford that, but I'd played with a virtual one once.

"Then let's do it, and be quick," I said, but before I could move the bowl, the ship gave a mighty lurch, more dramatic than the ones that had come before. We all staggered, and I lost track of the basin. I stumbled, caught Deilani, kept her upright, and grabbed the examination table.

It didn't stop. This was it. Time was up. The ship rocked around us. Salmagard had the power pack. Deilani had the lasers.

I shoved them both into the corridor and tumbled after them. The floor shook and jumped beneath us. Our boots' sensors didn't know what to make of this gravity or the tremors. The emergency lights flickered.

The ship was grinding and shifting; the ground beneath it was weakening. The shapes of the cavities beneath us made them structurally strong, but that couldn't change the frailness of the mineral or the weight of the freighter. We were sliding toward the edge, and this time we wouldn't stop.

I didn't let myself panic. I'd had to move fast under these exact circumstances before. Fear wouldn't help, only clear thinking.

Maybe this time that was actually an option.

Unsecured equipment was everywhere, falling out of cabinets that were normally held shut with electromagnets made useless by the lack of power. Crashes echoed through the narrow metal corridors, drowning out our footfalls.

It was a noticeably steeper climb to the bay, and it was getting harder to stay on our feet. Deilani tripped more than once, but Salmagard and I were there to keep her up. We burst into the open, hand-lights flashing madly over the crates. We could see the flyer's running lights. Nils had been shouting at us to hurry over the com; now he was making himself useful.

I took the surgical lasers and the power pack from Deilani, and pointed at the Avenger. "Get her ready to fly," I ordered, making for the bay doors. It was a long way, and anything less than a sprint wasn't an option. The deck tilted underfoot like a watercraft in a storm.

Things were breaking. Locks and safety seals couldn't handle this; the crates that dominated the cargo area were stacked high. They were falling, smashing open on the deck.

The noise was deafening, but the upside to having no power

was that there were no Klaxons. I didn't need more Klaxons in my life.

There was the crate of 14-14, pushed against the doors and secured with binders. Nice work, Nils. One of the doors was open, and a cylinder had fallen out of its clamps, threatening to go bounding across the rolling deck. I clutched the lasers and the power pack to my chest as I ran.

"Systems good," Deilani was saying. "Admiral, we're locked out of the systems!"

"Nils, do something about it."

"On it, sir."

"What are you doing?" Deilani asked the ensign.

"LT, please let me work." Nils' voice was strained.

"I don't think you're supposed to do that," she said.

"Deilani, let him steal the damn shuttle," I snapped.

I wanted to cry. I *needed* these kids to keep up.

"Oh," Deilani said. "All right. Well, strap in. No, don't raise the ramp yet!" she ordered.

"Thanks," I gasped. Maybe Deilani didn't want me dead anymore. That was progress.

No, I was just worth more to her alive.

"Sorry." Nils' voice came over the com. "Wasn't thinking." I could tell from his voice that he was hanging by a thread. I hoped Deilani wouldn't let him do anything stupid.

As the deck bucked, doing its best to throw me all the way back to the starboard bulkhead, I knew exactly how he felt.

I flung myself into the container with the 14-14, dropping to my knees. I'd never done anything like this with no light and no time before, but how hard could it be?

With shaking fingers, I tried to unscrew the casings on the surgical lasers. I pulled my knife and pried the panel off the power pack, searching for the right wires. I found the limiter and snapped it off, then broke the little crystal that would detect heat buildup.

There wasn't time to make this look good. I stripped and combined wires, hoping desperately that the light of my suit was showing me the real thing, and not just what I wanted to see. This wasn't meant to be done with gloves, and my fingers felt clumsy.

The pack was destabilized; I jammed the three lasers in where they wouldn't come loose, and wedged the power pack between two of the cylinders. It would go critical fast, and start to burn through the shielding protecting the 14-14. How long that would take, I wasn't sure. I'd never done a job this sloppy before.

I went for the door, but a cylinder broke from its clamps and struck me hard in the chest, pounding me back against the wall of the container, knocking more cylinders free. They crushed me to the deck. They weren't as heavy as power cells, but they were still a good hundred kilograms each, and I had about three on top of me.

I tried to lever myself out from under them, but it wasn't happening. The EV suit struggled to keep its form, preventing the cylinders from smashing me flat.

Ah, hell. What was the word for this? The Old Earth word? Karma.

It looked as though the admiral was going down with the ship. That was an Old Earth thing too, right? Or was it captain? I was seeing stars, I couldn't breathe, and I wasn't thinking straight.

Salmagard appeared in the doorway. She knelt and tried to lift one of the cylinders. I opened my mouth to say something clichéd, but the cylinder actually moved a little. She set her back to it and pushed. It tumbled aside, and she dragged me out.

It was easy to think of the gentry as a bad Evagardian joke. Ninth-tier genes? I was impressed.

I was too breathless to say anything, and so was she. She pulled me to my feet, paused long enough to see that I could stand on my own, and sprinted off for the Avenger. I staggered after her.

The deck suddenly tilted down in front of us; the front of the ship had begun its final slide into the chasm, and the aft end was rising.

The ship gave a sudden jerk, putting us into free fall. Salmagard was going too fast. I caught her hand before she could be thrown past the flyer, and threw out my arm for the landing strut.

The impact felt like it should've separated my arm from my body, but centrifugal force helped me swing Salmagard onto the ramp. She slammed a glove onto metal, put a cling charge into it, and reached out to help me on.

We clambered up; the angle of the ramp made for an almost vertical climb—then we were inside the flyer. Nils hit the ramp control, and it closed with a hiss.

He and Salmagard got me upright and hauled me to the cockpit, where Deilani hurriedly vacated the pilot's seat.

"Strap in," I wheezed, securing myself. I was seeing double. I focused on the controls.

The angle of the deck was too much; the Avenger's weight broke the craft free of its restraints, and we began to slide down the bay. We struck a stack of containers, which broke apart, beginning a chain reaction. Even more cargo crates rained around us, bursting on the deck.

The trainees all grabbed for handholds, Nils and Deilani swearing loudly.

If that pack didn't go critical and set off that 14-14—

I caught a flash from the crate.

"Close your eyes!" I grabbed the stick and hit the thrusters. There was a heartbeat's delay, and the Avenger blasted forward hard enough to throw me back in my seat, and get a startled cry out of Deilani. I hoped they'd secured the supplies back there.

Even with my eyes shut, the blast burned. Everything in the bay was instantaneously reduced to atoms, and the impact on the shuttle was substantial. I shoved the stick down to keep control, opening my eyes and trying to blink away the stars.

The glare cleared, and all I could see was green. It went on, and on, and then there were stars.

The Avenger's tactical screen automatically focused on what it perceived to be action, showing what was taking place below us. There wasn't much of the freighter left, only pieces. The chasm had tripled in size, and what I could see of its walls was glowing white, and bubbling from the heat.

The remainder of the freighter slipped into the darkness, sliding out of sight. It didn't fall over, or smash to the bottom of the chasm. The vast ship just vanished into the black void.

10

WE were above the mist. With a clear view of the stars, it was now possible to determine our approximate location in the cosmos. We could see the Demenis system, and that way—up and to starboard— was where the rest of our species was. Unfortunately, this flyer couldn't take us that far.

I slowed our cruising speed to make the most of the power we had. We'd used a lot of fuel making that spectacular, if poorly planned, exit from the freighter.

Deilani sat beside me, gazing absently at the stars. Since she'd just come from an imperial academy, maybe it had been a while since she'd had a view like this. Or maybe it was all just catching up with her. She looked boneless and tired.

"By the Empress," she murmured.

"And the Founder," Nils added. "Should we sing the anthem?"

Deilani snorted.

The odds had not been in our favor. The three graduates were new to making daring escapes, and they didn't know what to think or how to feel.

They were too shell-shocked to celebrate. It had been a rough couple of hours, and now they had to decompress. I didn't have the heart to remind them that we still had a long trip ahead of us.

And at the end of it—well, that was something I'd have to think about.

I had things to do, like keying in the coordinates Nils had come up with. Not an easy job without data for this planet in the Avenger's computer, but we could still draw a line and have the Avenger's AI follow it.

Once that course was set, there was nothing for me to do but admire the view and hope we hadn't traded the cell block for the gallows. It seemed straightforward, but there were a lot of things that could go wrong on an inhospitable planet, and our plan to reach the colony hinged on everything aligning perfectly.

That wasn't out of the question, but for me it would be a change of pace.

The Avenger's AI would keep us from running into a spire, and there was nothing else to hit. This planet had no mountains. Perhaps the spires *were* its mountains.

Monoliths protruded all over from the veil of mist that blanketed the planet. Some towered so high that their black tips appeared to be lost in the stars.

The mist was endless, and it kept rolling underneath us, rising and falling in waves. There were occasional gaps through which we could see the black surface. I'd seen planets with limited color schemes before, but never one quite like this.

The black ground was cracked and jagged, the mist emanating from the rifts and chasms that pocked the planet's surface.

It wasn't clear if the mist was vaguely luminescent, or if the light of the three feeble suns and the dozen or so moons was just bright enough to cause the green glow on this side of the planet.

If this system had a name, I didn't know what it was—but it was odd. Even with three suns, this planet still managed to have a dark side. That took finesse.

I was glad we'd landed on this side.

The stars did not move. Only the passing spires confirmed we were in motion.

I didn't care for it much. I preferred green grass and blue skies. Most terraformed worlds, especially Evagardian ones, were ultimately molded after Old Earth. Major cities would use light-enhancing fields to emulate the light and color temperature of Earth's sun. Common plants would be genetically engineered to survive new ecosystems, and introduced to create the illusion of evolutionary familiarity.

That would never happen with this planet. There was nothing down there but cold black rock. Crystals. Mist. You couldn't even land a ship on it safely. There was no future here.

I wanted a warm afternoon, a cool breeze, and a grassy hillside to lie on.

I'd spent a lot of time in my garden during the war. As much as I could spare. It had been a massive, decadently indulgent garden— but not such a convincing one that I could truly forget I was on a space station.

And with the war on, going planet side was no longer so effort-less. In fact, during the war it had been a hassle to go anywhere. Every government on alert, every spaceport on edge, every defensive agency watchful for spies. Travel, particularly to worlds with strategic value, had become an ordeal.

It was only slightly better with the cease-fire in place. If the Empress was able to finalize the Commonwealth's surrender, and drive a satisfactory peace treaty, maybe things would go back to normal. But the peace talks were still weeks away.

Not that there was any red tape to limit travel on this planet.

I watched the distance and power readouts for a moment, then made myself look away. No sense agonizing over those. All we could do was try to be ready. I hoped the crawler was snug on the roof of the flyer. We would need it sooner than I liked.

For the moment we could rest. I just had to try to keep my mind off my withdrawal. How long had it been since we came out of our sleepers? I hadn't kept track. It would've been nice to get out of my EV suit, but I'd just have to put it on again, and we hadn't brought anything else to wear.

Even all of that tumbling about and crawling around on the surface had barely marred the shiny white material. Evagardian technology was in a league of its own. I thought about what our experience on the freighter would have been like if we'd been forced to use Commonwealth pressure suits. Or worse, tech suits. This technology might have made the difference.

I smiled and watched it all flow by.

It was a dreadful planet, but there was a dark majesty to the spires and the deep shadows and the mist. It was hypnotic.

"Are you all right, Lieutenant?" Deilani was still wearing that glassy look. She was in unfamiliar territory.

"I am perfectly fine, Admiral."

I believed her. Or I believed that Deilani was as perfectly fine as the situation allowed. It was easy to get caught up in the triumph of our narrow escape and forget that our future was still uncertain. Were there enough power and air to get us where we were going? If so, what waited for us there?

Those questions rested uncomfortably at the back of every mind on the flyer.

The linear nature of our predicament, our lack of choices—it took some of the pressure off me. It was a shame about the trainees; this was no way to start a career in the glorious Imperial Service, clawing for survival on the surface of some worthless planet so far from civilization that nine-tenths of the galaxy would never even know it existed.

A struggle like this challenged the aesthetics of Evagardian thought, a way of thinking so deeply bred into these three that by now it was beyond changing.

Deilani had inadvertently revealed to me enough about her background that I could forgive her excessive vigilance.

Cohengard was more a ruin than a city. Not physically, of course. Mentally. Emotionally. Socially.

The wreckage that was left of the city was not a blemish for the Empress—more like a badge of honor. There had been a misguided, idealistic uprising. These things happened from time to time in the Empire. As progressive and admired as Evagard was, at the end of the day, behind all its layers and illusions of freedom and democratic process, there would always be the Empress.

People could get elected, they could bring about change, and they could achieve power. They could influence the Empire.

But the Empress could always undo their work, if she chose. Her word was still law. It was absolute.

There would always be a small segment of the population that didn't care for that.

Normally anti-Empress sentiment was harmless, ironically protected by the Empress' own laws concerning freedom of expression. But occasionally things got nasty, as they had in Cohengard. That particular movement had gained enough momentum that the Empress had to step in.

She issued a warning. The warning was seen as an ultimatum, a perfect example of the totalitarianism that these people found so objectionable. They didn't listen.

So the Empress struck them down mercilessly, killing some, punishing many, and wreaking havoc in what had been at the time a gem of her continually growing Empire.

The city was still recovering, even now. Things were more or less rebuilt, but there was no erasing the resentment. There was no poverty there—not true poverty, because that did not exist for subjects of the Empress—but Cohengard was not where you wanted to be born.

Most Evagardians took pride in their Empress' handling of the matter, but for the survivors and descendants, there was nothing but shame.

It was difficult for a native of Cohengard to gain citizenship; it was difficult for a native of Cohengard to do much of anything because of the stigma.

Deilani had fought for what little she had, and here she found me, a guy claiming a rank that I obviously had not earned. And there was Salmagard, who had likely been offered every opportunity from birth. Salmagard had never had to fight for anything.

So under the circumstances, I could overlook Deilani's ire.

Cohengard was still the home of the main body of imperials involved in the allegedly peaceful anti-Empress movement. It was easy for Cohengardian youths to get sucked into that morass of anger and self-pity because of the disadvantages that could come of being born there. It was hard for them to get apprenticeships, and there were fewer prestigious schools because of the location, which meant fewer slots offering good prospects.

In other parts of the Empire, young people worried about how they were going to excel. They wondered how they would distinguish themselves, prove that they were capable of great things in the hopes of having some value assigned to their genes. To gain that affirmation from society that they were contributors instead of parasites. To show that they deserved everything the Empress offered, that they were not the recipients of charity.

That was a steep hill to climb, even without a handicap. For someone born in Cohengard, it was more like a mountain. A lot of people saw that mountain and chose not to try.

But Deilani hadn't taken that route. She'd entered the Service and given her life to the Empress.

She had chosen to accept her situation.

Salmagard was no different. Her situation wasn't the same as Deilani's, but her acceptance was. Though she was a low-level aristocrat, socially she was the giantess to Deilani's tadpole. Both of them were, in their own ways, bearing it gracefully, in true Evagardian fashion.

Both of them were following the current, in their own way.

But Deilani would always have to swim harder.

Salmagard hadn't joined the Service to prove something. She'd just done it for the advantage it would bring to her family. She had still been required to show her aptitudes and prove her ability to serve, but the opportunity to do so had been handed to her.

Deilani resented that, but those feelings were tempered with puzzlement and respect. Deilani couldn't understand someone of Salmagard's birth being in negotiations, and she certainly couldn't find fault with it.

Even with Cohengard weighing her down, Deilani must have reached the front of the pack, because none but the best would be assigned to the *Julian*. The flagship would be a showcase of the Empire's finest men and women.

But mortal peril had finally let her look past all that. I hoped that would hold true until we got where we were going. Then all I'd have to worry about was the fact that she was convinced I was her enemy.

My arm still hurt from throwing it around that landing strut. I kneaded it irritably.

Nils cleared his throat behind us. "Er, Admiral, Lieutenant?"

"Yes, Ensign?" I asked, still massaging my arm. I was a little high on our narrow escape. It must've shown, because Nils was giving me a funny look.

"Well, sir—it's been a while since we've eaten, and I've got the combiner working. If you'd like something," he added.

Deilani and I exchanged a startled glance. "You brought a *combiner*?" she asked him, incredulous.

"It was only one extra trip, ma'am." He didn't meet her eyes.

Deilani buried her face in her hands. I wasn't surprised that Nils had risked some of our precious time in the hopes of having a proper meal. It was a little appalling, though. I got up and patted him on the shoulder. "Well-done, Ensign. Full marks."

We went back into the passenger area, where Salmagard was waiting with the combiner, which was perched on a seat and strapped in. So that was how they'd secured everything; I hadn't even looked when I'd been desperately trying to get aboard. These three were starting to grow on me.

"I only brought one bag of gel, but that should be at least one entrée apiece," Nils was saying.

I admired the little setup: neat wiring connected the device to a power cell that had been appropriated from . . . something in this craft. I wasn't sure what. I decided not to worry about it. Nils was gently feeding the bag of protein gel into the combiner. "Er," he said, eyes flicking between me and Deilani. The ranking officer, or the lady officer first? He settled on Deilani.

"Lieutenant," he said, poising his hands over the controls.

He didn't believe I was a real admiral. How could he? I couldn't hold that against him. If the time came when this had to be dealt with, he'd probably side with Deilani. As he should.

I'd worry about it then.

The lieutenant had her chin on her hands. She gazed at the combiner, expressionless.

"Can it do a spicy cohen? Like, toasted? Pork?"

I blinked. That was unexpected. The dish wasn't unique to her birthplace, but it was noted there. The sort of food that betrayed her humble origins completely.

She would never have asked for it in front of other members of the Service, never admitted to sentiment or a taste for something so crude and lowbrow. Salmagard showed no sign of surprise. Nils did, but he managed not to say anything.

I was shocked, but not in a good way; rather, it was a sinking feeling.

There had to be plenty of properly Evagardian dishes that Deilani liked—why expose herself to ask for a taste of home now?

Because she seriously believed this was her last meal. Whatever the request did for her image would be short-lived. The implications weren't lost on anyone, but subconsciously we'd all been thinking it. That was probably Nils' motivation for going out of his way to lug this combiner aboard. He didn't want the last thing he ever tasted to be imperial survival rations.

He dutifully called up the menu, searched, and punched in the codes for Deilani's request.

It was a novel sort of dish. Thin slices of protein, flavored after the flesh of certain Earth mammals, along with more slices flavored as particular bits of vegetable matter and sauces, and all of it between two slabs of products derived from wheat. It was a dish commonly associated with Cohengard's sustenance culture, because people living in sustenance housing ate almost exclusively from combiners.

The device produced the components, and Deilani assembled them in a businesslike fashion. She looked at the finished product in her hands with faraway eyes.

Nils turned to me.

"I'll have what she's having." He looked at me as though I was insane, but I didn't give a punch line, so he repeated the code.

"The same," Salmagard said.

Scowling, Nils delivered, then called up simulated marbled beef cutlets with Frontier-style fermented natural cabbage and sweet oyster sauce. A combiner couldn't really do a meal like that justice, but at least he was making an effort. I let him borrow my knife, but he had to break off the lid of the pod storing the O_2 masks to use as a plate.

This food wasn't what they were serving in the crystal ballrooms of the galaxy, but it wasn't so bad. Maybe it tasted good because it wasn't a calorie bar, or because of all that had happened. Whatever the reason, I felt like we'd earned it.

Salmagard seemed placid and neutral. Deilani was distant. Nils was actually paying attention to what he was eating, seemingly amazed to find himself enjoying it.

It was surreal. It was also a little somber. I was just glad I wasn't eating my last meal alone.

"Looks like we've got a bit left," Nils said, checking the combiner. "Dessert?"

"Have at it," I said, getting to my feet.

"Sir, I'll check on the oxygen conversion right after. Sir."

"I know you will. Thanks." I went back to the cockpit. There was no sense brooding; we'd already thrown the dice. There wouldn't be time to rest when we were on the surface, so I'd rest while I could.

The readouts on the console looked fine. The planet and stars were still spectacular, but unchanged. The shaking in my hands had come back, and my body was starting to ache. I had to conserve energy. I closed my eyes and settled back, wondering if this would be my last nap. If so, it had better be a good one.

The carbon shielding shattered like glass.

The massive cruiser punched through the armored plates as if they weren't even there. The impact was deafening, even from so far away. The forty-five-hundred-meter vessel was out of control, smashing effortlessly through the city. Buildings and towers were brushed aside like kilometer-high blades of grass, breaking apart and toppling in the distance. Glittering structures disintegrated by the dozen. Flyers veered, little more than points of light trying to avoid the destruction.

The ship crashed through tier after tier of raised highways and elevated train routes, sending it all spiraling away, pulled toward the breach.

Blue and green flames flashed around the cruiser's hull as coolant was burned off. The station was depressurizing, and the people and debris were like fine dust caught in the wind. Klaxons tried and failed to wail over the din. The ship reached the super-structure, crashing through and folding in on itself. The entire station shook violently, and the deck rushed up to greet me.

I woke when Salmagard came into the cockpit. A glance at the controls told me we had traveled some distance, but that I couldn't have slept for more than a couple hours. I didn't feel great, but I knew immediately that this was the home stretch. If I slept again, it wouldn't be here.

I took a deep breath and looked over at Salmagard. She had perched in the copilot's chair and was admiring the view. Her expression reminded me of Deilani's when she'd been looking at the food from her home.

I straightened, and she glanced over at me. I waved off her apology before she could voice it.

"I've been to a lot of places," I said, joining her in watching the mist flow beneath us. "But never anywhere like this."

"They're breathtaking," she said, eyeing the largest spire yet as we passed it.

"Do they remind you of home?" Some of the tallest buildings in the Empire were on Old Earth, after all.

She shook her head. "There's nothing like this."

Salmagard wanted to tell me something. I couldn't guess what it could be, though. There wasn't much to talk about. The way ahead was anything but clear, but all we could do was walk forward.

Some sort of confession? Or maybe she was finally letting her curiosity get the best of her.

"You never did tell me how they convinced you to enter the Service," I prompted, glancing back into the passenger area. There wasn't a sound apart from the mild hum of the flyer. Nils and Deilani were probably taking this opportunity the same way I had. Smart.

I expected her to look at me, but instead she just sat back and closed her eyes. I took a hasty mental snapshot of her profile against the stars, then made myself focus.

"I come from a humble family," I told her.

She looked at me in surprise.

"So I don't know what it's like for someone like you," I went on. "I guess you were obligated to take the Service route, since they'd already set it up for you. But you still didn't have to, did you? They couldn't force you."

She took that in, staring at me intently.

"The responsibilities of the first daughter have not changed in a long time," Salmagard said.

"Let's see," I said, rubbing my chin. "Your bloodline's tiered, so I assume you're valued enough for an arranged marriage?"

"I would be. But we don't actually have those where I come from."

I wasn't surprised. The Empire was large, and every city in every district in every province on every continent on every planet in every system was a little different. But in the dramas about aristocrats, it was always arranged marriages—usually the sons fled them to join the Service, and just before dying heroically in some righteous war, they would realize that they truly loved the girl that their parents wanted them to marry.

In some imperial dramas the line between art and propaganda was thinner than others.

"So you didn't join to get out of a marriage," I said.

She shook her head. "There are three suitable candidates in my district," she said. "One seven, one thirteen, and one nearly fifteen. I was prepared to marry any one of them."

"Why not two? Or all three?"

"I'm not disposed that way."

I leaned in a little so I could see her eyes. "Is that a hint of judgment for the girls that are?" She gave me a surprised look. There was embarrassment there. "I knew a girl once, who was disposed that way, as you put it. I'd hate to think you were looking down on her."

"Certainly not," she replied, looking flustered.

I put up a hand, smiling. "Relax. I'm just giving you a hard time. But you still walked away from it. I know joining was a way up, but an upward marriage will get your line to the next tier just as quickly. And it won't kill you as fast. You could've had a rich, peaceful life on Old Earth. But you went along with this. You're here. Nobody forced you."

"I never resented my responsibilities. Not at first."

I didn't know the details; I'd never taken the time to learn—but I knew those responsibilities were substantial, particularly for a first daughter. "My—my particular role," Salmagard went on, gesturing at her face, "was not revealed to me until shortly before I was of age."

I winced.

At first this program with the faces of the heroes had struck me as typically Evagardian, but the more I thought about it, the more twisted it seemed. Salmagard went on, voice even. "When it was made known to me, I saw it as an opportunity. Escape, so to speak, had never occurred to me before."

Of course it hadn't. She was too well-bred.

"I never looked for a way out. I was ready to marry, ready to safeguard the bloodline, ready to do all of it. But when they *handed* me a way out"—Salmagard shook her head—"I had to take it."

"So you didn't want to stay on Old Earth forever. I guess that's not so strange for someone who grew up there. It's the people who don't that won't understand."

Salmagard found guilt in it though; this *was* a confession. She felt as if wanting to do anything but her duty was wrong, like her desire to get away made her a bad person. Or more accurately, a bad daughter. That was a big deal for an Evagardian aristocrat.

I tried not to smile. "You know there's historical precedent for women wanting to do things with their lives. The Grand Duchess was kind of a champion in that field, wasn't she?"

"Yes, I suppose."

"And now you're in the Service. And headed for the *Julian*."

She scowled. "That berth was guaranteed me from the outset."

That didn't surprise me. It was a bribe, and Salmagard knew it. "Don't dwell on it. Every recruit in the Service would give their right arm to serve on the flagship. Maybe you don't appreciate the honor."

"What honor? I haven't done anything. And that's not the problem, not the real problem, anyway. Nothing is real aboard the flagship. It's all aristocrats and bloodliners, all playing soldier." Here was the young woman behind the mask. I wished she'd come out more often.

"They're all trained," I replied. "No different from you."

"Do you really think it's fair?" she asked. "That it's really merit that put so many liners on that ship for its maiden cruise? It's all for show," she said, frustration evident in her voice.

"It'll show you the galaxy."

"Nothing but our allies' capital ports," she said, waving a hand.

"In other words, it won't go anywhere interesting."

"Unless there's war."

"Surely you're not hoping for that."

"No. But it would be something real."

I was beginning to understand. You couldn't give a girl the genes of the Guardian and expect her to take gracefully to the sheltered and choreographed life of a high lady. It was easy to understand how she might view the rituals, traditions, and conventions of the Earth-born aristocratic lifestyle as false and hollow. It *was* a sort of show.

But it had a purpose. The Empire's caste system wasn't meant to keep people down, or to separate them. Anyone could move up if they had the inclination—and the exaggerated privilege of the high bloodlines was supposed to be the incentive. It let people see what they could strive for. The wealth of the Empire was there for the taking.

Salmagard had grown up on the inside of it, though. To her it was just a joke.

"You're not trapped," I pointed out. "If you serve well and mind your record, you can get assigned wherever you like. Even a fringe colony, if that's what you really want. Free Trade space probably wouldn't bore you, plenty of imperial presence there. All the border stations have big garrisons. You're probably a little overqualified for most of the station security posts out there, but they'd be glad to have you if you wanted to get away from ship duty."

She shook her head. "My family will find a way. They're terrified."

"For you, or of you?"

"Both. They won't let me reenlist."

"They can't stop you."

"There are ways."

She was probably right. "Then fight back," I said. "Your family only has as much authority as you give them. Tradition is only tradition, not law. They can find a way? *You* find a way. Outplay them. From a daughter like you, they'll never see it coming. And don't act like you don't have it in you. You've already taken the first step."

Salmagard looked genuinely taken aback. Maybe she'd never thought along these lines before. Or maybe these things just sounded strange coming from me, but they shouldn't have. It was the first solution to occur to me, but I'd made a career out of thinking for myself. She hadn't.

I let her consider that for a moment, but it would take more time than we had for her to really wrap her head around the idea of rebellion. I hoped I wasn't leading her astray. I wasn't trying to sabotage her sense of propriety; I just wanted to remind her that she had options.

"I suppose you won't have to worry about it if we haven't brought enough air," I said.

"No, I daresay not." She smiled. Then her expression grew serious. "I'd like to ask you something."

"I was afraid of that." I'd actually been sort of trying to avoid that by making conversation. Salmagard hadn't taken the hint.

"May I?"

I resigned myself. "You don't need my permission. Just don't be surprised if I refuse to incriminate myself. That is a fundamental Evagardian right, after all. I'm in enough trouble already."

She hesitated. "Quite."

I tried to look open and approachable. Salmagard deliberated for several moments.

"If we *do* reach this colony," she began, and I nodded encouragingly. She licked her lips. "If we do, how will you hide your identity? You'll be recognized straightaway. I can hardly believe the lieutenant hasn't recognized you," she added in a low voice.

"You don't see what you're not looking for. I won't hide it." I shrugged. "That's how we're going to survive."

She looked confused. "I don't understand."

"What's not to understand? I'm our ticket."

"But the penalty for defection." She spread her hands. "We'll be detained for planning your extraction. We'll be taken for spies."

I stared at her, dumbfounded. Defection? Extraction? What was she even talking about?

Salmagard could see the way I was looking at her. We were both intensely confused, and looking to each other for answers.

I started to laugh. I covered my mouth and leaned back, closing my eyes. When I finally got myself under control, I grinned at her.

"You're serious," I said.

Her mask of placid calm was back in place, and I realized I'd upset her.

"I'm sorry," I said quickly. "That was rude, but you caught me off guard. Very off guard."

She said nothing. She simply gazed at me. I didn't know what she was thinking. She was probably a little offended. She wasn't used to being laughed at. I sighed, then glanced back into the hold. It looked as if my laughter hadn't woken Deilani and Nils.

I took a deep breath and faced Salmagard.

"I think I've got it," I said. "Just a little misunderstanding, that's all. Look, how can I say this? I'm not who you think I am. I'm not *what* you think I am. Nobody's talking about defection. Not the Ganraens, not the colonists. To have defection someone's loyalty has to change," I said. "Right?"

She nodded slowly.

"I'm the same guy I've always been. I've had a little work done," I admitted. "But you do what you have to, you know?"

Her eyes widened. *Now* she understood.

"By the Empress," she said. "I don't believe it."

"That's up to you. But don't worry about the colonists—even if I was what you thought, they can't connect me to anything. They're not going to be suspicious of *me*. We've got our cease-fire, but the capital was destroyed. As far as anyone's concerned at this point, I'm a simple refugee. You guys are just helping me out. We might have to think of a cover story to explain how we got here, but I'll handle that side of things. Just let me do the talking. I'm good at it. Of course, I'll have to get into character again." I sighed. "But there's no helping it."

"Why didn't I see it?"

"You weren't looking. But isn't it better this way?"

"Infinitely," she breathed. That was gratifying. "I feel rather foolish."

"Don't. You were right about what mattered." I paused, searching her face. "You were right to trust me."

She nodded, still looking troubled. "Have I interpreted the situation aboard the freighter correctly?" she asked.

"You mean the sabotage?" She nodded. I sighed. "Probably."

"And the capital?"

I hesitated. "Yes."

"Who is responsible for the sabotage?"

I smiled. "Better if I don't speculate on that."

Salmagard turned a shade paler. "It's monstrous," she said, and there was a flash of anger in her eyes.

"Which part?"

"What they're doing to you."

I wasn't pleased that she knew the truth, but it was better than her thinking that I was some kind of traitor. "Don't worry about me. Worry about all of us. We still have a long way to go."

"I know." She looked tired.

"You're doing well," I told her. "I don't know what that's worth, but all three of you, you especially. You're trainees, but you're holding it together. I'm impressed, if that matters."

"You think I'm suited to this?"

"I think you'd be suited to anything you put your mind to. You've got the genes and the drive. I can see you commanding a fleet."

One corner of her mouth quirked upward. "Really?"

I shrugged. "Why not? Admirals and tetrarchs are just people too. Nobody doctored the Grand Duchess' genes. She wasn't the one they built for her job, but she got it anyway. Genes aren't everything. She was just a woman. Hell, she was just a girl. Remember everything she did."

"How could I forget?"

I blanched. "Sorry."

She shrugged. "I'd imagine that you can relate, can't you?"

"I suppose we do have that much in common. Neither one of us likes mirrors. Does it ever get to be a problem in day-to-day life?"

"Occasionally."

I knew how she felt. "Look on the bright side. At least the Duchess wasn't ugly," I said.

She laughed.

I cleared my throat. "And with that in mind—and the looming threat of death—do you think a high lady could, under these circumstances, overlook a small impropriety?"

She looked at me quizzically. "I'm not a high lady."

"Compared to me."

"Under these circumstances I think any lady could overlook just about anything."

I leaned over and kissed her. I meant it to be a brief kiss, one without too much subtext.

But it didn't stay brief. Salmagard was initially shocked, but she didn't resist, and when I finally let her go, I thought that for the briefest second, she looked vaguely disappointed. Maybe that was wishful thinking.

Then the blush faded from her cheeks, and her mask of Evagardian calm slid back into place.

Unreadable.

11

WITHOUT the looming threat of a cold and lonely death on the surface of an alien planet, it might have been a pleasant flight. For me, at least.

With the taste of Salmagard's lips still fresh in my mind, Nils and I confronted the problem of getting oxygen from our tanks into the super-concentrated cartridges used with our EV suits. We had fully charged spares, and when they ran out we'd have to refill them. The obvious way was to fill them at normal pressure, which would result in a substantial loss of O_2 in the process.

We couldn't just cobble together the equipment needed to charge the cartridges, but perhaps we could refine the obvious route a little. By using the pressure from one tank to increase the pressure on a second, we could potentially force slightly more oxygen into a cartridge, though we'd also lose more. It would be a lot of work for a small gain—ten or twenty percent at most was our estimate—but maybe even that one breath might make a difference.

We kept trying. Deilani did her best to make herself useful, but her technical knowledge was of a different sort. Between Nils' brilliance and training, and my experience with making technology do things it wasn't supposed to, we finalized our system with something like confidence. It wasn't a guarantee, but at least we knew we'd done all we could.

The flight would have been dull under different circumstances, but now it was over too quickly. As I switched off the critical emergency lights activated by the power cells being at their absolute end, I could see that the trainees were ready to leave the flyer. We were all handling this differently, but no one wanted to drag it out.

I didn't land the Avenger; the AI didn't need my help. The flyer set itself down on the surface without even a bump.

We stood in the passenger bay, enjoying what might be the last things we ever saw that weren't through the faceplates of our helmets. We divided the work of detaching the crawler, and breathed the last of the air that could be provided by the Avenger's recyclers, which would die when the power cells did.

"There was a time," I told the trainees, "on Old Earth, when a drive in a ground crawler through the rural countryside was considered diverting. Even a luxury."

"And the scenery here is so charming," Deilani said, massaging her temples and taking long, steady breaths.

We activated our helmets, and Nils lowered the ramp, depressurizing the flyer. Thin tendrils of green mist began to curl up and around our ankles.

The surface of the planet was as inviting as ever. The black mineral felt strange underfoot, and the shifting mist played tricks on the eyes. This deep in the mist, we couldn't even see the stars overhead.

We were on the clock. As we detached the binders that held the crawler to the top of the flyer, I used them to fasten the O_2 tanks to the chassis of the vehicle as Salmagard and Deilani tossed them up to me.

We worked efficiently, but it still felt tedious. We wanted to hurry, but exertion would demand more oxygen . . . It was better not to get mired in thoughts like those.

Soon the work was done, and the trainees had strapped in. Apparently I was driving. No pressure.

"How do we get it down?" Deilani asked over the com, and I glanced over at her, though all she could see was my helmet. I hit the throttle, simply dropping off the flyer. The crawler wasn't a heavy vehicle, but even this impact drove its wheels several centimeters into the planet's black surface, and created some alarming cracks. I got us away from that spot, adjusting to a more fuel-efficient cruising speed.

The trainees stood up in their seats, hanging on to the chassis as they turned to watch the Avenger, sitting alone, ramp down, fade into the mist.

The crawler was perfect. It was blind luck, but it was true. In the light gravity, we skimmed more than we rolled—the only problem was the mist. We wouldn't get much distance out of the crawler if I crashed it, and visibility was poor.

There were chasms that had to be avoided, but no mountains that I could see, unless you counted the spires.

In the Avenger we'd flown past them quickly. On the ground,

even cruising briskly, it took forever. The scope of the spires was never clear until you were close to one. We'd been lucky that the one to fall on Tremma's freighter had been merely staggeringly large—because some of the ones out here were so great that they would have simply smashed the ship flat, or buried it.

Gentle hills and small slopes occasionally brought us out of the mist, and we were steadily climbing. Soon we found ourselves above the green haze completely, rolling on smooth black ground that shone dully under bright starlight.

We could see valleys full of mist, some of them long and winding. I soon realized the mist wasn't really green—it was tinted that way by one of the dim suns in the sky. The effect was compounded by the reflected light from a dozen or so small moons that were scattered across the ceiling of stars.

Nils was beside me with Tremma's reader in his lap, keeping us pointed at our destination. There was no indicator of distance; at this point we could only guess, but Nils was keeping track somehow. He couldn't help it. It was a good thing he was there, because it was too easy for me to look up and get lost in the cosmos and forget our situation. It was something I hadn't done nearly often enough in the past.

"I thought the *Julian* would be an easy post," Nils observed idly, taking his eyes off his screen to join me in admiring the stars.

"It would've been," I assured him. "Not much for a tech to do on a ship like that but look good, and keep your quarters ready for inspection. You'd have to spend a lot of time training."

"I think I could've managed," he said wistfully.

"Which lab did they promise you?" I asked Deilani.

"Atmospheric sampling."

"That's awful."

"I'd still rather be there than here."

"Yeah. What about you, Private?" I asked.

"The Empress," Salmagard replied. "Honor guard."

Of course. "Do you think she's really aboard?" Nils asked.

"Why wouldn't she be?" Deilani replied.

"Nobody's ever seen her. Everybody says she uses a double for this stuff."

"Nobody's seen her without her mask. Doesn't mean it's not her under it," I said.

"It could be anybody under there," Nils said.

"But it's not—it's the Empress," I told him. "Have a little faith."

"What's her name? How old is she?"

"We don't need to know," Deilani said. Her mind was elsewhere.

"She's got to be the thirteenth or fourteenth one by now," Nils speculated.

"Sixteenth by common reckoning," I told him.

"So where does the new Empress come from?"

"The bloodline, obviously. It's the direct bloodline of the Grand Duchess," Deilani said.

"What about the fathers?" Nils asked.

"There are no fathers. They use the DNA of the Heir."

Deilani was giving these answers as though they were facts. To many people, facts were exactly what they were—but in truth, it was speculation. Nobody knew the first thing about the Empress for certain. Not even me.

Was she really aboard the flagship? Excellent question. Another interesting point was that if the bloodline was intact, which seemed likely, then it was probable that under the mask, the Empress looked quite a bit like Salmagard, who was modeled after the Grand Duchess herself, the first true Empress.

This discussion was using up valuable air, but it was also taking our minds off things. Besides, I didn't mind talking about the Empress. I decided to let it go.

"They say she's got a harem," Nils said. "So they probably know what she looks like. I'm surprised nobody's leaked anything."

"Nobody's seen the harem," Deilani countered, probably on principle. "That's a rumor."

"Well, you wouldn't, would you? I wonder if it's guys or girls. Or both."

"The Empress of Evagard shouldn't need companionship. It spoils the aesthetic."

"She's still human."

"But is she really female?" I asked idly.

"How would we know?"

"She's supposed to be."

"There'd be a son here and there, wouldn't there?" Nils said.

"No, she's totally lab-grown using genetic material from the Heir." There was no doubt in Deilani's mind.

"That's impossible—if it was always material from the Heir, it would mean that every single Empress has the same father. It's incestuous."

"It's all in a laboratory."

"It's still un-Evagardian. I don't know how they do it, but it's not like that. I'll bet it's the genetic material of the best and brightest from one of the core bloodlines, rotating by generation," Nils said.

"That would make more sense," I agreed.

"But you never hear anything about the *father* of the Empress."

"The father doesn't know he's the father; our genes are all on file. You could be the next one for all we know," I said to him.

"No, I only share one marker with a family that only shares two with a distant removed old Rothschild, not even one of the important ones."

"It could still be you if you distinguish yourself. A lot."

"I'm not aiming that high. I just want a ship that can keep me away from my family. I want to get paid. I need citizenship."

It sounded as if he meant it. I wondered what kind of situation he came from.

"Hear, hear," Deilani said, sighing.

"I'll bet she's cute," Nils said.

"The Empress? If she is, why's she wear the mask?" I was just trying to get a rise out of Deilani, but she didn't bite.

"The same reason we do. It's tradition. She's always worn it. The only pictures of the Grand Duchess are from when she was a teenager," Deilani said.

"Even that's too much," Nils said. "When we were in training on those Trigan mining ships, hands on—we stayed in a hotel on the station called the Grand Duchess. Supposed to be high class and exotic—I guess it seemed that way to galactics. Anyway, it's got this huge mural of her in the lobby. They had no idea how disrespectful that was. And most folks don't know better out there." Nils shook his head in disgust. "I mean, I'm not one of these people who gets offended about stuff like that, but there's something vulgar about using her face that way. Especially since they were outsiders."

"Were they happy to see you?" I asked.

"Real imperials? On their humble station? Yeah, but the officers escorting us got all the attention."

"Naturally. My class went to Earth and to the Union," Deilani said.

"To study disease?"

"Mostly. It was wretched."

"What was the problem?" I was curious. Someone of Deilani's origins should've luxuriated in traveling abroad.

"Our lead specialist—the one in charge of the curriculum—took ill."

"You're kidding," I said.

"She was the only one with clearance to get us out of the embassy, and she was in stasis while they tried to figure out what was wrong with her."

"Was it serious? How could they not know?"

"Well, that's the thing—she wasn't ill. She'd been poisoned."

"You're joking." Now I was really interested.

"I'm dead serious. The war was still on, and security for six bio students wasn't all that much. Somebody found a way to get to her." Deilani shrugged.

"But you guys were a long way from the war."

"They said it was probably a noncombatant sympathizer."

"Did your teacher pull through?"

"She did, but only because she had medical training; she put herself in stasis the moment she realized something was seriously wrong. Anybody else would've died."

"Stranding the rest of you," I said.

"Yeah, but we'd have been stranded anyway because as soon as they realized it was poison, they locked down the embassy."

"What was there to see?" Nils asked.

"On Earth? Everything. On the Union we couldn't have gone

anywhere. But on Earth . . . It was a disaster. You never saw six more furious people. And our element leader was *determined* to add an Earth girl to his collection, so he kept trying to break out. He didn't handle rejection well. I had to break his nose. Twice."

"You're not an Earth girl," Nils pointed out.

"When he realized he wasn't getting out, he decided not to be choosy. I could've had his commission for that. Probably should have, in retrospect—but I was worried about what it'd look like that I'd struck him."

I couldn't see Nils' expression, but his faceplate was pointed at Deilani. "Is Cohengard as bad as they say?" he asked her.

"Worse," I said.

"How do you know, Admiral?"

"Call it a hunch."

"I didn't know officer training was so colorful." Nils shifted the topic back, sounding impressed.

Deilani shook her head. "It was ridiculous. It was a joke. There was trouble every step of the way. The best bit was on the way back from Earth, just before she went into her sleeper, my roommate's implant malfunctioned."

"Oh, no."

"It nearly killed her. They're still trying to get her hormones back under control. And it happened because of a scan we had after the embassy—looking for dangerous implants." Deilani sounded contemptuous.

"Well, that's the military. Get used to it." I didn't have much sympathy for her.

"Incidentally, she was my main competition for this posting."

"How convenient," I said.

"I never really thought about it until now, though. I do feel badly for her. She'll lose her eligibility on medical grounds, but they'll give her full citizenship and preferential hiring for civilian work, I'm sure."

"Then she's coming off better on that deal."

"Most likely."

"I can beat that," Nils said.

"I already know about the thing with the dreadnought cannon."

"Oh, you heard?"

"That wasn't you, obviously."

"No, but he was in my wing." Nils was disappointed that he didn't get to tell his story. Even I had heard the one about the Evagardian cadet who vaporized himself.

"How could something like that happen?" Salmagard asked. I was glad to hear her speak up. I was willing to bet she had some stories to tell about her own training.

"Too smart for his own good," Nils said.

"I think anyone else would call him too stupid," Deilani countered.

"But he couldn't have gotten in there without bypassing maximum clearance locks. He was the *best*."

"And now lost to our gene pool forever."

"Well, like you said—his DNA's still on file." Nils was grinning inside his helmet.

"Can't see anyone taking much interest," Deilani said, looking over to watch the surface of the planet roll past. "I wouldn't go near it."

"The desire to show off: poor evolutionary trait," Nils said.

"Quite," Deilani sniffed.

"It has its uses," I said.

"Like what, Admiral?"

"You've got to impress girls somehow," I said. "Doesn't matter where you come from. That's a universal constant."

"There are better ways," Deilani said firmly.

"Oh, you know about this?"

"What? No."

"Then you wouldn't know," I told her.

"How did your gender stay on top for as long as it did?" she snapped.

12

WE only got about eight hours from the crawler before it finally rolled to a stop.

The screens vanished, and the warning lights went dark. It wouldn't move another centimeter. Several moments passed in silence. We all climbed out.

Our O_2 tanks had gone away amazingly quickly during the ride. We were down to nothing but the fresh cartridges we'd been saving. That was good; I was beginning to feel my withdrawal again, and carrying heavy O_2 tanks wouldn't make the most of the energy I had left.

Walking away from the crawler wasn't as easy as driving away from the Avenger had been. We were all tired of riding, but none of us wanted to see the vehicle go.

The planet that had flowed by so effortlessly suddenly seemed huge and daunting. I didn't ask Nils how far we'd come. Knowing wouldn't change anything.

It had taken longer to drive past the spires than to fly past them; now that we were on foot, it took ages. What did it look like, four figures in white trudging across the black planet? We were lucky to be above the mist for the moment; it would have made for uncertain footing that would have cost us time we couldn't afford.

I thought about the oddest things: how to breathe most efficiently; wondering what the best gait would be in this situation. Ridiculous things, but I'd take anything to keep my mind from wandering.

". . . what about you, Admiral?"

"What?"

"You may as well tell us who you really are," Nils said, walking just ahead of me.

"It's not important," I said.

"I don't think anyone believes that."

"You're happier not knowing."

"Then you really are our enemy," Nils said.

"I'm not *your* enemy. If I wanted to hurt you, I think I had plenty of chances. More air for me. I'm a friend."

"But you're not an admiral," Deilani said.

"It's an honorary title."

"You're not an officer."

"Even an honorary admiral is still an officer."

"You're not an imperial," Nils pressed.

"I *am* Evagardian," I said patiently.

"What could you possibly have to gain by hiding it now?" Deilani asked.

"Maybe I haven't given up on us living through this," I told her. "I wouldn't have bothered with all this nonsense if I didn't think it at least gave us a chance. You think I'm leading you on for my health? It's all well and good to be prepared for the worst, but you guys are ridiculous."

Salmagard snorted, and quickly cut her com so we couldn't hear. Nils actually turned and looked over his shoulder at me.

"What? Can't I stay positive?" I asked.

"You're just trying to change the subject. What kind of secret could you possibly want to take to the grave this way?"

"Nothing special. You're better off living not knowing. You're better off dying not knowing," I said. "Has it occurred to you that I'm doing you a favor?"

Deilani's sound of derision was transmitted clearly over our helmet coms.

"You don't have to believe me; you just have to keep walking."

"If we are rescued, you're done for," Nils said. "You have to know that."

"Not true," Deilani told him. "He thinks the Ganraens will protect him."

"What about us?"

"We'll be hostages, I expect. As far as killing us, he's telling the truth. If he wanted us dead, he wouldn't have brought us along. I'm starting to see what he's up to. We've played right into his hands."

I didn't let myself laugh. It would be a waste of air. "Lieutenant, you are a girl of wonderful insight. Sometimes."

Nils cut in, perhaps hoping to avoid another argument. "We

never did find out what happened to the captain. What was going on with you guys when you were in Medical?" he asked.

I considered that. "Something was alive in there," I told him.

"That's impossible."

"That's what we said. We think it was a hamster."

"A what?"

"Earth mammal. Common pet," I explained.

"But Medical was three decks down, and a long way from anybody's quarters."

"We're open to suggestions."

"You said you'd seen a survey," Deilani said to me.

"I heard about the survey. I never *saw* anything," I corrected.

"They concluded there was no life here, didn't they?"

"I think so—but how they could do that with faulty scanner readings, I'm not sure. I don't know if they came down here and looked, or even sampled for microorganisms."

"That's what I was thinking. Suppose there *is* something alive here," she said.

"I've been supposing it. I'm still not sure I buy it. This place is barren. Even if there were small organisms, say the size of the thing we trapped—I think we'd still see some evidence of them. We didn't see anything when we went underground."

"We should never have gone down there." Deilani shook her head. "That was stupid."

"I know, and it's my fault. But we didn't see anything. And if they're not up here and they aren't down there, where are they? I don't think we had a local."

"What *could* live here? There's no atmosphere," Nils said.

"There's some pretty hardy stuff out there. Life's adaptable. But like I said, I don't think there's anything here. There's got to be an explanation for what we found in the lab. What about some kind of rogue prosthetic? Part of an artificial hand?" I said.

"That would make sense." Nils liked that explanation.

"It would be a pretty small one," I added.

"Maybe for a woman?"

"The crew was two men," Deilani pointed out.

"Might not've been; I know Tremma was a guy, but he could've had a different pilot officer. Hell, a malfunctioning prosthetic could actually explain that stuff with the incinerator."

My brows lifted. That was actually a plausible explanation. I imagined that the copilot had a prosthetic hand. Something went wrong, causing the copilot to lose control of the hand. They went to Medical and switched it out with a backup—then they went outside with the 14-14. They came back in, and the backup hand had the same problem, except this time there was an incinerator involved. And for some reason, the safety tab had been removed.

It was thin. A lot of things would've had to line up just right to get the outcome that we saw, but it wasn't impossible.

"Are you sure *you* didn't kill them?" Deilani asked.

"Yes," I said. "What's the matter?"

"I'm just thinking about the thing you caught. We didn't see it, but we heard it. What if you had something like that in your suit? Would you panic?" She looked back at me. "Could explain what happened to them."

"You couldn't have something like that in an EV."

"But the men in the airlock were wearing tech suits; plenty of room in there for a stowaway," she pointed out.

I shuddered. She was right. "I don't even want to think about that." It was a nightmarish idea. I looked down and focused on walking.

"What do you have to worry about? You're wearing an EV."

"It could still get in the helmet."

"Can we talk about something else?" Nils asked.

We walked on. It was endless. Sometimes we waded through the mist; sometimes we felt as though we were swimming through it. Sometimes there was no mist at all, and we were just walking on the vaguely reflective black surface. It was all the same. Hills were always gentle, and valleys never went too deep, except for the occasional crevice, but these were never substantial. We could usually jump across.

Conversation eventually trailed off, and we walked in silence.

Things took a turn for the grim every time one of us had to switch out an O_2 cartridge. We left the spent ones behind, a trail leading back to the crawler that we would never use again.

I could sense the trainees' spirits darkening with every passing kilometer.

Things came to a head when we reached a crack in the ground that wasn't so easily jumped.

Nils stood at the edge, looking down into the dark. "What if we just got it over with? What if we just dropped them all in here?" he asked.

"What?" I didn't understand what he was saying.

"Drop them in, eject the ones we've got. It'd be over fast."

"Why not just jump in and see what's down there?" I asked, spreading my arms.

He turned to me. "You really want to just walk this out?"

"What have we got to lose?" I didn't wait for an answer. "Do you have a better way you could be spending your time right now? I've got places to be, Ensign. If you want to stay, give them your cartridges first." I got a start and made the jump, barely.

Deilani ran past Nils and jumped as well. Salmagard made it look easy.

The three of us looked back at Nils over the gap. Shaking his head, he backed up a few steps, then jumped, but either he miscalculated, or his heart wasn't in it. Deilani and I were there, though. We caught him by the arms and hauled him up.

"Everybody's told a story but you," he gasped as we lifted him to his feet.

"Is that what it's going to take for you to stop talking?" I started to walk again, telling myself not to be bothered by the delay. "Let me think of one." I sighed. I wasn't really in the mood. The detox wasn't making me any cheerier. I didn't know what was worse: the withdrawal, or not being able to get out of this EV suit.

"Don't make it up," Deilani said.

"I wouldn't do that."

"Tell us a spy story," Nils said.

"Do I seem like a spy?"

"Not at all," he admitted.

"What *do* I seem like?" I asked Nils.

"I don't know. Sometimes you're like this rich Ganraen. Sometimes it's like you know what you're doing." He shrugged. "I'm not worrying about it anymore."

"I wouldn't expect a spy to be such a pretty boy, but I don't know much about spies," Deilani said. "You're the first one I've met."

I felt myself bristle, and decided this wasn't the time for it. "I don't know any spy stories. But I do remember something from when I was a kid."

"In Ganrae?" Deilani asked.

"Never mind where it was. When I was away from home, sort of unsupervised for maybe the first time ever, I met a girl."

"Oh dear," Deilani said.

"Don't interrupt. This girl and I got along. That was kind of new to me; it had never happened before. I really liked her. But like I said, I was away from home. And I had to go back." I ignored their exaggerated noises of sympathy and cleared my throat to shut them up. "But we stayed in touch, sort of as good friends. She liked me. A lot. And I knew it—and I was glad—but I didn't want to change the status quo, so I just played it like I didn't know."

"That's terrible," Deilani said.

"Will you let me finish?"

"I don't like this story," Nils said.

"You make your bed and you sleep in it, Nils."

"Fine."

"Thank you. I lost track of her. I don't know how; I don't remember. Maybe I started taking her for granted. Knowing me, that was probably it. Anyway, I found out that later on she'd taken some wrong turns and ended up in a less than desirable spot. I told myself for a long time that it made me miserable because I thought that if she'd been with me, she might not have made some of those decisions. Of course that wasn't true; I was really miserable because she was with someone else, and it killed me to think about it. I was really young when all that happened. Like twelve. I mean, I was twelve when I lost track of her. I was older when I found out the rest."

A pause.

"That's the story?" Deilani said, incredulous.

"That's it," I said.

"That's terrible. That's the most depressing thing I ever heard," Nils said, disgusted. "Why would you tell such a downer?"

"It's not as bad as it sounds," I replied. "In retrospect—logical, grown-up retrospect—she and I weren't remotely suited to each other, so at least in a way, it's just as well that we were never together."

"That isn't very romantic," Deilani noted.

"*That* is the truth. Doesn't make it hurt any less—it's just a thing. But it's not a depressing story—it's relevant. It's about having things to live for."

"How do you get that from that story?" Nils demanded.

"Because there's no one to blame but me. I have to better myself and move on; I have to get past it, and I can't do that if I'm dead. I have to put her to rest."

"Is she dead?"

"No. You know what I mean."

"*I* thought you meant you could die here with no hard feelings, because that would put it to bed for you," Nils said.

"No, that would be cowardly. Hardly befitting an imperial admiral," I added.

"You do carry yourself like an admiral sometimes," Deilani admitted. "But we all know better."

"You seem awfully sure of that. You all have stuff you want to do, right? Don't tell me they teach you to give up at your academies."

"You'd know if you'd ever been through one," Deilani pointed out.

I groaned.

Space sparkled above. The black planet didn't sparkle back. The light of the suns grew slightly brighter, bathing us in a green light that shone on our white EV suits as we walked.

We passed chasms that might have gone to the core of the planet, and spires larger than space stations.

The time came.

I ejected my spent O_2 cartridge and snapped in my last full one. I paused and looked back at the trainees. "Last one."

"I'm already on mine," Deilani said. Nils was putting his in as we spoke. A look at Salmagard told me she had already done the same.

Then this was it.

We started to walk again.

"Ensign," I said.

"Yeah?"

"I'll bite. How far have we come?"

"We're there. I mean we're here," he said.

"What?"

"We are. We should be well inside their perimeter. We should have seen probes. They should have picked us up on their scanners. We should be able to see the colony, and they should have come out to get us long ago."

"Why didn't you say anything?" Deilani asked.

I knew the answer.

There was, of course, nothing here.

"Have we passed the reception point?" I asked.

"No, but we're close."

"You're sure?"

"There are a lot of things I'm not good at, Admiral. But I know math." The ensign just sounded tired.

"You do. I'm sorry."

He was right. There should have been a visible perimeter, and lights. There were none.

It was small consolation that if there *had* been a colony, my plan would've gotten us to it. We had come a very long way.

"There's nothing here," Nils said. "How long are you going to keep going?"

"Until I run out of air, I guess," I said without looking back.

Deilani collapsed first. Her breathing had been getting increasingly ragged. I looked back and saw her white form sprawled on the black stone. I jogged back and turned her over. I pulled the cartridge from her neckpiece and took a deep breath.

"What are you doing?" Nils shouted, grabbing my shoulder.

I locked my cartridge to Deilani's and equalized it, halving what I had left. I plugged her back in, then myself. She started to breathe after only two pumps to her chest.

She couldn't walk, so I picked her up.

"Looks like you two have to put the chairs on the tables and turn off the lights," I told Nils and Salmagard.

They didn't say anything to that.

"Either of you have any theist beliefs? Any spiritualism?" I asked, trying to keep the strain out of my voice. Deilani was as tall I was, and I wasn't even close to being at full strength. And full strength for me wasn't anything to brag about.

"No," Nils replied.

"Judeo-Christian," Salmagard said quietly.

"You want to rethink that, Ensign?" We were approaching the edge of a cliff.

"I already am. What about you?"

"I try not to worry about the afterlife. I have enough problems in this one. And I know exactly where I'm going."

"Where?"

"Down there."

I had stopped. Nils and Salmagard caught up, also halting. We were at the edge of the most breathtaking chasm yet.

At the bottom was the colony.

13

THE Ganraen colony ship was twice the size of an imperial destroyer, and twice as heavy. It had met the same fate as our freighter; of *course* it had.

The ship was the shape of a shallow dome, and substantially larger than Tremma's freighter. The hull of the colony was dull gray and rusty brown in typical, unattractive Ganraen style. There were viewports and bay doors, landing pads and vehicle launch exits with steeply sloping ramps leading up to the surface.

The planet had tried to swallow all of it. This was why we hadn't seen the lights, though we could see them now.

There were temporary structures on the surface, and vehicles. Work lights and power cells—everything that we should have passed on the way. It was all down there, a hundred meters below us.

Yet there weren't *enough* lights. The plastic survey tents were all dark, and they didn't look sealed. None of the vehicles was moving, and only the ship's visibility lights were glowing.

It looked as if the colonists were on emergency power, but that was still enough. We didn't need a luxury resort; we just needed life support.

I had fallen in with the trainees' way of thinking. Once I put in that last cartridge, I was just running down the clock. That had just changed. My calm resignation turned to something like panic. I resisted the urge to look at my O_2 readout. We had to get down there, and it wasn't going to be easy—especially not with Deilani.

"By the Founder," she breathed. I set her down, and she leaned on me. "It's really here."

"Can you climb?" That was a long way down.

"Yes." She wasn't as sure as she sounded, but we had to try. I grabbed her wrist and ran a line to her, connecting us. She didn't protest. That was all I could do; I'd be lucky to make this climb myself, so I couldn't carry her.

"Nothing to say here, guys—go."

We started down, not even knowing if it was a feasible climb.

I went first, with Deilani just above me. I would be the safety net, and Deilani wouldn't risk taking Salmagard or Nils down with her if she made a mistake.

The gravity was light, but not so light that a fall from this distance was survivable.

The silent world of our helmet coms, broken only when one of us breathed particularly loudly, had been our universe since we left the Avenger. It was just me and my withdrawal. I wished I'd asked Deilani exactly what she had given me. My limbs had started to feel like lead.

Time had stretched and twisted as we walked. I hadn't kept track. It had been hours, but I didn't know how many. Walking had seemed unbearably slow, but climbing was even slower.

There had been a time when humans on Earth climbed rocks just like this. Like the fabled drive in the countryside, it had been a form of recreation. I smiled behind my face mask. Those people had some peculiar ideas about what was fun.

Salmagard was light, but not light enough. We were halfway down when she chose a foothold that immediately gave. The rock crumbled, striking Nils, who slipped as well. Salmagard caught herself, but Nils fell free with a cry, knocking Deilani loose even as he secured himself. I reached out and grabbed, catching her neckpiece, but the weight and the sudden jerk were too much for my remaining handhold, which broke away. For a moment I was in free fall.

Nils' glove closed around my wrist. He couldn't have held us both, but it bought me the time I needed to shift Deilani and jam my arm into a crevice.

It wasn't the same elbow that I'd bashed on the landing strut, at least. The bruises I would have after this would not be flattering.

We were all still there. Somehow.

It took precious minutes to get Deilani back to climbing, and now she was below me for better or worse.

It took a long time. No one spoke.

Deilani finally detached her line from mine and dropped the final few meters to land on the rubble, falling to her hands and knees. I touched down next.

We'd done it. We'd done it with minutes to spare, too. If Nils hadn't believed in a power higher than the Empress before, he did now. Together, we made for the nearest airlock.

The colonists were in for a shock. We all waved at the camera mounted over the blast shield.

"Open channels," I said.

"We're on it," Nils told me.

"Then we should've heard something, shouldn't we?" Deilani's voice was weak, but high.

"Yeah." Nils started to fidget.

"Something's wrong." I didn't understand. Why wouldn't they open up? And where was everybody? This wasn't a planet where everyone would be strolling about, but there still should've been some movement.

"We don't have all day for them to notice us," Deilani pointed out, still sounding feeble.

That was true. Especially for Deilani and myself, as we were on half rations.

"They're obviously conserving power. They could've disabled their security if they're having reactor issues," Nils suggested. "Could explain it. I mean—why watch the surface of a planet like this? They're not exactly expecting visitors. Maybe sensors are so bad here that they just don't bother."

That was a good point.

"Then what do we do? Knock?" Deilani asked.

"You guys are too polite." I walked up to the emergency access, smashed the safety shield with my elbow, and jerked down the lever. I got ready to get into character, mentally rehearsing my story. I put on my smile, and adjusted my posture. I worked my jaw, ready to slip into the right voice.

The blast shield lifted, and the outer airlock opened.

"They're not going to like us for this," Nils fretted as we jogged up the ramp and into the blinking red light of the small personnel airlock.

We all froze. The inner door of the airlock was jammed halfway open, and horribly mangled. There were some dark smears on the bulkhead, and peculiar burns. Against all odds, the colonists had found a way to surprise me. I stared.

"What in the Empire," Deilani said.

I didn't say anything. I just slipped through the doors and into the ship. The outer doors closed behind us. Nils reached for his helmet control, and I caught his wrist. "There's no atmosphere in here."

He blinked at me through his faceplate. Then he groaned. Nils was the last person to make such a mistake; it just showed how frayed we were. We were exhausted and dehydrated.

"Then we're still dead," he sighed.

"The hell we are," I said. "Emergency power's on. We just have to get this place to autoseal and restart life support."

"The whole ship can't be depressurized," Deilani cut in. "That's ridiculous."

"This corridor's an artery. If there's no air here, there's none on this deck. We have to get to engineering, or find the colonists."

I didn't wonder why the outer door was intact and the inner one wasn't. I didn't care why life support was down, or why no one had picked us up on sensors, why no one seemed to be bothered by us breaking into their ship. I wanted air. Everything else could wait.

"You saw the size of this ship," Nils said. "How much have you got left?"

"A few minutes."

"We have to move."

"I know. Think fast."

"What?"

"Ensign! We're on a ship. Life support's down, but there's still air. We just have to find it. Deilani and I need it *now*."

"Oh, Founder." Nils stepped back, rapping on his faceplate with gloved knuckles. "I don't know anything about Ganraen colony ships . . . This is a lower deck . . . We might be near the reserves, but I don't know how to find them."

"What about emergency masks?"

"The temperature's equalized. It'd buy you a few minutes at most, but it wouldn't help us solve anything. The exposed skin would freeze. I don't know if your suit could maintain your core temperature. You'd lose half your face."

"Wait a minute," I said, turning around. "We just came through an airlock. There have to be pressure suits."

"Oh!" Deilani understood.

The life of a colonist inevitably involved the occasional trip outside. On a planet without atmosphere, most of the colonists would have their own suits, but there still had to be something for general use. There were large lockers for emergencies in an alcove just to the left of the airlock's inner door. Two of them. Perfect.

Deilani and I wrenched them open and pulled the suits out.

"A suit in a suit," Nils said, but the relief in his voice was evident. He'd been afraid we were going to drop right in front of him.

As Deilani and I clambered into the emergency pressure suits, I knew this was yet another temporary fix. Salmagard and Nils would need air next. I got the helmet settled in place, pressurized the suit, and disengaged my EV helmet. There. I was safe for the moment, and a look at Deilani told me she'd managed as well. The

SEAN DANKER

Ganraen suits were primitive compared to Evagardian ones, but we weren't complaining.

Besides, playing dress-up was my specialty.

"Now what?" Nils asked, looking around at the bleak Ganraen bulkheads and ceiling.

The interior of the colony ship was more inviting than Captain Tremma's freighter. There were fewer sharp edges, padding on the bulkheads, and the deck was solid plastic instead of metal grating that rattled underfoot. It still wasn't as elegant and comfortable as an Evagardian vessel, but after the freighter it felt like unspeakable luxury. And there was power.

"Something's obviously wrong here. Security should be all over us. The damage in the airlock looked serious, but if we've still got power, we've got options. Do the guide paths work?" I asked Nils.

"Do Ganraen ships even have them?" He sounded dubious.

"A colony ship would. It's too big. People couldn't get around without them. There's a console— Nils, you do it. I can't with all these gloves."

"Will it still work on emergency power?"

"If you want to live, you better find out."

Nils fiddled with the Ganraen console. "I don't know these systems," he muttered. "This is stupid. Why would they make their emergency systems so counterintuitive? And why's it so slow?" He prodded the screen and swiped through menus, making his selections.

In time he was able to make a blue line light up on the deck. We followed it. The bulkheads were light gray, which wasn't very cheery, but it was all clean and new.

"This is starting to really bother me," Deilani said.

"Wearing two suits?"

"That there's no one here," she snapped. "Reckon they abandoned this unit when it sank?"

"I didn't see the others," I said.

"Probably because of the mist," Nils said. "Maybe they all sank."

"What others?" Deilani asked.

"A Ganraen colony is actually four ships; they split apart on the planet's surface. The manufacturing ship, the mining ship, the science ship, and the executive ship." I paused in a junction, looking in either direction. Deserted corridors stretched away, littered with debris. This didn't look right. It couldn't be good.

"Which one is this?" Deilani's voice was small, almost hesitant. She was trying to stay in the game, but she couldn't forget that she'd been only minutes from suffocation. I felt the same way. Detached. The empty ship couldn't mean anything good for us, but I hardly felt worried. I was just glad to be breathing.

I was looking at this situation as if it was someone else's problem.

"I don't know. This is a weapon burn. What are these marks?" I ran gloved fingers over the blemishes on the bulkhead, lit up by soft glow panels on the ceiling.

"Something's corroded the plastic," Nils noted. "What did they build this ship out of? Are the Ganraens really that broke? Kind of sad. They better hope the cease-fire holds."

The trainees had been expecting, in the best-case scenario, a cool welcome from the Ganraen colonists.

But finding no one at all—this was unthinkable. The damage to the ship and occasional bloodstains weren't helping.

"Looks like there was some civil disobedience," Nils said,

nudging some shredded and bloody clothes with his foot. There were signs of violence and mayhem everywhere, but no bodies. Grav carts were overturned in the corridors, hatches were left open, and the carbon shields over emergency Klaxon releases were broken. We were looking at the aftermath of some kind of major incident, but for the life of me, I couldn't guess what kind.

"These people are animals," Nils said.

"The colonist life isn't easy," I told him distractedly. His theory wasn't crazy, but I didn't think he was right.

Nils looked through an open hatchway, then back at me. "You think the people on this ship got out of hand, and leadership depressurized it to get them in line?"

"To get them in line they'd have needed to *re*pressurize it at some point," I said.

Nils swallowed. "I guess so. What is this stuff?"

"It looks like ash," I said, kneeling on the deck. My joints ached from the withdrawal. Grimacing, I ran a gloved finger through the stuff on the floor. "Or something like it."

"What were they burning?"

"How could they burn anything? Where's the fire-suppression foam? None of this makes sense." I got up, shaking my head. I turned and looked back down the long corridor. It was a mess—a mess like you'd expect to see in a loss of gravity. But we were on a planet. This gravity couldn't be switched off.

"Where's security?" Nils demanded suddenly. "I *want* to be detained."

I put a hand on his shoulder. "Easy."

"I just want to see another person," Deilani said. "I keep thinking about how Tremma ended up."

I was thinking the same.

"I've got a weapon on the deck," Salmagard reported, and I turned to look. A pistol from a Commonwealth maker lay beside two heavy plastic impact cases, probably containing survey tools. It was a compact handgun, not the kind that the ship's security would've carried. It was something a civilian would have for self-defense.

"Leave it—we don't want them to think we're hostile."

"There's nobody here to think it," Deilani said, sounding lost.

"It's a big ship, Lieutenant. Look, there aren't any bodies—so if there was a fight, someone's cleaned up after it."

"Doesn't look cleaned up—did you see those rooms back there?" she replied. "Either there was a war in here, or somebody picked up the ship and shook it. It's a disaster."

"It's a disaster with power, and we're guests in it. Do we need to take this lift?"

"No, we should be able to get to engineering from down here."

"Did you set the path right?"

"How should I know?" Nils sounded disgusted.

Our confusion only grew when we reached engineering. We'd assumed there had to be a maintenance reason for the depressurization—perhaps temperature control—and I'd hoped to find techs in pressure suits working to get things in order.

Instead we found nothing but empty rooms and unmanned consoles. The hatches to the reactor chamber stood wide open. Aside from a few items knocked about, everything seemed to be normal. There was no blood, and no sign of weapons fire. Everything that mattered was in its place. Even the chairs at their stations looked neat and orderly.

"Can't we get a break?" Nils groaned.

"This is a break, Ensign. The consoles are online. Activate the seals and get some air in here before you run out."

"Can we do that?"

"I don't see anybody telling us not to." I shrugged. "If anybody tries to stop you, let me know. I'll talk to them."

"I'm not even going to think about the political ramifications here. I'm just following orders."

"Do what he says," Deilani told him.

"Following orders," Nils repeated firmly. "That's what I do. Because that excuse has worked so well throughout history."

I let him whine; it was his way of coping.

I turned to Salmagard, catching her eyeing her readout. We were cutting this close. I could only hope Nils could figure out the Ganraen systems before he turned blue.

"Private, are you all right?"

"Just conserving oxygen, sir."

"Keep an eye on the ensign while he works. Lieutenant, with me."

"Where are we going?"

"We need to look around a little. Keep in touch."

There were tools left out as if forgotten. A broken monitor. There were dents in some of the bulkheads near the airlock, and it was nearby that we found the body.

"He can't be alive, can he?" Deilani said.

We stood in an open hatchway to a control room. In a chair on the far end was a figure sitting up, his back to us. We'd have missed him if I hadn't seen his limp hand dangling over the armrest.

"Not unless he's wearing an invisible pressure suit," I replied.

"He must've been dead before they depressurized."

"Safe bet. There's a suit over there." I pointed.

"I'm in the system, Admiral," Nils reported over the com.

"Keep at it, Ensign. Are you all right?"

"Got a few minutes left," he replied distractedly.

"What about you, Private?"

"Four percent."

"Deilani, take this suit to them. I'll find another one."

"What about this guy?" she asked, taking the suit from me.

"He's not going anywhere."

"You found someone?" Nils asked, sounding hopeful.

"Just a body. Stay focused."

"What is going *on?*" he moaned.

"Focus. Take that to him. There'll be another one in the next core chamber. I'll get it." These suits were meant to protect techs from radiation if something went wrong, but they'd work well enough for getting breathable air to Nils and Salmagard.

Deilani and I split up. I resisted the urge to enter the control room and examine the body; there were more pressing things to do. I found another suit, but before I could return to the trainees, Nils let out a shout of triumph over the com, and the doors dropped, sealing me in.

"I've got it!"

"What have you got?" I asked warily. I noticed my right hand reaching back, like I was wearing trousers and a jacket, and I had a waistband with a pistol in it.

But I was wearing a pressure suit, and I'd gotten rid of my gun hours ago.

I swallowed, looking around the chamber. There were only two sets of doors, both firmly sealed. I might be able to get out through a maintenance hatch, but even if I did, I'd still have Private Salmagard's combat scanner to think about.

"The diagnostic's running. It's deciding which parts of the ship are compromised," Nils said.

Ah. So he hadn't sealed me in deliberately; this was just part of the system. That was a good decision on his part; the suit I was holding was his lifeline. I let my breath out slowly. I wasn't sure when the trainees would've found the time to make a plan to detain me once we got here, but they were resourceful. They could've done it.

But they hadn't. Maybe we finally had trust.

"I've got it spiraling out from engineering . . . recyclers online. It'll take a few minutes to get air pumped in, but we should be all right. It'll take even longer to get the temperature back up, but I can deal with being cold. I think we're good, Admiral. We're in business." Nils was elated, and I didn't blame him. For the first time since we'd come out of our sleepers, things were looking up.

"Contact the bridge. Let them know we're here, and why we've done this—we don't want them to shut it down."

"On it. Um—wow, I don't even know what to say. Uh, reactor section to bridge. Reactor section to bridge, we're a little low on air down here, so we're . . . Admiral, there's no one on the com. I'm showing no active stations," Nils said. "My terminal is the only one on this entire boat that isn't idle."

"That can't be right." I looked around as though there was someone I could glare at for an explanation. It would take time to kill that sense of entitlement.

"Where could they be?" Deilani asked.

"Town meeting?" Nils suggested.

"Try the security net, look through the feeds. Find me *some-one*," I ordered.

"Security systems are locked. Or down. I can't tell with this thing. Admiral, these systems are ridiculous."

"Is it because we're on emergency power?"

"I don't think so. I'm getting an error code. But I can't tell if something's broken or if I'm just locked out."

The doors reopened; this part of the ship had been declared intact, and life support was back online. I checked the Ganraen suit's atmosphere gauge. It still wasn't safe to breathe, but it would be soon.

"If this is a ghost ship," Deilani was saying, "how did it get this way?"

"Something must have gone wrong, something that made the colonists relocate to one of the other ships. Crowded, but better than whatever's the matter here?" Nils speculated.

"We've got air and power. What more do you want?" I asked, making my way back through the gray corridors.

I found them all clustered around the console, looking intently at the readouts. They were as anxious as I was to get their helmets off. I dumped the suit over the console and waited with them. Why not? They weren't going to be able to concentrate until the helmets were deactivated anyway.

I couldn't make sense of what we'd walked into. Even I couldn't have predicted exactly how the colonists would have reacted to us—but I'd been ready for anything. Finding *no one* was about the only thing I didn't have an answer for. Typical.

My suit declared the air safe to breathe, so I broke the seal and stripped out of the Ganraen pressure suit. Deilani was doing the same, and Nils and Salmagard had already collapsed their helmets back into their neckpieces. It was freezing cold, but none of us cared.

How long had we had those helmets up? Twelve hours? Eighteen? More? I didn't know. The others breathed deeply and appreciatively. I did too, and rubbed at my face—I always seemed to develop an itch when I had a helmet on. It was cold, but it would warm up quickly.

"I can't believe it," Nils said, looking down at his gloves. "We made it."

Deilani was giving me a funny look, and Salmagard was smiling.

Finally, they appreciated me. Then Deilani's expression became one of suspicion, and the moment was gone. I cleared my throat.

"If there's no security, we just have to get creative. If there's anyone else on this ship, they must be in pressure suits, so track active suits."

"You got it, Admiral." Nils grinned at me, popped his knuckles, and turned back to the console. This from the guy who'd been ready to throw in the towel just a few short hours ago? Good. "The only active suits I'm showing are in this room."

"Then there we go. We've got the place to ourselves. And the other ships don't know we're here, because in a place like this, who would just come walking up to the door? Security's down because it doesn't need to be up, that's all."

"Supposing there was some kind of conflict," Deilani said. "And these people fought among themselves—what would they do with the bodies?"

"Each ship will have an infirmary and a morgue," I told her. "There, or incinerated—depending on how long ago this happened."

"How can we tell?"

"We can't unless we can get into the computers. If it's been in vacuum the whole time, it'll be preserved. But that fellow in the other bay didn't make it to the morgue. We should probably go see why," I suggested.

"Is that safe?" Nils asked.

"How long are your decon nanomachines good, Lieutenant?"

"A while longer. Let's have a look."

We retraced our steps, this time with Salmagard and Nils in tow. The body hadn't moved. Nils stayed by the doorway. Squeamish?

The sidearm hanging from the Ganraen's hand didn't leave much uncertainty about how the hole had gotten in his head. He had been about Nils' age, and his uniform was that of a tech.

"Why?" Deilani asked, turning very pale.

I looked at the console in front of the dead man. "I think he's the one that vented the ship."

"He'll thaw out now. Should we do something with him?"

"Leave him. The colonists wouldn't like us touching their people, but they must have left in a hurry if they didn't take him with them."

"What do we do?" Deilani was looking to me for an answer.

"We get to the bridge and see if we can get in touch with the other ships."

The trainees were starting to realize that maybe we weren't out of danger yet. The urgent but straightforward threat of asphyxiation had been replaced by a new threat, this one more ambiguous. Were we in danger from the colonists? Ordinarily we wouldn't be, but circumstances on this ship were anything but ordinary. These people *could* be a threat, and if they weren't, what about whatever had driven them off this ship? We didn't know. During our trek across the surface, this colony had represented safety.

Now that we were here, we weren't feeling very safe.

14

ON the way to the bridge we saw more of the same general disorder that characterized the ship's corridors and common areas. There were some stains that had to be blood, but not enough of it to account for even a fraction of the crew.

There was more evidence of weapons fire, and more structural damage—though the parts of the ship that were seriously compromised were sealed off completely to preserve atmosphere.

We saw more of the inexplicable burns and corrosion. Through a window into a sealed area, I could see damage that looked as if the colonists had literally torn the walls open.

There were no bodies, but there were occasional indicators of how suddenly the trouble must have struck. Objects thrown aside, hatches left open, and even a frozen, half-eaten calorie bar lying on the deck.

The shields over emergency alarms were smashed everywhere.

This was the colony's science vessel, and according to Deilani, the ship's infirmary had seen some use.

The trainees were distracted from the possible danger by the fact that they were strolling through an enemy ship as though they owned it. Even with the cease-fire in place, no one was going to just forget about the war. Even if the Empress' peace talks went as well as they possibly could, there would still be bad blood for a very long time. For the talks, the stakes were high.

There was more to worry about than just preventing the war from flaring up again here and now—there was also the danger that we'd just have another one in ten years when encroachment into Free Trade space became an issue again.

It wouldn't be enough to call off hostilities. Relations had to actually heal.

And that wouldn't be easy. I could see the trainees' prejudices, and it went without saying that they were mirrored by their counterparts, young people entering the assorted branches of the Commonwealth armed forces.

The Commonwealth was not happy, and neither was the Empire. The Empress had a big job ahead of her.

What surprised the trainees most was how things weren't that different from what they were used to. The colony ship wasn't as pretty as an Evagardian vessel, but it wasn't as much of a step down as they expected.

Cash-strapped Ganrae had never been able to do much about imperial propaganda during the war. Now the trainees were seeing firsthand that maybe reports about the primitive Ganraen way of life might have been exaggerated.

The bridge was on the uppermost deck. It was smaller than an

Evagardian bridge, but it had all the same action stations, even if they were in different places. The chairs were empty, but the screens were glowing.

"Ensign, get on the com. Open up a channel to the other ships."

"Where are they?"

"They can't be far." I went to the viewport and switched it on. There was nothing but green mist. The valley was full of it. I hadn't seen any mist inside the ship, though it had been essentially sitting open. Perhaps without the light of the green star, the mist was colorless, and less noticeable.

"Admiral, I'm not familiar with these systems."

"None of us are, Ensign."

"I mean I'm not a bridge officer, sir."

"And I am?" I shot back. Deilani gave me an arch look. "Honorary title," I reminded her. "Just figure it out, Ensign." The withdrawal was starting to get the best of me. I caught myself irritably reaching up to brush back my hair again. I gave my hand a little shake and folded my arms.

"Yes, sir."

"There's no hurry now."

"Right." He cleared his throat. "Uh—attention, Ganraen colonists? This is Evagardian imperial personnel aboard your science vessel. We're not here in a hostile capacity. Uh, we'd like to talk to you. Please respond." He took his hand off the screen and waited. There was nothing.

"Did you send?"

"I was sending. Everybody on this rock should've heard it. Provided our array's up, and it's all green, which it is." He leaned over, keyed a second time, and repeated himself. No reply.

"Find us a red line and put us through to somebody directly," I said, feeling my heart sink.

"I can go straight through to the executive ship. It's an emergency code, though. They might not like that."

"It'll be the least of their worries. If an empty ship isn't an emergency, I don't know what is," I told him. "Do it."

Nils did something, and the screen resolved itself into the image of a bridge not too different from the one we were standing on. The Ganraen Royal crest was clear on the bulkhead behind the empty command chair.

There was no one there.

"Is that live?" Deilani asked.

"It ought to be," I said.

"But even the Ganraens keep . . . Hey, we've got charts," Nils said, tapping keys. He'd been about to say that even the Ganraens always kept someone on the command bridge. The practice was more or less universal. Obviously there was no one, a fairly damning indication that things were every bit as bad as they looked.

"Put them up," I said.

He did so. We all moved closer to the large screen. "Then that's the executive ship, about two kilometers north of us. Well, it's not north—no, I don't care. It's north if I say it is. And there are the other two—what are they doing over there?" Nils pointed.

"Shouldn't they be closer together?" I asked.

"Much closer together. Much, much closer," Deilani said. "This makes no sense. This isn't how you set up a colony. I don't care where you're from."

"What were these people doing?" Nils squinted at the screen, zooming in on the valley. "Look at this. There's something at the edge of the valley, they were setting up around it. Look at the sampling tents."

"Forget that. Ensign, set that message to repeat at interval, then if our beacon hasn't been activated, get it online."

"Yes, sir. That was the first thing I did. It's active now."

"Good." I blew out my breath. "We might get off this rock yet. Now, why would the ships be so far apart? That hardly seems efficient."

"Seismic activity," Salmagard said, surprising all three of us. "They wanted stable ground."

"That's the only explanation," Deilani agreed. "They wouldn't set up like this unless they had no other choice."

I nodded. "The ships are more or less self-contained, and they would have brought plenty of vehicles. So the distance would be an inconvenience, but not a deal breaker. Then where'd they go?"

"Where is there *to* go?" Nils asked.

"Nowhere," I said, shrugging. "Yet they aren't here."

"Sabotage," Deilani said. "Or terrorism. Mutiny. Something from the inside."

"Like what?"

"A chemical weapon. Something to instigate . . . unruly behavior. That could account for the damage and inconsistencies. There are a lot of bioweapons that can do it, and plenty of precedent."

"But there would be both bodies and survivors. There were twenty thousand colonists on this planet, probably four thousand on this ship, and we have one—*one*—dead engineer. And if he hadn't strapped in before shooting himself, his body might've blown out when the ship depressurized."

"That could be something," Nils pointed out. "A lot of evidence could've been lost that way. Sucked out of the ship. We weren't looking for it out there."

I knew exactly how easily humans could be swept up and carried during a violent depressurization.

"I think you're right. But we've got what we've got, and that's a planet that looks to me as though it's found a way to make a lot of people disappear."

"Not us," Nils said, swallowing.

"Not yet. We've only been out of our sleepers for a little while, so don't get comfortable."

"Why not? We've got control of the ship," he pointed out. "And the beacon's on. All we have to do is wait. Admiral, we have to sleep."

"Not until we clear the ship," I told him. It hurt, but there was too much wrong with all of this.

"Of what?"

"Of suspicion. We're going to look around."

"That'll take ages," Nils complained.

"You were about to die a few minutes ago, and now you're going to complain about this? We need to make sure we're not missing something. Security's offline. That means we do it the old-fashioned way. I know we've done a lot of walking, but this is the Service. Come on."

"He's right," Deilani told Nils. "Can't let our guard down until we know what happened."

"It'll go faster if we split up."

"But we're not splitting up. We need rest, I know. And we've been stuck together for a while, so a few minutes to ourselves wouldn't hurt, but not until we know where we stand. Then we can borrow some living quarters and take it easy."

Together, the four colony ships were the size of a space station. Apart, they were still massive.

There were closetlike living quarters for single colonists, cramped rooms for couples, and tiny apartments for families. Every deck contained a certain number of each, along with communal features, like recreation and VR rooms.

It was harder to colonize a world like this, where people needed suits to go outside. It took time to build structures and expand the safe zone, and even longer to put up atmosphere domes and start true terraforming. This colony hadn't been here nearly long enough. Everyone would still have been living exclusively in the ships.

The science vessel boasted an enormous medical bay, and a huge battery of laboratories. The faster the colonists understood their new world, the faster it became home. The science vessel was the core of the colonial tetrad.

Colonial authorities tended to be wealthy businesspeople and aristocrats; the colonists themselves more often came from humble birth. Sometimes you'd have a colony that was widely coveted, like on an attractive world that supported human life easily. In that situation you'd have qualified and overqualified people lining up to come along.

But a lot of the time, choosing to become a colonist was a last resort.

In most cultures, joining the military was often a career move reserved for people without better prospects. Only in Evagard did military service offer the level of prestige and reward that made it attractive to even the best imperials.

Colonization was a similar situation—the colony would be founded by someone wealthy, but the colonists themselves were usually people from a much lower social stratum, recruited with modest incentives. It was often a one-way trip, or at the very least carried a long commitment, so the types of people who signed up for these things usually came from a scenario that wasn't overflowing with options.

Much of the galaxy viewed becoming a colonist as being only one step up from selling oneself into indentured servitude, which was legal in Free Trade space.

I didn't think it was so bad. Being a first-generation colonist offered a lot of upward mobility, if you had some patience. Someone had to do it, and for every colony in a terrible place like this, there was one someplace promising. No one really appreciated these people, but they were doing a good thing.

And for many of them, even life aboard a ship like this was an improvement.

One deck was much like another. Some areas were pristine, seemingly untouched. The deck itself was often marred, though we still weren't sure what was doing it. Carbon plating wouldn't corrode like metal, and it couldn't be burned—but something had been eating at it all over the ship. If it was just in one place, that would be a chemical spill—but it was everywhere.

There were also signs that I secretly believed pointed toward a full evacuation. A hasty one. I didn't want to scare the trainees. If there *had* been an evacuation, what had caused it? It could hardly have been completely successful, but in that case, where were the people who hadn't made it?

We didn't find any more bodies, but we weren't trying to be thorough. I had my suspicions about what we'd find if we went through every cabin. What puzzled me the most were the dusty clothes lying everywhere. Boots, personal devices, even weapons. There was no pattern; it was all just scattered around.

"One dead guy," Nils said, shaking his head. "Why would he kill himself?"

"I don't care where they went anymore," Deilani said. "I just want to know why they left."

"They were afraid. Maybe afraid the ship would fall like ours did," I said.

"Then why'd that guy vent the ship before he shot himself?" Nils countered.

That was a good question. We moved on, but Salmagard stayed behind.

"Private?" She was still standing in the last junction. I watched her gaze intently down the cross-passage. "What is it?"

"I thought I heard something, sir." She said it without looking at me. Deilani and I exchanged a glance. Nils didn't look pleased.

"Let's have a look," I said. We followed the passage all the way to the next junction, but there was nothing to see. Nils called out, but no one replied. We stood in the intersection, listening to the echoes of his voice fade away. There was more mysterious damage to the ship, more corroded panels, more mangled doorways. A couple of lights were out, which I didn't care for.

There was a plush toy on the deck, a chubby lobster. I nudged it with my toe, exposing a dark stain.

"You still have your scanner?" I asked Salmagard, who nodded.

I watched Deilani open a hatch and peer through. She looked back and shrugged. Nils didn't look good. The circles under his eyes looked bad, but I probably didn't look any better.

"Go ahead and put it on," I told the private. "Someone did

this. And just because we haven't seen them doesn't mean they aren't still here."

"Yes, Admiral."

We finished our sweep without finding any answers. More than once we heard noises from other parts of the ship, as though there was someone moving around. We searched, but didn't find anything.

I wasn't going to broadcast my suspicions, but I didn't think we were alone. I hoped my withdrawal wasn't making me paranoid.

In space, on colonies—anywhere far enough from what was considered civilization—you would find plentiful amounts of superstition, even among Evagardians. It was especially prevalent on long deep-space journeys. I'd never had any patience for it. Reality was dangerous enough without making up new threats to justify the strain of isolation.

All the evidence suggested that we were alone, even if my instincts thought otherwise. We had to stay focused.

As we made our way back to the upper decks, I gave the trainees their orders. "Nils, you're our new com officer. Find a reader and keep it with you. If anything bites on our surface broadcast, I want to know about it. Same for the beacon. Otherwise"—I looked at my chrono—"I say find something to eat, get some rest—whatever you want to do. Let's meet here at, uh . . . fifteen hundred. That'll give you time for a nap before we look deeper. We good?"

"Admiral, I want to go to the med lab and see what I can find. They were treating people there. I want to find out for what."

"Do what you want, but don't push yourself. You dropped from oxygen deprivation an hour ago. You probably have brain damage."

"Then we have something in common."

"Just be careful. We all need rest." Me especially.

"I'm just going to have a look at the overseer's notes. I expect them to be revealing." Deilani was rubbing her gloved hands together.

"I expect you're right."

Nils was looking at Deilani thoughtfully. He turned to me. "I want to look at the systems one more time, too."

"By all means. I wouldn't dream of holding you back. God-speed. Just—if you do run into anybody, don't do anything that's going to mess up the cease-fire."

"Yes, sir."

Salmagard and I watched the two of them trot off. I wasn't surprised; they were too spun up. Walking around this huge ship wasn't enough to unwind them after our brush with death. They'd need more time before the exhaustion could set back in. And if they wanted to do the legwork, I wasn't going to complain. I wanted to know what was going on as much as they did. If they could get answers while I rested, I could live with that.

My feet hurt, I was hungry, and I was in withdrawal. I needed a lot of things, but I could start with sleep.

I was also alone with Salmagard. This ship was not dead silent, as the freighter had been. Even with only emergency systems, there was plenty to hear. The hum of consoles, vents cycling, and the distant sounds of automated systems.

It was big and empty, and we could both feel it.

"How about a bite?" I asked Salmagard. Rest would have to wait.

One corner of her mouth curved upward. "By all means, Admiral."

We made our way into the nearest galley corner, which boasted a single Ganraen combiner. We had some fun figuring out how to use it; Ganraens had completely different codes for their foods, but there was a nice interactive menu. Our little picnic on the shuttle had been the first time I'd eaten food from a combiner in quite a while.

The product was surprisingly good. I was guessing they used a better grade of protein gel than Tremma had stocked on his freighter. They also had a beverage dispenser that offered some variety, along with a selection containing actual ethanol.

"Is that wise?" Salmagard asked, eyeing my cup.

"It's been a long day. And I'm not exactly known for wisdom. I have to stay in character."

"A trifle late for that, I expect."

"You never know. But I don't think anyone's going to come along and see. Maybe we really do have this place to ourselves."

We were seated at a tiny table for two, which folded down from the bulkhead. The galley was little more than an alcove, and it was open to the corridor. It wasn't intended to be used as a place to eat. Colonists would come for food, which they would eat in their quarters, or the larger communal eating area one deck down.

"What do you think about the *Julian* now?" I asked after a drink. The colony ship was clean and new, but no less cramped than Tremma's freighter. The cargo bays and the bridge were the only parts of the ship that didn't feel claustrophobic.

"I think this experience has made me less particular," Salmagard replied. "I think any assignment with oxygen will do. Regardless of where it takes me, sir."

"That's the spirit. But like I was saying, don't roll over. You can handle anything anybody throws at you—you just have to put some thought into how you fight back. I mean, look at Prince

Dalton. He's a Ganraen Royal. Plenty of expectations on him, but he still finds ways to be different. To do more or less whatever he wants." I shrugged. "He even denounced the war."

"Imagine that," Salmagard said, smiling at me.

"If royalty can make that good a show of independence, you can too."

"Rebellion is not looked on kindly on Earth," she said, keeping her eyes on her food.

"Or anywhere in the Empire. But we're talking about personal freedom, not treason. Bloodline or not, you have the same rights as all the Empress' other subjects. More, since you're a citizen. If you want to see the galaxy, no one can stop you. Get transferred to a frontier ship if you want to see things. And there are other ways—apart from the Service. How long are you in?"

"The minimum."

"Then you've got time *and* options. It's a blank ticket. It won't be easy, but you can work with the Service. Believe me." She gave me a look. "Yes, sometimes you'll get assignments that you're not exactly thrilled with. But that's the cost of doing business."

"That cost is higher for some than for others, clearly."

"Yes. But that's what you'll deal with serving anywhere. Surely you're willing to brave a little risk for the glory of the Empress."

"I'll do anything for the glory of the Empress," Salmagard replied softly. "Anything at all. It's the glory of my family name that I'm not quite as keen on."

"I don't know anything about your family," I said honestly. "I don't know anything about Earth, or what it's like to be you. But even if you don't see eye to eye with your folks, go easy on them. You'll miss them when they're gone. Do you *know* that they gave you that face with mercenary intentions? What if they did it to open more doors for you?"

"This face only opens one door," Salmagard replied grimly, looking down at her reflection in her cup of water.

"But it suits you."

She seemed heartened by that, though we both knew she had an uphill battle ahead of her. Old families like hers wouldn't allow their first daughter to break from the mold lightly. It would take some perseverance and ingenuity if Salmagard wanted to go her own way.

Her smile, and the way she was looking at me, seemed promising. I leaned a little closer, but the com came alive.

"Admiral, we've got trouble," Nils said, but in almost the same instant, on another channel, Deilani was speaking: "Admiral, we're in trouble."

15

"TALK. Deilani first," I replied over the open channel, putting down my drink. I gazed at Salmagard, swallowing my disappointment.

"Mine's more urgent," Nils cut in. Deilani spluttered, but I overruled her.

"Go ahead, Ensign."

"There's someone in maintenance."

"Send again," I said. The com was perfectly clear, but what he was saying needed to be repeated.

"In maintenance, there is someone," he said, more slowly.

"How do you know? Where are you?"

"I'm on the bridge. Since security's down, I'm using maintenance systems to put up a safety net."

So *that* was what he'd wanted to do. Nils was paranoid; he

knew something must have made the colonists abandon this ship, and he couldn't relax until he found out what it was.

"How are you tracking this person?"

"Just movement. There are air density sensors, and there's no mistaking this. There's someone moving around down there in the crawl spaces. A ship with a small crew might have androids, but this is a colony. They had plenty of people, and they wouldn't waste space on robots."

"Which level?" I asked, thinking hard. I'd heard this before, and we'd gone chasing shadows before. But we couldn't ignore this, as much as I'd have liked to.

I was turning into an irritable mess. And this was withdrawal still in its early stages.

"Sub four—there's a lot of damage down there. Maybe they're making repairs."

"He'd have to be in a suit. There's probably coolant down there," I said. "So it's got to be venting all the time since we're on emergency power."

"Yeah, the temperature's crazy—and that's in line with nobody being here to regulate it. I don't know these ships, but with ours if you have a power loss, that takes your main cooling systems with it, so you have to be really careful while it's down. That's where these guys are, and that's what this guy has to be doing. They abandoned this ship, but they don't want it melting down."

"Get a fix on his suit. Patch us through to him."

"That's the thing," Nils said, and I felt my heart sink.

"What?"

"I'm not reading a suit."

"Then it's another ghost story. We're the ones that sealed the ship. It was depressurized, so if there was someone still here, they'd have to be suited up. Or they wouldn't be moving."

"I know," the ensign said. "But it's right in front of me."

Salmagard frowned. "Putting air aside, to be performing maintenance without proper cooling systems, they would have to wear personal protective gear."

"Exactly," I said. "Forget it, Nils. There's nobody down there. Something tripped your net. There's a lot of stuff on this thing that still moves."

"I *know*," Nils said, exasperated. "But there's something you're not thinking about. What if he's from one of the other ships? Those suits wouldn't be registered to this system. It would explain why I can't track him or reach him. He's moving, Admiral. He's moving right now. This isn't a loose panel."

"Could be one of those little rolling things that buffs the floors," I said, though that was wishful thinking. I just didn't want to get up. "But you're probably right—we need to check it out. What *is* it, Lieutenant?" I couldn't ignore Deilani's impatient sounds any longer.

"I know what killed the colonists!" She nearly shouted it.

That got me. "What killed them? They're dead?"

"What *was* killing them. It's all here in the medical logs—well, not all of it . . . but, Admiral, you've got to get down here. There's *life* on this planet." Deilani sounded breathless.

"Wait. We got hostile locals?" I was stunned.

"He's moving," Nils reported. "Guys, this isn't a real security system. No sensors, no reading. If he leaves the coolant grid, we lose him."

"Son of a bitch." I gave Salmagard an apologetic look. She looked very grave.

"All right—look, the guy in maintenance might need help. Especially if we've got hostiles. He's alone. Right, Ensign? We can't ignore him. Everybody get down there. Deilani, we'll worry about your stuff after we check this out."

"All right," she said, sounding dubious. "But why would someone be making repairs on a ship this torn up? And how did it get this way? Obviously the ground giving way accounts for the exterior damage, but what about what we're seeing inside? This doesn't add up, Admiral. Even with what I've just learned."

"Could your hostiles be responsible?"

"Absolutely not."

Fantastic.

Deilani reached Nils only moments after we did.

"Show me," I said to the ensign, who pointed at the screen he was carrying. "I'll be damned. Let's get down there and see what it's about."

"We'll need O_2."

"Then we'll have to borrow suits again. Uh—all right, everybody hand over your cartridges to Nils. Ensign, find a way to get these filled—we may need them. Go now. Lieutenant, watch this feed and guide us while we're down there. Private, find suits."

Nils gave up the reader to Deilani, and jogged off with the empty O_2 cartridges. Salmagard was already gone.

We were beneath the main body of the ship. These were sublevels, where system hardware and heavy machinery were housed in maintenance canals. The layout was intended to distribute the weight of the vessel's heaviest components practically. This part of the colony was more reminiscent of Tremma's freighter. Ganraen engineers had no desire to impress their techs with attractive design.

This part of the ship was meant to be worked on, not seen. There was metal everywhere. Red foam padding covered certain sharp edges, but it was yet another place you'd hate to find yourself with no gravity.

"Something's wrong here," Deilani said to me under her breath as we struggled to muscle the hatch open.

"You think we've got a local down there?" I grinned at her.

"Of course not. But why would there be one man on this ship, and here of all places?"

"You heard the ensign's theory. I don't buy it, but it's plausible. It's not crazy."

"It doesn't work."

"We're here to get answers. There was only one dead body. There should be a lot of colonists left. Maybe this guy knows where they're all hiding."

"I don't think it's that simple," Deilani said, straining to lift the hatch.

"Careful. Lock it open. And let it vent—it shouldn't bother you up here. Use the force screen if you have to."

"Got it," Deilani said, repositioning the pin that locked the hatch open.

Salmagard returned wearing a pressure suit, and dragging another. I wasn't looking forward to experiencing a suit within a suit again, but there was nothing for it; my EV had no air left for me. I donned it and looked at Deilani, who pointed, her eyes on the reader.

"Go right," she said.

I clambered down, and Salmagard came after me. "How soon

until it vents?" I asked over the com, turning right and panning my light down the corridor.

"Four minutes."

"Give us a warning, will you?"

"Of course."

"This way."

I hunched over and started in the direction Deilani had indicated. Here was where the greatest differences were between Ganraen ship design and Evagardian. An Evagardian vessel has few crawl spaces—and those are perfectly smooth and white, with clearly labeled panels that can be removed for easy maintenance. They're also very well lit.

Down here it was a mess. These were the ship's innards, just out in the open. An Evagardian vessel would never be so immodest. I pushed aside a bundle of cords and tubing, holding them out of Salmagard's way so she could get through.

"Deilani, can you brighten it in here?"

"What have you got?"

"Yellows every three meters. It's bad."

"I think I can turn on the emergency ones. Nils should be doing this."

"Just do it."

Red lights began to flash.

"Turn them off," I groaned. "Surely flashing red lights would be more distracting than helpful in an actual emergency," I grumbled as we continued. "This is what happens when you let the government design things."

"But they make it clear there *is* an emergency," Salmagard pointed out. "Commonwealth logic."

And Evagardian prejudice.

"Right. Which way?" I asked Deilani.

"Don't turn yet. Move up to the next junction."

It was slow going, walking in a crouch. "Deilani, tell me what you found."

"The mist out there—it's not mist."

I'd been expecting that. The stuff had never behaved like mist, and the planet had no atmosphere. "Microorganisms?"

"Yes. The Ganraens were exposed. Their decontamination wasn't enough. They're lethal."

I stopped, blinking rapidly. "Well," I said stupidly, "I can see how that would pose a problem for a colony."

"Yeah, kind of a deal breaker," Nils said over the com, laughing nervously. "Why would they settle here? Could they seriously not tell? Were their scans that far off? If you can't properly survey a planet, you can't colonize it. Even my three-year-old niece knows that."

I shook my head, and started to move again. "They came here blind."

"Why, though?" Nils was baffled.

"I don't know. Maybe the Royals forced them to. There were a lot of questionable things going on in the capital before it was destroyed. Internal stuff. It was out of control."

"How would you know that?" Deilani asked.

I ignored her, trying to think. But I didn't have an answer. "Maybe they knew—maybe they knew, and they thought they could handle it. I take it your nanomachines are protecting us."

"For now. They won't last forever, though. That decon was nearly eighteen hours ago, Admiral. We haven't got much time before we go the same way the colonists did."

"How does it kill?" I asked, not really wanting the answer.

"That's not clear from the notes—I'm reading between a lot of lines here. They didn't last long enough to map this thing out completely. The organisms transform cells into something similar to the mineral that makes up this planet."

"Turns you to stone?"

"More like dust. That's what we've been seeing. It's not ash. It's people."

I blanched. "That's not very hygienic."

It explained all the clothing we'd seen lying around.

"All right, stop. Your man's on the move. Funny, I'm picking up even more movement now." She sounded puzzled.

"Which way?"

"I'm not sure. This isn't very precise. He's moving fast. Stand by."

I motioned to Salmagard, who put her back to mine. We kept our lights pointed outward, down the paths that intersected on the junction. Nothing appeared to be moving, but our lights and the shadows gave our imaginations plenty to work with.

"Go left," Deilani said. "Hurry. Maybe you can cut him off in the drainage tank."

"Is it safe?"

"As long as you get there before we vent."

"That gives us about two minutes."

"I'd get a move on," Deilani said mildly.

I motioned to Salmagard and got moving. If we did manage to pull some confused colonist out of this place, he'd better be grateful.

"We're here," I reported as we emerged inside the tank.

"Well?"

"There's nothing here." I climbed down into the shallow basin, sweeping my light around. "It's empty. How long have we got?" There were no lights to speak of down here. Technicians performing maintenance would be wearing tech suits with their own lights.

"Another minute yet. He stopped in there. There's no doubt."

I swept my light over the ceiling, the floor, the walls. Pipes, machinery—it was all a dark tangle of Ganraen ugliness. I didn't have a clue what I was looking at.

But there wasn't anyone there.

"You got a bad reading," I said, shaking my head. I was anxious to get clear. "Back up, Private. Let's get out of here."

"I think you're right," Deilani said. "Now I've got movement all over the ship. But that can't be right. I think Nils must've miscalibrated this thing."

We made our way back up the side of the tank, into the crawl space.

"Now he's moving again," Deilani said.

"There's nobody there," I told her. "And if there is—well, he's on his own. That room's about to be full of coolant. It was nice knowing him."

"Admiral, if *these* sensors are malfunctioning, nanomachines could be the least of our problems."

"Can our problems wait until we're topside?"

"I guess they'll have to."

"Ensign, you got that O_2 worked out?"

"Yes, Admiral. I'm filling them now. I can get them almost to full capacity. Shame we didn't bring our empties. Sorry about the false alarm," Nils replied over the com.

"My fault—but we shouldn't need them. And no harm done, I suppose."

Salmagard and I climbed out of the maintenance hatch, and Deilani sealed it behind us. As we stripped out of our Ganraen suits, I returned Deilani's gaze.

"There *wasn't* anyone there."

She still looked dubious.

"Tell me what you were going to tell me."

She sighed. "It looks like the microorganisms penetrate the skin and contaminate the blood, leading to circulatory arrest. Then they permeate the body, reducing it to this. It's everywhere."

She held out her hand, and I considered the fine gray ash in her palm. I didn't know what to think.

"All of our colonists?" I asked, looking at it sadly.

"Hard to say. It's actually a lot like ash. There's some calcium in there. I don't have the full makeup, though. The colonists didn't understand how they were doing it either."

"I need you to do better."

"At a molecular level it's got some similarities to carbonate, according to the Ganraens. I haven't looked for myself. The remains essentially disintegrate. When the ship depressurized, the bodies went with the air, along with clothing and anything else that might've been left behind. They must have done a true vent with the airlocks to get this kind of air movement in here."

"How does that explain the damage to the ship?" I asked impatiently.

"The exterior damage . . ."

"From the planet. I'm talking about the doors and the shooting. Some of the marks on the walls make me think someone drove a cargo loader through the corridors or something. Your microorganisms didn't do *that*."

"That I'm not sure—there could have been a disagreement about how to deal with this crisis. It's possible that the introduction of the alien organism to blood flow in the brain might have had something to do with it, influencing behaviors. They might've tried something crazy to fight back against it. Plenty of options," Deilani said. "People get strange in deep space. There isn't always an obvious explanation. There's stuff out here that we don't know about or understand, Admiral. Signals, radiation. When things get strange, it's not always an easy answer. We've seen a lot, but we haven't seen it all. That's what makes deep-space colonization dangerous."

"Some of this damage," I began, but didn't finish. Some of this damage didn't fit those theories.

Nils returned, looking pale. He'd been listening over the com.

"Don't panic," I told him, pointing a warning finger. "Let's get up to Medical. You can show us what you've got, and we can figure out what to do." I gave Salmagard what I hoped was a reassuring smile. She was visibly exhausted. I didn't want to think about how bad *I* probably looked.

It was not a cheerful walk.

Deilani had made herself at home in medbay. There were several glowing readers showing half a dozen reports, casting blue light across the room. "The colonists didn't get far before things went to hell," she told us. "None of this is complete. One doctor was convinced that the mist wasn't actually microorganisms, just a larval form of something else. The geological survey—which might have touched all this off—showed that the farther down they went, the larger the subterranean cavities became."

"That doesn't make any sense," I said. "This stuff isn't strong. Is the whole planet unstable? How does that even work?"

"It doesn't make sense to *our* thinking, but the galaxy doesn't have to play by our rules of structural engineering." There was a light in Deilani's eyes that I hadn't seen before. Her inner scientist was coming to the surface again. "I'm going to guess that the makeup of the mineral is different deeper down, though."

"How did they get these readings? I thought scanners were no good."

"They sent a team to blast their way down. When they returned, that may be how they compromised the ship. Bringing the mist aboard."

"That would count for *one* ship," I pointed out. "Not all four."

"I'm not saying I have the answers," Deilani said, leaning on the table. "Just what I've read here. I'm still working the data."

"Could the mist be behind this? Could a—a swarm of these things account for the readings just now?"

She shook her head. "Completely undetectable. The whole ship's probably contaminated. But our decontamination nanomachines won't let them bother us—until they run out."

"How long do we have?"

"Not quite two hours."

I winced. "So that green mist out there is actually a massive crowd of microorganisms. Or larva."

"That's what the Ganraens thought," Deilani replied.

I swallowed, feeling ill. We were breathing that swarm right now.

"They did try to decon, right? Wouldn't that be protocol for colonists?"

"Probably. But they don't have nanotechnology on their side, and we've seen that this planet has its own sensibilities. Commonwealth tech wasn't up to the job."

"Wouldn't be the first time." I folded my arms and thought. "Somehow, all four ships were compromised, there was shooting, and everybody died. Or left."

"That's how it looks."

"When did all of this happen?" I asked.

"According to these logs, over a month ago."

I nodded. "So they'd pretty much just gotten here."

"Looks like everyone was wrong about this planet."

Nils shook his head. "Worst colonization program ever."

"Yeah, like nothing ever goes wrong on imperial colonies," I replied.

"Not like *this*."

"Fine," I said. "Back to our first plan. We'll stockpile supplies and establish a clean zone before the clock runs out. It'll have to hold until help comes, and we'll need a way to communicate with whoever does show up so they can avoid contamination. It's a lot to do, but everything we need is on this ship, and this time we've got power. We don't have a lot of time, but we'll manage."

"I'm not saying it's impossible," Deilani said. "But that won't be easy. Another option is to go back to the freighter for more nanomachines. There should be long-range flyers somewhere in this colony."

"That was my first thought too. But for all we know, now the freighter could be at the center of this planet, especially if integrity actually lessens as you go down. Who knows if we could even reach it, much less get inside? The flight would take more than two hours anyway, so we'd have to think of something to keep ourselves alive that way too. I think we're better off here. This tech is a step down, but it's a step up from no power. Besides, the freighter could be on its side or something."

"This ship already sank once," Nils pointed out. "What's to say it won't end up just like our freighter? I hate to be that guy, but I don't even want to think about what a ship this size weighs."

"I'm not worried unless we do something to shake things up, which I don't plan to." I rapped gloved knuckles on the bulkhead and thought hard.

"That's another thing." Deilani showed me a reader, looking elated.

"What am I looking at?"

"A mineral formation."

"Doesn't look like one." The image showed a massive shape, partially buried in the rock of the planet. It jutted from the wall of the valley, as though it had been exposed when the stone had been knocked away by the ship when it sank. There was also a sliver of the colony ship in the frame, for scale. The formation was probably forty meters across, and roughly cylindrical. It emerged from the stone, curving down, and disappearing into the valley floor.

"What is it?" I asked.

"I don't know. What bothers me is the shape—it reminds you a bit of a pipe, doesn't it?"

"Like an L junction," Nils said.

"Yes, but it's clearly mineral. It's probably coincidence, but it's *not* the same mineral as everything else. The colonists were interested in it," Deilani said. "So maybe we should be too. I checked the status of the ship itself. We're half buried. This thing's partially covered, so we can assume it's part of a larger formation in the ground. I don't see how that's a problem, but . . . I don't like it. We don't understand this planet, Admiral."

We certainly hadn't seen anything like that formation on the way here. I looked closer. I could understand Deilani's concern, but it was just part of the scenery.

"That's an understatement," I said. "The clock's ticking. Unless anyone objects, I say we draft ourselves a clean room and make it happen. You don't want to go out like the Ganraens, do you?"

"No, sir." A chorus answered me.

"Good. Nils, hit the plans and find us a room. Deilani, containment measures are up to you. The private and I will stockpile supplies. Lieutenant, give us a safety briefing."

"Hurry," Deilani said.

"You heard her. Questions?"

16

"ADMIRAL," Nils said over the com. Salmagard and I paused in the corridor.

"Yeah?"

"About your plan."

"Yes?"

"It sort of counts on us getting rescued, doesn't it?" There was something in his voice I didn't like.

"It does, Ensign. That's what the beacon's for."

"That's the thing, sir. It's active, but I think it's buried."

I recalled the image of the landslide that Deilani had showed me, and the strange mineral formation.

"What? Would that be an issue?"

"It might, considering what this planet does to signals," Nils said.

"You getting this, Deilani?"

"I'm listening."

I rubbed my eyes, glanced at Salmagard, and spoke into the com. "Can we clear it?"

"I don't know. We might do more harm than good. It could already be damaged."

"It received your ping, didn't it?"

"That could've been any one of these ships. They all have com arrays, and I don't have any reason to think they don't all have power. Admiral, if we're not broadcasting, we could be waiting for rescue for a very long time out here. Call it a hunch, but I don't think this planet's the first place they're going to come looking."

"How do you want to handle it?"

"I'd better get out there and have a look."

"Not by yourself." It pained me, considering our tight schedule, but safety had to come first. "Change of plans. Nils, put down paths to the smartest airlock."

"All of us?"

"Yes, everyone. I don't want anybody alone out there or in here." I didn't want to share the details behind my concern, but the situation inside the ship still didn't add up. Until it did, I'd stay cagey.

This was time we didn't have. The trainees knew it too. It was a good thing both Nils and Deilani had chosen curiosity over rest, or we'd have been in real trouble.

In the airlock we all inserted the recharged O_2 cartridges that Nils had brought, and deployed our helmets.

"Hit it," I told Deilani.

"Already started the cycle. There's an automatic decon—just

not a very useful one, clearly. This chemical mist." She put out her glove, rubbing her fingers together. "For all the good it seems to do. There must be something about the matter on this planet that reacts to our materials and corrodes it. I think that's the cause of these burns, and some of the ways the ships have been compromised."

The outer doors opened, immediately letting in tendrils of green mist.

"As long as this stuff can't get through EVs. There's probably a better way up, but we don't have time to argue over the map. Let's just go." I activated the charge in my gloves and began to scale the side of the colony ship. We were starting from an upper deck, but it was still a long climb.

The mist was thin at the top of the ship, though we were still far below the surface of the planet. I looked around at the distant walls of the valley that had been created when the Ganraen colony sank. There wouldn't be any climbing out of this basin; we'd need a vehicle, but the pilot bay was blocked by collapsed rock. It was just as well; if there was no one left on the other ships, there was no reason for us to visit them.

The damage to the ship, and the large amount of debris that had collapsed onto it, was evident when we reached the top. We were half buried.

"Oh, hell."

"What, Ensign?"

Nils pointed. "The array is in there somewhere."

"No way we're clearing that. We could blast it."

"We could destroy it, though. And there's no time to excavate it."

"And that means no rescue."

"Not until the Ganraens get suspicious about how quiet things are out here—they probably are by now. They'd have to be."

"They might've written it off," I said.

"What? How do you know that?"

I blinked and turned toward him, looking at him through his faceplate. "I told you," I said. "Colonial safety isn't high on the Commonwealth's list of priorities right now. This colony launched at a bad time, and right now the Ganraen systems affected by the war just want to recover. Besides, there's a good chance these people were separatists. A lot of people jumped ship during the war, and it's one reason they might've risked a planet with sketchy surveys."

"You don't think they'll send anyone?" Nils was incredulous. Spoiled by the Evagardian way of doing things.

The words hung as we all stood on the sloping side of the colony ship, surrounded by the vast emptiness of the misty valley.

"I wouldn't count on it. Especially if some of the colonists escaped," I said finally.

"Then we're here until our people come looking," Deilani said. "It could take them a while to find us. Maybe Galactic Rescue will come."

The lieutenant was right. But it wouldn't be Galactic Rescue. It would be Evagardian Intelligence. Or Imperial Security. Or both.

"I don't think the GRs mobilize for stuff like this," Nils said.

"They don't," Deilani replied. "I was joking."

"Back inside," I said. "We haven't got all cycle. Oh. Hello."

I stopped. Nils froze. Salmagard gave no indication of surprise or alarm, but Deilani let out a cry.

The thing was clinging to the side of a thruster that we'd

absently walked past to reach this point. We must have been within a meter of it. Now, facing this way, it was impossible to miss.

It was quite obviously a life-form. An indigenous life-form. The thing's black limbs stood out clearly against the gray metal, but it was the same color as the planet. It would be . . . invisible anywhere else.

Nobody moved.

I struggled to keep my bearing. "First time seeing a xeno up close, Lieutenant?"

"Yes—yes, sir."

"Mine too. Don't panic."

"Yes, sir."

"I don't suppose anyone brought a weapon?" Nils' voice broke.

With its legs outstretched, the thing was nearly three meters across. It reminded me of pictures I'd seen of Old Earth arachnids and crustaceans—but those organisms were built with a meticulous symmetry. Artistry, even. This thing had none of that. The jagged, bizarre angles of its limbs made it one of the most intensely hideous things I had ever seen. I didn't see eyes or a mouth, nothing but joints and the lumpy carapace.

Where the spindly legs touched the metal, the metal was smoking faintly.

Deilani's readings hadn't been faulty. Something like this would have been tough to spot on the ceiling of that coolant tank, among all the piping and wires, even if you were looking for it. And we hadn't been.

"You told us not to touch weapons," Deilani said. "Didn't want us to seem hostile." She sounded distant.

"Right." I swallowed. "No reason to think we might need them, anyway. This fellow might be friendly."

But he wasn't. This was how the inside of the colony ship had gotten to this state; suddenly the weapons fire and damage all came into sharp focus.

"He's killed thousands of colonists," Nils pointed out, a distinct quaver in his voice.

"Colonists," I said slowly, beginning to back away. "Who were trespassing. For all we know, this ship might've fallen on his home. Anything he's done has been perfectly justified by Evagardian law. And Commonwealth law, for that matter."

"So the mist is the larval stage of *this*? This *thing*?" There was no point telling Nils not to panic now. He already had.

And if what he said was true, it explained more or less everything, even Salmagard's allegedly faulty scanner readings. I saw her switch her scanner back on, and immediately look sharply over her shoulder.

"Contact?" I didn't take my eyes off the creature.

"I'm reading movement all over this valley."

I began to swear internally.

"There's one over there," Nils said, pointing. His finger shook.

Now that we were looking for them, they were very obvious.

"Guys," I said. "Let's go inside."

We started to make our way toward the edge of the ship, giving the creature a wide berth. I started a controlled slide down the slope of the hull. I reached the airlock and started the cycle.

"Incoming," Salmagard reported, touching down beside me and looking over the railing.

One of the creatures was scuttling determinedly up the side of the ship. It wasn't as large as the one we'd seen up there, but it was still more than a meter across, and apparently very keen to meet us. Deilani backed up until she hit the bulkhead. She wouldn't be any help.

There was no atmosphere out here, nothing to conduct sound. The thing was coming at us in absolute silence. I wondered how much we'd been oblivious to as we'd just climbed into this valley and approached the colony.

We hadn't been looking.

Salmagard vaulted over the railing to crouch on the hull. She pulled up a release for a maintenance hatch and raised the panel a few centimeters, staring the thing down as it got closer. It clambered onto the metal sheet almost faster than she was ready for, but she jerked it out of its clamps and gave it a hard shove, sending the panel and the xeno sliding down the side of the ship to disappear into the mist.

The airlock was open. I pulled her back over the railing, and we joined the others inside. Nils hit the seal, and the doors closed. The dim airlock filled with the impotent Ganraen decontamination spray.

"Did I just fire the first shot?" Salmagard asked worriedly.

"The colonists did. These guys were prejudiced against us before we got here. I bet four big colony ships crunching down like this killed a lot more of them than us. Halt that cycle—we need to talk."

"I'm reading them inside the ship," Salmagard reported.

"No doubt; the hull's breached in a dozen places. This changes things. Now, not only do we have no functioning beacon, but we've got active hostiles. Our clean room won't stay clean for long with these guys running around—were any of you looking at his feet?"

"I saw," Deilani said, nodding. "There was some kind of reaction with the metal."

"Hiding ourselves away and holding out isn't an option anymore." I looked at the trainees, then at my chrono. "We have to get off this planet before our nanomachines fail."

"Shuttle," Nils said immediately. He was right. It wasn't polite to just swipe a transport, but there was no one here to object. "Most of the vehicles probably aren't on this ship, but there have to be some shuttles. Is the bay buried?"

"A colony ship has its atmosphere bay on top, so I doubt it. Or at least not *so* buried that we can't get the doors open. We'll get into orbit, hit the shuttle's subspace beacon, and go to sleep. And hope for the best. Questions?"

"You trust Ganraen sleep tech?" Nils still seemed dazed.

"More than I trust their decon. Ready?"

"Let's do it." Deilani hit the release, and the inner airlock doors hissed open.

Nils went to the nearest console and keyed in a path to the flight bay. He seemed reluctant to disengage his helmet. I reminded him that his air supply was finite, and he shut it off.

"I didn't think I could hate this planet even more," Deilani muttered. "These larger ones must have hit the colonists suddenly, because there's nothing about them in the logs."

"I know why security's down," Nils said, looking up from the console, realization dawning. "The security office is smashed all to hell. Someone must have tried to make a stand there."

"That's where I'd have done it." I kept moving.

"It didn't end well."

"Don't be fooled," Deilani said. "The larval ones are the most dangerous. The mist. They can't be fought at all without a compound that'll kill them, or at least nanomachines to hold them back."

"You didn't seem too bothered," Nils said to Salmagard.

"I'm from Earth," she replied distractedly, busy with her scanner.

"So?"

"You've never seen a Nipponese spider crab? Delicious."

The fact that she was making jokes meant she was every bit as rattled as the rest of us.

The ensign shook his head. "Mad. The lot of you."

"It was one of these—a little one, back on the freighter. In Medical," I said, tugging at my collar. "Not a hamster. But how'd he get in?"

"What?" Deilani looked at me.

"The hull breach was at the other end of the ship." I folded my arms. "How'd he get from there to Medical?" My eyes caught on a Ganraen vent cover. I felt ill, and this time it had nothing to do with my withdrawal.

"Got the atmosphere bay—two decks up. Let's go," Nils said, disconnecting from his terminal.

"Private?"

"I'm not reading anything nearby."

"Then let's move. I doubt there's much reason for there to be many in here, but when we repressurized we sealed them in with us. I think just now we might've agitated them."

Now that we knew we weren't alone on the ship, its vast emptiness took on a new significance. There couldn't be *too many* of them in here with us, but that wasn't very comforting. I was looking around in a decidedly paranoid fashion, even when I knew that Salmagard would pick up anything nearby long before I'd notice.

As we ran through the deserted corridors of the colony ship, I knew how Captain Tremma and his pilot officer must have met their end. By blasting the spire, they had stirred up the locals. They must not have been quick enough to decontaminate when they got back aboard; that explained the mishap with the incinerator. Blind panic. I didn't know what it would feel like to have these things inside my body, turning it into their mineral—but I could imagine that it would be distressing.

There were no more mysteries, but that was small comfort when there were so many crises. On the other hand, if all went well, we'd be off this rock in a matter of minutes. I could pilot a Ganraen shuttle, and it wasn't as if I could make Deilani's suspicions *worse*. Hoping for the best in Ganraen sleepers powered by a Ganraen shuttle carried some risk, but no more than we had here on the surface. It wouldn't be my first time.

We *would* be picked up. The question was by whom.

None of us had come up this way since our initial sweep, which had been cursory at best. The damage to the ship was no longer puzzling, but we didn't like the story it told.

There had been some sizable specimens running amok in here. We just had to hope the big ones had all gone back outside. Or was it the small ones we needed to worry about?

I was worried about all of them. I was used to human beings as my enemies. This was completely new to me.

We reached the bay, stopping short.

"Little roomier than it needs to be, isn't it?" I said, feeling detached. My voice echoed in the cavernous chamber.

There were bays for several shuttles. They were all empty.

Rubble was strewn about the deck; the bay doors had been open—probably when the colonists had made their escape. This was why there was so little evidence: most of the colonists hadn't actually died here.

"At least we know what that guy was doing in engineering," Nils said, face white, eyes wide. "He missed his ride."

17

NO shuttles. Not one. Of *course* they'd evacuated. Anybody would, and I'd seen the signs.

"We're not alone," Deilani said.

"I'm not picking up anything," Salmagard countered.

"It's not moving." The lieutenant pointed. There was something dark on the ceiling of the bay. It was well over a hundred meters away. The fact that we could even see it at this distance meant it was at least twice the size of the one we'd encountered outside.

"Don't panic," I said.

"Too late," Nils replied.

"Back in the lift." I hurried them out of the bay. Once we were safely in the lift with the shield closed, I rubbed at my eyes. I opened my mouth to ask Deilani how much time we had, then thought better of it. "Do or die, guys. How do we get off this planet?"

"We're on a ship," Deilani said.

I shook my head. "It takes a crew to fly, and a hundred techs to keep it flying. Even if we had the training, we couldn't budge it—especially not knowing how badly damaged it is."

"I looked at the overall diagnostic," Nils said. "The damage is substantial, but as far as we're concerned, nothing that would keep us here."

"Moot point. We can't fly it. Next idea."

"There could be more shuttles on the other ships," Deilani said, looking hopeful.

"It's possible, but not likely enough to gamble on. They've all evacuated. It would be worth a look if time wasn't so tight, but we're at the bottom of a valley. We'd have to secure some kind of vehicle, then navigate. I don't think there's time."

"Then I'm out of ideas," Nils said. "Those were the only space-worthy options on this ship. If our ECs won't get us into orbit, Ganraen ones sure as the Empress won't."

"Wait a minute." Deilani put her hands on her hips and stared at her boots. "Wait a minute. This is the *science* vessel."

"Yeah," I said, raising an eyebrow.

"So this is where the satellites are."

I wanted to kiss her. "This is why I keep you around, Lieutenant. Nils, find a console and locate the ballistic launch bay."

"They'll already have put their unit into orbit," he said, shaking his head.

"There'll be more than one."

"There *has* to be one in orbit—that's how they got their charts."

"Not important, Ensign. Do it."

Nils hit the release, and the lift started to move. "Survey satellites aren't meant to be manned," he pointed out.

"It's worth checking out. We might have to get creative." I was thinking fast.

"I've heard that before."

The launch bay was more like a silo. A narrow, retractable corridor led to the satellite itself, which had already been loaded for launch. Nils immediately went to work on the control panel.

The maintenance cavity in the satellite was cramped, but not as cramped as I'd feared. We could all fit inside, and there would be room for supplies as well. It would be a brutally awkward and intimate fit, but I'd been worried that we wouldn't all be able to come along.

"It hasn't even got a recycler," Deilani said. "It can't support life. It's like going into space in a metal box."

She had a point.

"We'll think of something." I ducked through the hatch to get inside.

"All we need to do is stick some sleepers in there," Nils said, grinning. It was a joke, of course. Maybe we could fit Evagardian sleepers, which were relatively compact—but not Ganraen ones.

We couldn't cram much air in there, either. Not more than twenty-four hours' worth for the four of us. We needed more time than that. And we'd need a way to keep the temperature up. And at least *some* kind of ventilation.

Deilani was right—this wasn't a good solution.

"Getting off the planet's all well and good, but not if we're just going to die in orbit," Deilani said. "This won't work. It's not made for passengers. This space is only here so a tech can get in there and fix it when it breaks."

Nothing I didn't already know. "Asleep won't work, and neither will awake. What does that leave? How about medical stasis?"

Deilani blinked. "Does the Commonwealth even have it?"

"Of course."

"Do you trust it?"

"Do we have a choice?"

"EMS can't support you for more than a couple hundred hours at most. It's called emergency stasis for a reason. You don't even want to know what it'll do to you if you stay in there too long."

I shrugged. "A couple hundred hours is longer than we'll last down here. And we won't need air or heat."

She gave me a calculating look. "You want to stick four stasis modules in there."

"You and I could share one."

Her eyes narrowed. "We are about to be *dead*."

"Not if I can help it. We can rig up some kind of power supply— hell, can't we divert some of the satellite's systems for it?"

"Maybe." Nils folded his arms. "But I don't know these systems. If something goes wrong, we'll all wake up in plastic coffins, watching one another suffocate."

"It'll be dark," I told him. "We won't have to watch."

I clapped him on the shoulder and climbed out of the satellite, starting back down the corridor. "What do we need to do? We need to prep the satellite for launch, secure four stasis modules, and find a way to keep them powered up. What else?"

"That's pretty much it," Nils said, glancing at Deilani. "We might be cutting it close, but it could be possible. It might not," he added. "I can't make promises about coupling Ganraen tech—I'll have to make it up as I go."

"You didn't get assigned to the *Julian* because you were bad at your job." I waved him off. "Lieutenant, where do we get the EMS units?"

"If this was an Evagardian ship, there would be at least one mobile unit on every deck. But there probably isn't, and I wouldn't know where to look."

"Medbay, obviously."

"No." Deilani chewed her lip. "Those are stationary units. You can't move them. All right—this is a colony. They must have surface craft for workmen and surveyors. Those flyers and personnel carriers will have mobile units in case there are injuries on the surface. Colonists have accidents all the time. It's kind of their thing. We'll use those. Those vehicles should be in the bay underneath the one we just came from."

"Will they be hard to move?"

"I don't know. Who can tell with these people? They should have their own grav pallets."

"Let's get down there and have a look. Can we actually fit four of them in there?"

Deilani scowled. "Depends on how bulky they are. We could fit four of ours."

The planetary survey vessels were all there in the bay, looking almost pristine. It was a lot of vehicles, and the vast space almost seemed full. The floor and walls were like a massive gray grid, stretching into the distance.

We appeared to have the bay to ourselves. "There," Deilani said, pointing. "The big ones—those are for long-range work crews. They'll have EMS." She jogged off across the deck. I didn't have that kind of energy. My withdrawal was getting worse.

I looked over at Salmagard. "Private?"

"There's movement under the floor, Admiral."

Movement *under* the floor didn't worry me. I hurried after Deilani.

The long-distance crawler was the size of a small spacecraft. A big colonial seal was printed on each of the six massive wheels. There were some dents in the gray chassis, but no serious damage.

Deilani was lowering the ramp. She'd been right: there were two EMS units—one on either side of the cargo hold. "They aren't as big as I thought they'd be . . . but I'm not sure we want to trust our lives to these," she fretted.

"You'll have to. How do we detach them?"

She shot me a look. "We need to be gentle. Two to a pallet. We'll have to make another trip." There was a hiss, and the float pallet lit up. Deilani seized the controls and lifted it off the deck, moving it gingerly away from the bulkhead. Nils took over for her, and she went to work on the other one. "Six hours on its internal charge. Then it'll need power."

"Six hours? That's terrible," Nils said, appalled. "What's the point?"

"There are power docks here, but they're for use with this vehicle. It's Ganraen; what do you expect?" Deilani snapped.

Nils was looking at me worriedly. I knew what he was thinking. These units might not buy us as much time as we'd hoped. But until someone thought of a better plan, it was still full speed ahead on this one.

Deilani detached the next unit, and I grabbed the controls. "Go," I said, and she joined Nils in moving the first unit down the ramp. Salmagard helped me steer my pallet.

The temptation to rush was strong, but these Ganraen lifts weren't as responsive as Evagardian ones. In the long run, a spill would cost us more time than a deliberate pace.

"Admiral, are you all right?" Salmagard asked me quietly. We were several meters behind Deilani and the ensign. She could plainly see how bloodshot my eyes were. They were burning. And I could feel the occasional muscle spasm.

"The drugs the lieutenant gave me are wearing off," I told her. "It's making it hard to focus."

"Is there anything we can do?"

I shook my head. "Ganraen pharmaceuticals aren't on our level. If they had a cure, I wouldn't be blazed in the first place. Don't worry. I can stay in it a little longer." This side of things had slipped the lieutenant's mind completely, but I couldn't distract her with it now. Our survival was more important than my comfort.

It was a long walk, but I was getting used to crossing bays on foot. That didn't make my feet hurt any less.

"It's following us," Salmagard whispered to me.

"What?" She looked down. I looked down at the deck too. "Vibration? Heat?"

She shrugged. "The more we move, the more I read. We're attracting them."

"Get ready to fight."

"I am. Are you?" She looked concerned.

"I don't like fighting."

"Sir?"

"Don't worry about me," I told her. It would be enough for me to stay lucid. I'd leave the fighting to Salmagard.

"Take the first lift," I called to Deilani. "We'll use personnel instead of cargo—one at a time, it's still faster. Can't fit both of these in there." I waved her on. "Just go." We were lucky the lift was big enough for one unit. It was tight, though.

"Copy that." Deilani and Nils disappeared through the hatch.

Salmagard opened the pouch at her hip and situated a Ganraen sidearm inside so it would be easier to get at.

"That's against orders," I said lightly. I hadn't seen her pick it up.

"They didn't seem to *me* like faulty readings," she replied without meeting my eyes.

"Maybe we do need more people with your genes on the enlisted side." The lift doors opened, and we pushed the EMS unit into the cramped carriage, tilting it up to fit. The ride up took only a moment.

The doors had barely opened again when there was a shout over the com. Salmagard flew out of the lift so fast that I was suddenly left with the full weight of the EMS unit, vastly reduced by the grav pallet, but still considerable. I eased it down and stumbled after her.

Deilani was dragging Nils away from *three* xenos. One was so large that it seemed to fill the whole corridor, and the other two were just big enough to give me nightmares.

All three were advancing. Nils was hurt; there were smears of blood on the deck and on his suit.

Salmagard got between them and the xenos, the Ganraen side-arm extended in one hand. She fired at the nearest one, which was scuttling toward her at an alarming pace. The projectile, intended to be safe for use on spacecraft, fragmented on the thing's carapace. It barely seemed to notice. And it was one of the little ones. Salmagard's eye twitched, and she took a step back.

I helped Deilani pull Nils back toward the lift, but we couldn't outrun these things in such close quarters.

Salmagard seemed determined to keep them from getting at us.

She took another step back, then pointed the weapon at the bulkhead and fired several times in quick succession. It looked random to me, but it was precision shooting. A panel broke free and fell to swing, held up by only one fastening, revealing piping and wiring. Salmagard didn't see what she wanted, because she blasted another panel off the other side of the corridor, then fired a final shot.

There was a small explosion, and the corridor was suddenly filled with scalding steam. I triggered my helmet, and Deilani reached down to hit the ensign's. We got him into the lift, which was crowded with the EMS unit still in it. Deilani shoved it out, and it thudded against the bulkhead, drifting crookedly through the corridor. Salmagard dodged it narrowly, sliding into the lift and hitting the release.

"Down," I said, disengaging my helmet, and we started to move. "Did it work?"

Salmagard nodded.

I turned my attention to Nils. There were serious burns on his back, each focused around what looked like a deep puncture. His white suit was streaked with blood. He looked terrible; his EV wasn't bothering to mend itself; it knew he needed treatment first. "We need Medical."

The steam had been good thinking on Salmagard's part. Brilliant, really. There was no atmosphere on this cold planet, so it was unlikely that locals would have evolutionary defenses against heat.

Deilani and I carried Nils into the Ganraen med lab, where we found no fewer than a dozen of the things, all less than a meter across, and all clinging to the walls and ceiling. The lieutenant and I held up, blocking Salmagard.

"I think you've upset them," I said to her.

"Oh, Founder." Nils closed his eyes.

Salmagard was bouncing on her toes to try to see past us. She spotted the things on the walls, and motioned for us to get out of the way. Deilani and I backed up; Nils was still bleeding. This was *bad*.

One of the Ganraen tech suits we'd discarded earlier was lying a few meters away. Salmagard picked it up and started to pull it on. She got the helmet sealed, and pressurized it. The suit more or less shrank to fit her, and she removed the safety tab from the wrist-mounted incinerator.

She marched into the med lab, and the door closed behind her.

Nils stared after her, uncomprehending.

"The Empress only negotiates one way," I reminded him. "Don't tell me you forgot."

About thirty seconds passed. The door opened, and Salmagard beckoned us in. The med lab was covered in burns, and I could see several shriveled carcasses. There was a lot of steam, but the emergency sprinklers had stopped.

"Clear," Salmagard said.

I couldn't help but think of how many hiding places there were, but the private sounded sure of herself, and she had her scanner to back her up. We laid out Nils, and Deilani bustled away, but was back almost immediately. "Turn him over," she ordered, and we did so. Salmagard was stripping out of the pressure suit.

"Better keep that on," I said over my shoulder.

"No use, sir. It's out of fuel."

Deilani jabbed Nils with a hypo, then moved a digital lens over his wounds. "It's already affecting him. We have to slow it down." She switched cartridges and jabbed him again. Nils swore loudly. "Shut up. Get me that cutter." That was directed to me. I grabbed it and threw it to her. She used the beam to slice away the back of Nils' EV suit, revealing wounds that looked, even to me, extraordinarily ghastly. The skin around his punctures was purple and black. There was a dark foam bubbling from the wounds.

"How soon before he's dust?" I asked, squeezing my eyes shut. I was seeing double, and I felt light-headed. My heart rate was up, and that was making it all worse.

"I'm right here," Nils moaned.

"I don't know," Deilani said distractedly. "These Ganraens weren't very creative. Ensign, I'm going to slow your metabolism. I need to shut down your heart for a second because this chem needs to be localized. If your heart's beating when I do this, it's going to go places you don't want it to go. Don't panic."

"Wait—what? You're gonna kill me?"

"Dying's easy," I said.

Nils gagged, face white.

"Don't panic," Deilani repeated, attaching leads to his exposed skin.

"Oh, Empress," he gasped.

I looked around to see that Salmagard had disappeared from the lab. I hadn't seen her leave. I shook my head, but it wouldn't clear.

"Hold him!" Deilani ordered.

"I got it, I got it."

"I'll say one thing for your plan," Deilani said, the cap of yet another hypo held in her mouth. She spat it out. "He'd have to go into stasis anyway."

"See? I plan ahead. I bet you guys thought I've been winging it this whole time."

She looked up at me sharply. "Did you take something?"

"No, I'm drying out. It's almost as good."

"Oh, Empress. Just help me. I'll get to you."

"No hurry."

"Take your hands off." I pulled them back, and she ran a current through the ensign. He started to seize. "Grab him."

"Are you going to bring him back *today*?" I asked, holding him down more with my weight than with my muscles.

"You want to do this?" She sprayed some foam on his back, muttering about Ganraen medical technology. "Pull that third lead and juice him."

"What?"

"The *blue* one."

"Oh. The blue one." I tried, but my hands were shaking too badly. Deilani saw me and blanched. "All right, just back off."

"I can hold him."

She yanked the third lead from his back, checked the other two, and zapped him, then immediately hit him with another injection. He gasped and began to swear in between groans of pain.

"Don't be a baby." She pulled a black spine the size of my finger out of his back and tossed it aside, then sprayed on more foam, which seemed to help. "We need to seal him so he has EV integrity; it can't repair a breach this big in time. Where's Eyelashes?"

She meant Salmagard. "I don't know." I keyed the com. "Private, where the hell are you?"

"Clearing the satellite launch corridor, Admiral."

Well, that was something that needed to be done—and damn it, she was thinking more clearly than I was. My presence of mind was coming and going as it pleased, and we were running out of time. "Be careful."

"Sir, the first unit's damaged. We'll need another. But I've got ours in there." Wasn't that a nice thought? Of course two people could not share one unit. She meant the one that we'd been moving together. Now we were out one unit, and . . . I stopped thinking about it. "Carry on, Private."

"We're not getting off this ship, not with those things all over," Deilani stated flatly.

She was right. We had enough of a hill to climb without hostiles. But I couldn't wish them away.

"Stay positive," I told her. "We'll make it work. So far I'd say that negotiations are going well."

"I think I like you better this way," she said.

"I've heard that before."

Deilani had sealed Nils' back nicely, and turned him over. "Listen, Ensign. I've put you on a cocktail that'll kill you in less than twelve hours—thankfully, we'll be in stasis by then, or dead anyway. This is a stimulant. It's going to make you forget that you're dying. Don't forget that you're dying. Do you understand?"

"Yes, ma'am."

She shot him up one last time, and got him into a sitting position, where he began to cough. I understood what she was doing. Not medically, of course—but we needed Nils. We weren't getting off this planet without him, so no matter how radical the treatment, she had to keep him in the game. This was the first time I'd seen Deilani really doing her job; her assignment to the *Julian* made more sense now.

"How do you feel, Ensign?"

"Who the hell . . ."

"Give him a minute," she said.

"We don't have a minute."

"Good point. Help me get him up—he's not going to be mobile. We'll have to park him in the satellite and bring the work to him. What about you? Are you up to this?"

"I'll manage," I said.

18

WE were losing time. We had to get back to the satellite.

Deilani and I spilled out of the lift to find Salmagard with her back to us, facing down the largest of the three creatures that had jumped Deilani and Nils. I didn't know where the other two had gone. The steam had cleared; the ship's computer had recognized the breach and cut it off.

Salmagard was right. Something *was* attracting the xenos to us, and the big one was advancing on her.

In her arms was a device nearly as big as she was, and I didn't recognize it. It looked like something you'd see held by someone in a tech suit doing major work on a ship's hull.

Deilani and I backed into the lift. It probably wasn't a good idea to walk Nils into this situation.

"Um—Private?"

"Clearing the way, Admiral."

She started to advance, and that halted the creature. I wondered if it was puzzled to see something so small refusing to run away. The creature was so big that it had difficulty fitting in the corridor. Its legs were spread over both walls, and it less walked than dragged itself toward her.

"Is she going to be all right?" Deilani hissed.

"I don't know. Private, fall back!"

She didn't reply, but instead set her feet and readied her—her thing. Weapon, presumably. She knew we had to secure this corridor to reach the satellite.

It was almost on top of her. I saw the xeno arch its back, revealing more spines and smaller limbs on its underside—so those were what had done that to Nils' back—and that was what Salmagard was waiting for. The front of her device lit up, and she lunged forward, ramming it into the creature's underside.

It was a magnesium cutter. Like most things Ganraen, it was bigger and more primitive than what Evagardians were accustomed to. The light was blinding—then the tip was buried in the xeno, which was trying to scramble away from Salmagard. She pushed the thing back, past the corridor to the satellite. Deilani and I immediately started forward with Nils.

We moved him down the narrow approach passage and into the satellite, propping him up against the EMS unit we'd already placed.

Salmagard appeared in the hatchway, flushed, but unharmed. It wasn't a look of pleasure or elation on her face, but rather one of deep satisfaction.

Instead of looking for weapons, she'd gone looking for tools. Smart. The lance was gone; maybe she'd left it buried in the thing.

"Did you get him?"

She shook her head. "But he shouldn't bother us again."

"What about the other ones?"

"They've gone off, Admiral. We're clear for the moment."

I let out my breath, trying to collect my thoughts. I just wanted a minute—*one minute*—but we didn't even have that much to spare. I rubbed at my eyes, opened and closed my hands a few times, and focused.

Deilani and Salmagard were watching me worriedly, but I was more concerned about Nils. Without him, we weren't going anywhere. We had to keep him safe. His eyes were closed, but he was conscious, taking deep breaths.

"Guys, we need to own this deck. Or at least the ground between here and the lift. I'm going to need both of you in play, so the ensign has got to be safe. Private, get out there and lower every pressure door you can find. There's nothing here but this and the lift. Got it? If it doesn't come off the lift, it's not getting in here."

"Yes, Admiral." She jogged off.

"You're fading fast," Deilani said. "I can give you a stimulant. It'll set you back, but it might get you through the next few hours. You look weak."

"What do you need to do?"

"I need to check your blood first, or I could kill you or put you in a coma."

"No time." I shook my head and led her back down the corridor. "We've got work to do. Find Nils whatever he needs, and help him. Get him set up; do what you have to do. You work for him now."

"What about you?"

"The private and I are going to try to find three more EMS

units. Look—I'm not—I can't be trusted to cover the details now. You have to make sure we don't forget anything, all right?"

Her gaze flicked back toward the silo. "If we don't put him in stasis soon, he's not going to make it."

"If he doesn't prep this launch, none of us will."

I tracked down Salmagard, who was making certain she'd been thorough in sealing off the silo passage. Together, we took the lift down and made for the vehicle bay.

The gray padded Ganraen corridors were starting to blur together.

"You're tired, aren't you? Do you need a stim?" I asked her.

"Evagardian ladies are expected never to rely upon chemical assistance, Admiral."

"That's your way of saying you need one, right?"

"No, sir." She said it with a completely straight face.

I wished she'd shown this side of herself before things had gotten this bad. It was probably the adrenaline.

"We'll get you one from Deilani when we get back up there."

"You need it more than I do, sir." She meant it seriously.

"Yeah, but I can't have one. It's karma."

The lift doors opened, and we moved into the corridor. "Movement in the bay," Salmagard reported.

"We have to go anyway."

"Naturally, sir."

"I don't suppose you've got another cutter handy?"

"No, sir." There was excitement in her voice.

"I'll run interference. You move the units," I told her.

We entered the bay, and I spotted half a dozen xenos of varying sizes, none smaller than two meters across. They hadn't been there twenty minutes ago. "You really have upset them," I said.

"How?"

I decided to let her work that out on her own. I started to jog in the opposite direction. I climbed into a bay skiff and started it up. It was a small, lightweight vehicle that techs could use to move around the massive bay quickly.

I drove it straight at the nearest xeno on the ground, veering off at the last moment to give it a scare. I circled around and made for another one, hoping I would be more interesting to them than Salmagard. I wasn't in too much danger as long as I was mobile. On foot I wouldn't last long.

The one I was charging down was on the small side, standing a mere meter off the deck. I smashed into it, flinging it against the bulkhead.

I wheeled around to look for another victim. One of the creatures crashed heavily into my roof, its hooked legs ripping easily through the thin canopy. It must have dropped from the ceiling. I released the controls and dove out, rolling to my feet. The skiff continued to skim, taking the xeno with it, but I wasn't alone. I barely dodged as a smaller one lunged for me. I backed away, but a look over my shoulder told me I had company behind me as well. I started to run.

"All right, Private?"

"Nobody's bothering me, sir."

Great. I couldn't outrun the big one behind me. I dropped into a slide that took me beneath a ground-crawling personnel carrier. I scrambled up on the other side of it and took off running again.

There were more xenos in this bay than I would've expected to find on the entire ship, now that it was sealed. The satellite launch corridor was secure, so Nils and Deilani didn't have to worry unless these things sorted out how to use the lift.

There was Salmagard, pushing an EMS unit across the wide expanse between the hulking survey flyer and the nearest bay door. She looked clear. All the same, I angled away from her.

At least their hard carapaces made the xenos easy to hear; their clattering echoed around the walls of the bay, a constant reminder that they were after me, and still very energetic.

"Private," I gasped into the com, twisting to put another vehicle between myself and my pursuers. "Private, I want you to open the big doors." There was one right above me, clambering over the top of an unmanned survey robot.

"But we still need two more units, sir."

"Open them and close them again. Quick."

"Yes, sir."

I wasn't sure how much more running I had left in me. The withdrawal was sapping my energy. If the private didn't do something, they were going to be all over me. There was a grav cart ahead. I powered it up, turned it around, and shoved it at the nearest xeno. The cart struck home with a satisfying crash, but I was already fleeing again.

Emergency lights began to flash. I deployed my helmet as the Klaxons started to wail. Salmagard was working fast. The lights on the doors came on. I knelt down and put both palms flat on the deck, putting a cling charge into my gloves.

The air was sucked abruptly from the bay. The smaller xenos were picked up and hurled toward the opening doors. The larger ones didn't seem fazed, but they weren't the ones running me ragged.

Almost immediately, the doors began to close. Several xenos had been pulled out; others smashed into the door with enough force to kill an unarmored human, but they were a hardy bunch.

I detached from the floor, switched off my helmet, and ran for the nearest survey crawler. It was big and sturdy—much sturdier than a skiff. I reached the hatch and searched for a way to open it. The little ones would've been all over me during this pause if Salmagard hadn't thrown them all to the far end of the bay with the doors. She'd bought me the time I needed, and unquestionably saved my life.

I got the door open and climbed in, sealing it behind me.

Something heavy thudded onto the top of the vehicle. I could hear them crawling on the metal.

I dropped into the pilot's seat and powered up the heavy crawler, then opened the viewfinder to see the deck. I released the brake and shoved the throttle forward, accelerating after the nearest xeno and heartlessly running it down. This wasn't very sporting, but my back was against the wall. My karma was already shot.

Besides, it wasn't like these things were endangered. They were everywhere.

After I flattened the third one, they got the message and started to flee. I went after them, taking down three more before ramming the crawler into the wall to smash the hind legs of one a full four meters across that was trying to crawl to safety. I backed up and it fell to the deck, twitching madly. It didn't seem right to just leave it there crippled, so I did the compassionate thing and ran over it a couple of times, then turned the crawler around to survey the bay.

The remaining xenos were all out of reach. I rolled the crawler to the middle of the bay and idled there. My vision was a little blurry, but on the whole I felt good. Piloting this crawler was a lot easier than running around out there.

"Private?"

"Yes, Admiral?"

"What's your status?"

"We've got the second unit tucked into the satellite. I'm on my way back down for a third. Ensign Nils is completely immobile, but the lieutenant's following his instructions. He doesn't look good," she added.

I sighed. "I'm going to cover you. I've got a survey crawler, and it's working pretty well out here, but you're on your own in the corridors. Keep your scanner on."

"It is, Admiral."

I leaned back in my seat. My joints ached. How many minutes were ticking by, and how many did we have left? I looked at my gloved hands. I couldn't see anything, but they were swarming with the nanomachines that were keeping me alive by keeping the mist out.

Mist that wasn't mist, just larval xenos. It was hard to imagine, hard to wrap my head around the notion that the ubiquitous mist was made up of tiny organisms that might ultimately grow into these hulking creatures.

Technology every Evagardian took for granted had saved our lives without us realizing it. Deilani's faithfulness to surface decon protocol also deserved credit. Her overly developed sense of duty had been a thorn in my side earlier, but now I owed my life to it.

I looked at the big doors, and thought about the planet beyond them. I felt bad for the colonists, but it just wasn't meant to be. This planet didn't want to be colonized.

It was already occupied, after all.

A stealthy local had come down to the deck, and I saw on my monitor that it was approaching my crawler from behind. No matter how you looked at it, *this* was a hunting tactic. It hadn't evolved out of nowhere. What did these things normally hunt?

This was supposed to be a dead planet? No. It just looked dead, and with typical human arrogance, we'd taken that at face value. Maybe there were whole worlds underneath that black and rocky shell.

I put the crawler in reverse and ran him over with a series of horrible crunching noises. I almost felt bad about it. A couple others that had been edging downward hastily scuttled back up the walls.

I had a nasty thought, and popped the hatch long enough to sneak a look at the ceiling. Sure enough, half a dozen of them were clustered directly overhead. I moved the crawler away. I couldn't stop them from doing that, but I could make them work for it.

The larger ones could tear this crawler apart if they wanted to. It was sturdy, but not armored. I hoped that wouldn't occur to them.

Salmagard appeared, looking very small at this distance, jogging across the deck. The xenos didn't all rush for her like I'd feared—they seemed wary. With good reason; in typical Evagardian fashion, Salmagard hadn't shown their kind any more mercy than I had.

She ran up the ramp and disappeared into another flyer.

A xeno dropped onto the flyer and crawled in after her. I'd barely opened my mouth to warn her when it came scuttling out, trailing pink smoke. "Ah—uh, Private? You all right?"

"Yes, Admiral." She'd used a flare launcher to scare it off. Clever. I put the crawler into gear and ran down the flaming xeno. "Admiral?"

"Yeah?"

"What's the situation overhead?"

I took her meaning; they would drop on her when she came

out. I looked up at the xenos poised over the flyer. Was there a way to scatter them? Did I *want* to scatter them? "All right, Private— you need to come out as fast as you can. If they drop, then at least it won't be on top of you, and I'll have a chance to try to help. How many flares have you got?"

"Two more."

"Then we're in business. On three." I released the crawler's manual brake and put my hands on the controls. "Three."

The float pallet with the EMS unit came hurtling out of the flyer; she must have backed up all the way to the cockpit to get such a running start. It flew down the ramp and skimmed smoothly across the deck. Not quite in the right direction, but that wasn't important. Three xenos dropped down, their reflexes fast, but not fast enough, and I was right on top of them. I rolled over two, but the third went off after Salmagard more quickly than I was ready for.

"Behind you," I warned, throttling up.

She twisted and shot it with a flare, but another clattered to the deck in front of the grav cart. Salmagard couldn't reload. All she could do was angle the cart away and put on some extra speed. I had caught up now, and I smashed into this newcomer, even as more landed.

The wide, open bay truly was the perfect place for irresponsible driving. Finally, something I was good at.

I wheeled the crawler around recklessly, and several xenos backed off, but some were still heading determinedly for Salmagard. I charged at them, and they scattered. That bought the private another few moments. By staying close to her, I made the creatures warier.

We were nearly to the hatch. With some threatening acceleration on my part, they held back long enough for her to get through.

I let out a long breath as I saw the doors close behind her, and sat back, watching the things mill around on the deck. I wondered how they were getting into the bay, but there wasn't anything I could do about that.

"Private, you all right?"

"Yes, Admiral."

Well, that was something. I rubbed at my eyes, then put my hands back on the controls. I couldn't let the xenos get too comfortable, not while we still had work to do in here.

I went after the ones still on the ground, and they were learning to get out of the way before I ran them down. I chased them back up the walls.

From the crushed and mangled carcasses strewn about, I knew I'd substantially reduced their numbers, but there were still so many.

I got up from the controls and went into the passenger section of the survey crawler. I found a small handheld launcher, and plenty of flares. I tucked them into my pouch. It wasn't the ideal weapon, but it was something. Salmagard was good at improvising with these things, but for my part, I hoped not to use it. The survey crawler itself was still the best piece on the board.

I went back up and checked the screens. I had xenos on the ceiling and walls. This wasn't going to work.

Last time's plan wouldn't fly. There were too many, and they were adapting to my tactics too quickly. Salmagard, for all her competence, wouldn't last ten seconds in this bay outside a vehicle. But we still needed one more unit. How would we get it out of here?

"Deilani," I said into the com. "Give the private a stim whether she wants one or not."

I'd just have to think of something.

19

"PRIVATE, we're going to have to do this a little differently."

"Agreed, Admiral. The third unit is secure."

"How's Nils?"

"Still awake."

I grimaced. "Where are you?"

"Just outside the door, sir."

"Here's the plan: I'm going to give you a lift to the last flyer."

"I'll just jump on your vehicle then, sir?"

"Right. I'll let you off at the flyer, and try to cover you while you get the ramp down. Once you're in there, raise it. Can you handle it?"

"I like a challenge, Admiral."

No hesitation at all.

"Then I'm coming for you now. Raise the pressure door on my go. How's Deilani holding up?"

"I think she's come a bit unhinged, sir."

Who could blame her?

"All right, get in here." I slowed the crawler, but didn't stop. It was slow enough already. Rolling over so many xenos had taken a toll on the wheels and underside of the vehicle; by now they were heavily damaged, and probably weakening by the minute. Nothing seemed to be immune to the corrosive effect these things had on plastic and metal.

The door shot up, and the white figure of Salmagard darted into the open. Xenos started to drop.

"I'm on!"

I accelerated toward the flyers, narrowly missing a row of skiffs.

I couldn't see Salmagard at all; I had to take her at her word that she was aboard. I braked hard at the flyer, and saw her drop away on my screen, hitting the deck and rolling into a sprint.

I put the crawler in reverse and backed over the smaller xenos out in front, then charged straight ahead at the ones dropping on and around the flyer. I smashed the one nearest to Salmagard, popped the hatch, and leaned out with my flare launcher to fire at one that wanted to rush her down.

The ramp was halfway lowered; Salmagard jumped, caught the lip, and hauled herself inside. A moment later it started to rise again. None of them managed to slip in, though one nearly lost a leg. That just left me. I ducked back inside the crawler and sealed the hatch yet again.

"All right in there?"

"Quite snug, sir. How do I get out?"

"You don't. You're going to taxi back to the door and unload there. I know you're not a pilot," I said before she could protest.

"But you don't need to be one to point that thing and make it go. Here's what you need to do. More or less." I explained it to her while watching the xenos swarm over the flyer. It didn't seem to occur to them to try to break in.

"And that means it's powered up?" Salmagard was more confident in her ability to fight than to pilot.

"Yes. You have to release the binders next."

"There's something wrong; I've got all these warning messages," she fretted.

"That's because there's xenos crawling on the wings. Don't mind them. Just bring it around."

I watched the flyer begin to inch forward, then turn. It crunched into the flyer beside it, smashing several xenos. "Oh dear," Salmagard said.

"Ignore it. You need it to take you about a hundred meters; it doesn't matter what kind of shape it's in when you get there. I won't tell anybody."

"Yes, Admiral." The flyer was moving along now, and the xenos suddenly seemed very keen to get off. I didn't blame them; the grace that characterized Salmagard's body did not extend to the flyer. She rolled right over the row of skiffs that I'd avoided earlier. Machinery was crushed, and metal and polymer were sent flying. Oil and coolant spilled across the deck. Well, it was all Commonwealth property anyway.

It occurred to me that I'd better follow, but the crawler didn't respond when I tried to accelerate. I looked at the plentiful emergency lights and blinking warnings on my readouts. This technology was meant for exploring harsh new worlds; it was supposed to be tough. I didn't have any sympathy for it. I pushed the throttle forward, and there were only sounds of mechanical agony. Metal screeched.

The corrosion had done its work. I wasn't surprised, but the timing wasn't ideal. I was stranded in the middle of the bay, and the locals were getting curious.

Salmagard had reached the far end, and was maneuvering to shorten the trip from the ramp to the door.

The xenos were teeming on the walls.

"Private?"

"Yes, Admiral?"

"I'm a little stuck out here. Can you give me a lift?"

"Yes, sir. On my way."

The flyer awkwardly changed direction, beginning to roll toward me. I didn't realize what she had in mind until she was only meters away. I grabbed for the straps, knew there wasn't time, and just braced myself against the console. It was only a bump, but it felt as if I'd just been hit with heavy weapons fire. My head swam and pounded. My arms burned, but I held on anyway.

Salmagard pushed me with the nose of the flyer, the ruined underside of my crawler grinding across the deck, leaving deep gouges in the metal.

"Thank you, Private," I said, jaw set as the crawler shook madly around me.

"Not at all, Admiral."

She pushed my crawler up against the bulkhead, then maneuvered the flyer around a second time, and came to a halt. Already the xenos were closing in. Now that we'd been stationary for a few moments, I saw a couple of them drop to the roof of the flyer.

"What now, Admiral?"

"I'm working on it." She was counting on me to get her out of this. Our strict timetable was at the front of my mind. Fire seemed to be our go-to weapon, and I didn't have a problem with that. Fire was easy to come by. We needed something flammable. What was flammable? What was flammable and could be found in quantity *here*?

"End of the line," I said, hoping I was thinking straight. "We fight our way out. Find the biggest oxygen tank on that craft, probably the one used to refill the pressure suits. Detach it. Lower the ramp, bleed it, and throw it out. I'll light it with a flare. That might push them back, at least for a second. You take off, and I'll draw fire. Got it?"

"Yes, Admiral." Salmagard didn't sound entirely convinced, but she didn't have a better plan offhand, and we didn't have time to think of one. I broke open the flare launcher and loaded it, then got it ready and put my hand on the hatch release. Several moments went by, and I pictured Salmagard in the flyer, wrestling with a big O$_2$ tank.

"Ready, Admiral?" She sounded breathless.

"Whenever you are, Private."

I waited. The ramp started to lower, and the xenos became noticeably agitated. A tank nearly the size of an EMS unit went banging down to the deck, venting visibly.

I threw open the hatch and straightened, taking aim. My hands shook, but it was an easy shot.

The tank went up with a modest fireball. The blast rattled my bones, and the heat and shock wave washed over me. I saw stars.

Shaking my head, I saw that it had worked better than I'd hoped. Salmagard was already down the ramp and on the move, nearly halfway to the doors. I clambered down, blinking away the streaks and lights, and fumbling another flare into the launcher.

The xenos were recovering, but not fast enough to catch me, and certainly not fast enough to stop Salmagard.

I made it through the hatch and sealed it. A black leg as big around as the flyer's landing strut punched through, tearing the metal as if it was sheet plastic—but it pulled back.

Salmagard was already pushing the last EMS unit into the lift. I got in and sagged against the wall. She looked at me and blanched. Did I look that bad? I was sweating even more than the situation warranted, and my EV suit wasn't sure what to do about it. It was giving me med pings, telling me to seek attention immediately. I muted them, feeling cold.

Salmagard, on the other hand, looked great. She was red-faced and sweaty, but her expression was triumphant.

"This is number four, right?" I gasped.

"Yes, Admiral."

Then it didn't matter. We were almost done.

The interior of the satellite had been transformed. Now there were three EMS units standing in it, along with a mess of cords and equipment, most of which I realized had been removed from the walls of the satellite itself. Several panels were missing, and a lot of things looked broken. All we needed was for the thing to keep the units powered up, and to send our SOS. The satellite's normal functions didn't matter, and I was confident Nils wouldn't order Deilani to break anything too important.

Nils himself looked terrible. His skin was gray, and his eyes were sunken and unfocused. Deilani looked ragged too. Evagardians weren't supposed to be seen in this state. We weren't even supposed to *be* in this state. But as much as the Empire would like people to forget, imperials were still just people.

"Do we have power?" I asked, stepping aside so Salmagard could move the final unit into position. There was barely any space left. This was going to be a tight fit.

"Yes."

"And the beacon?"

"Functional," Deilani said. She sounded breathless.

"What about the launch?"

"We've got it figured out," Deilani said, but I could tell there was bad news coming. "But we've got problems."

"What kind?"

"The rocket needs fuel."

"Rocket?"

She shrugged. "Ganraens. They're still burning chemicals to propel the unit up. It's a highly concentrated fuel, so we only need a few liters of it. Not too different from 14-14."

"I take it there's some aboard?"

"Yes."

"What else?"

"We didn't stop to think." She gave me an odd, slightly disturbing smile, and pointed up. "We're completely buried. We need to clear the launch hatch."

I took that in. After a moment, I sat down and rubbed my face. A part of me had been thinking I might get out of that bay alive, come up here and go into stasis, and my problems would be over. At least until I woke up.

At least then I'd be rested—well, not exactly. I would come out of stasis feeling exactly the way I felt the moment I went in. That was the point.

But still. It would've been sort of like a break.

My eyes were sandy, and they stung. I couldn't think straight. I couldn't even breathe properly. I didn't want to move. It had taken everything I had just to stay on my feet long enough to close out the business in the hangar bay.

Those were my limits. This was beyond them. Every part of me hurt.

"How much time have we— Wait. Never mind," I said, seeing Deilani's expression. She knew exactly how much time we had, and I didn't want to. "All right—all right, then we have to get on it. Where's the fuel?"

"A couple decks down."

"Great."

"It's sealed off; that part of the ship is depressurized."

"Of course it is. What about the silo? How do we clear it?" Muscles in my neck and back twitched painfully.

"It'll have to be with explosives, won't it?" Deilani shrugged. "There's no time for anything else." I looked to Nils for confirmation, and he nodded weakly.

"Explosives, explosives. Feels like all we ever do is blow things up. Not very Evagardian."

"Or extremely Evagardian, depending on your perspective," Deilani said. I was amazed she had the energy to get cute, but it was probably a good thing.

"We'll think of an elegant strategy next time." I continued to rub at my eyes, though it wasn't helping. "You two get the fuel. I'll clear the silo."

"We should stick together," Deilani countered. "You won't stand a chance out there by yourself."

"There's no time. But I'll need your help. I'll need you to open the big doors in the vehicle bay for me."

"What for?"

"So I can get outside. I'll get some seismic charges from one of the survey vehicles. Where do I blast?"

"If we knock out some of the rock under the grav drive chassis, most of the stuff covering us should just slide off the hull." Nils handed Deilani the terminal, and she showed me. "This thing." It was the odd rock formation we'd noted earlier. Well, it was hard to miss.

"Got it. Here, you guys should take some flares." I handed over my pouch. "We know there are plenty of these locals still running around the ship, and there's bound to be more where there's no atmosphere."

Salmagard opened my pouch. "You'll need some too, sir." She gave me a concerned look. She didn't like the idea of me going anywhere alone, and I couldn't blame her.

"Leave me a few."

"Pink or blue?"

20

"ANYTHING else?"

Deilani shook her head. "That's it. And, sir . . ."

Sir, eh? "Save it." I got to my feet. "No time. Let's get to it."

Salmagard returned my pouch. I attached it to my hip and straightened.

"The bay doors are opening," Deilani reported, handing the reader back to Nils, who clutched it weakly to his chest. "You'll need at least a couple of charges to guarantee it," she said to me. "It's a lot of rock. It won't be easy to clear."

"I know how to break things," I replied absently. I looked at the flare launcher in my hands. "Be careful," I said to the girls, then left the satellite. They were on their own now.

In the cramped lift, I leaned against the wall, forcing my eyes to focus on the flare launcher. I broke it open and tried to load a flare, but it slipped from my fingers, clattering to the floor. I knew better than to bend down for it. I took out another flare, and very carefully loaded it.

The doors opened, and I snapped the launcher shut.

The corridor hadn't changed. There was still a hole in the bay hatch, doing its best to depressurize the corridor. I activated my helmet and knelt to look through, bracing myself against the pull. I saw a few xenos, but none were nearby. My field of view wasn't good; there could have been some that were very close, but I couldn't confirm that without a combat scanner like Salmagard's.

I opened the hatch, dodged through the wreckage, and staggered toward the nearest skiff. Nothing dropped on me from above. With luck I could be halfway across the bay before they even noticed I was back.

We were certainly leaving this ship in a sorry state. There were vehicles smashed into everything, overturned, destroyed, flattened . . . carcasses everywhere.

What a mess.

This felt familiar. I was alone and at the end of my rope. Even if I got my way, someone wasn't going to like it. In this case, that would be the locals. This was no way to open relations between two species.

I powered up a skiff and took off. A smaller xeno dropped from the ceiling, but I avoided it. I needed a survey flyer, and there was only one left that was undamaged.

I could hear Salmagard and Deilani on the com. If they got into trouble, I wouldn't be able to help them. If they needed advice,

I wasn't in any state to give it. I barely had enough focus to keep the skiff level. I didn't need the distraction. I turned off the com and throttled up.

The xenos were closing fast. I leaped off the skiff, hit the control for the ramp, and got back on the skiff, narrowly avoiding the claws of a specimen so large it wouldn't have been able to fit into the colony ship's corridors. It must have come in through the open doors.

Through those doors, I could see the black walls of the valley, and the seething green mist.

I'd be out there soon enough.

I made a wide turn, almost reaching the wall of the bay, then changed direction sharply, heading back for the flyer. I took the skiff up the ramp and dove free as it crashed into the bulkhead, then rolled to my feet and pulled the hatch release. A large xeno had managed to latch on. I shot it squarely in what I hoped was its face with the flare gun, and it dropped free without a sound.

The ramp closed. They'd be all over the flyer, and I couldn't count on them being as patient with me as they'd been with Salmagard at the controls. I had to move quickly; for Salmagard it hadn't mattered, because she hadn't needed her flyer to fly. I did. I couldn't let them damage it.

I picked myself up and flipped on the cabin lights, powering up the flyer. I accessed the computer and checked the onboard inventory. Sure enough, there was a set of high-yield charges with the other survey gear.

I lifted off immediately, hovering over the deck. The backwash from my liftoff took care of whatever xenos were nearby, and wrecked the remaining vehicles. Purely from the feel of the flyer, I could tell that I had some passengers, but as long as I could move, I didn't care.

I took the flyer toward the open bay doors. These flyers were intended to taxi out onto the flight ramp, where they could take off safely. In here, my thrusters were wreaking havoc on the bay, blasting away the remaining equipment and xenos, and tearing up the deck and bulkheads. I couldn't hear the Klaxons from inside the cockpit, but I could see the warning lights on the walls giving their all.

I was past worrying about property damage. I hit the thrusters, and the flyer rose. I kept it slow and easy.

Once I was clear of the colony ship, I gained altitude more quickly, watching the survey screens. I needed to see the situation from above before I made my move.

I set the flyer to circle the ship from about two hundred meters, and dragged myself into the other seat to better concentrate on the screens.

There was an enormous amount of rubble on the hull. The wall of the valley had just collapsed on it. Blasting gone wrong? Seismic activity? It could've been anything—but it seemed as if it was related to the mysterious formation that Deilani had noticed.

I could see it clearly from here, but I still didn't have any idea what it was, or if it might affect what I was about to try to do. If it was substantially sturdier than the rest of this mineral, that could be an issue.

I thought about running a geological scan, but decided against it. There wasn't time, I didn't feel up to it, and the readings would be unreliable anyway. I could *see* what had to go away to get the rubble off the launch silo. All I had to do was blow it up. I'd just use more explosives to make up the difference. I gazed at the thing as I circled, hoping that would be enough.

It couldn't be a natural formation. It didn't look like anything else on this planet, not even the spires. Were locals going to come pouring out when I blasted a hole in it? Probably. Something about it reminded me of Old Earth insects and their hives.

There was the bridge—I could see the big executive viewports. That was the highest point on the ship. I couldn't just land the flyer anywhere, because it would draw xenos. I had to distance myself from it once I touched down.

I would use the flyer itself to draw attention away from me while I got down to business.

I went back to the equipment lockers to get my survey charges.

To cover distance, the only friend I had left was gravity. I could use the curvature of the hull to get down there fast. It was getting back into the ship that would be difficult if the xenos noticed me. I didn't know how to go undetected because I didn't know what senses these locals were using. Apart from a weakness to heat, I didn't even know which ones they *had*.

I couldn't account for all the variables. Actually, I couldn't account for any of them, and I was wasting time worrying about it. I set the flyer down, not very gently, but at least no one heard it. There can be perks to no atmosphere as long as you have a functioning EV suit. My helmet hummed into place when I activated it, and I disembarked.

I didn't waste time looking around to see if I had company. If they were onto me, there was nothing I could do about it.

The domed hull of the colony ship was so vast that it was like standing on a miniature planet. I jogged to the lip of the deck and dropped down, sliding down the hull for a rough landing in the rubble below. I could see movement in it: xenos only centimeters across. They were small, but for all I knew, their corrosive properties were no less potent than those of their larger counterparts. I had to avoid touching them, or I'd risk compromising my suit.

Up close the unusual formation was even larger than I'd realized. The surface was rough and pitted, but at a glance, it looked as if it had more in common with the xenos than the spires.

Whatever it was, I had no doubt I could blast it, but it was still awe-inspiring. If these creatures had built it . . . No, there were plenty of unintelligent life-forms able to show a remarkable grasp of structural engineering. It didn't mean anything.

But what about the spires?

A spasm of pain almost brought me to my knees, reminding me that I didn't have a lot of time before my withdrawal put me out of commission. I didn't know if I was going into shock, or a coma, or if my heart would just stop. I struggled to stay on my feet; falling down with all these little ones around was a bad idea, and getting up wasn't getting any easier.

I was in the rubble now, jumping from rock to rock as I approached the formation.

I ducked between two mineral shards that formed a sort of cave entrance, trying to find my way down. The lower I set the charges, the better the result would be.

Here was the planet at its most oppressive. The mineral walls soaked up my light, and there was virtually no ambient light from the surface. It would have been treacherous going for me even at my best. As I crept through the dark, trying not to slip on the sharp, crumbling rocks, I wondered if any Ganraen surveyors had come underground this way, investigating this formation.

And how many of them had made it back? Maybe that was what had touched things off.

I dropped onto a ledge and knelt, keeping very still. The cavity ahead had too many improbable angles. My light couldn't show much, but it looked to me like the walls were covered in xenos. The things were clinging to it, jagged, spiny legs jutting out and overlapping, creating a lacework of black limbs. My skin crawled. The silent world of my EV helmet only made it worse. Sweat stung my eyes, and I could feel blood thudding in my ears.

I pulled three charges off the belt, linked them together, set the timer, and threw it in.

I couldn't go any deeper and hope to get back to the surface alive. This was the best I could do.

I worried that even that small weight, just five kilograms, might knock something loose and bring down the locals on me. But if they noticed my intrusion, they didn't react. Maybe they were sleeping.

I turned and started to climb back toward the faint starlight above. That hadn't been so bad. I felt too weak to be climbing, but the thought of staying just made my skin crawl.

I clambered back onto the hull, putting some cling in my glove for extra purchase. Now I had to figure out how to get back inside. A look around showed me I was clear for the moment. I could see dark shapes crawling on the flyer. There was no hope of flying back in. I'd have to find an airlock.

Moving slowly, less with stealth in mind than my rapidly failing strength, I slid down the hull toward the nearest exterior walkway, but I immediately had to put a charge in my glove to stop myself. Massive legs emerged from the mist below me.

I was looking at a xeno over ten meters across. It mounted the hull and began to climb toward me. I scrambled up and away, but even with its leisurely stride, in my present state I was outpaced.

I took my hand away from the deck and faced the thing.

"You know the Empress only negotiates one way, right?" I took out another charge and thumbed five seconds into the timer. These surveying explosives weren't meant to be used as grenades, but I'd never been picky about these things. I tossed it.

There was, of course, no sound. I raised my arms to shield my faceplate. Pieces of the behemoth were flying away, their arcs made lazy by the mild gravity.

I groaned, picked myself up and shuffled along the walkway. There was another xeno on the side of the ship. It wasn't as large as the one I'd just dealt with, but it was still huge. It didn't seem to have a problem with me. Or maybe it had seen what I'd just done to its friend. Either way, it kept its distance.

I struggled down a ladder, across a set of handholds, then made a controlled descent to the same airlock the trainees and I had used to enter the ship in the first place. I'd come full circle without realizing it.

Inside, I deactivated my helmet and broke into a pitiful jog. That had gone well. Much better than expected. I still had a lot of ground to cover.

I took the strength I had left and tried to turn it into speed. I made it into a lift, and up, then down to the blue-level corridor, past the junction. Which way to the silo? There was no time for a guide path. These Ganraen decks were all alike. It wasn't far now.

I ran headlong into Deilani, who came out of a maintenance hatch so fast that the impact threw me against the opposite wall.

She was clutching some kind of cylinder to her chest, and for a moment looked like she might drop it. Her eyes widened in panic, but she held on, sagging against the opposite wall.

"Is that it?" I gasped. "Where's the private?"

Deilani shook her head. "She was—she tried to buy time." Her face was oddly blank.

I just stared at her. "Are you *kidding me*?" She opened her mouth, but I cut her off with a look. She flinched and backed away.

"The charges are set," I said. "Go get ready." She shouted something after me, but I wasn't listening, and there was an odd ringing in my ears that didn't bode well.

I ducked through the maintenance hatch and got moving. The air was flowing, so the area was breached. Deilani must have left a hatch open to the compromised part of the ship. All the better; it could guide me.

I followed the air, activating my helmet and pulling out the flare gun as I set my EV suit to home in on Salmagard's.

There was something wrong with the signal. I couldn't find her.

I stumbled through the hatch, and there was no light beyond. The ship wasn't going to waste power on sections of the ship no one was supposed to see. I turned on my suit's lights, and didn't look at my O_2 gauge. With the flare gun raised, I moved as fast as I could down the narrow passage. I reactivated my com.

"Private? Private, come in."

Nothing.

There had to be a way to track her down. They had used this corridor to get to the fuel, and the fuel was highly unstable. It had to be kept at a low temperature. Not lower than the temperature on the surface of the planet, but there would be some kind of temperature-control apparatus for wherever the stuff was stored . . . and that would need power, whether this part of the ship was sealed or not.

And power meant heat. I used my suit to track the temperature differential and made a guess. I took a left, then slid down a ladder, landing on top of a xeno the size of a one-man skiff.

I scrambled free and rolled over, taking aim. It reared up, and I fired. The flare lit up the crawl space, which was alive with xenos of all sizes. That sight gave me the strength to leap up and put a sealed hatch between myself and that part of the ship.

I found Salmagard at the bottom of the next ladder, lying in the gloom. The smoking carcass of a large xeno was beside her.

There was blood everywhere; her EV suit was dark, damaged somehow. There were large tears in it. I knelt beside her, quickly applying sealing gel to the most obvious ones. I pulled her up. She was completely limp. Her wounds made Nils' look mild by comparison. This was why Deilani hadn't wanted me to go after her.

She was dead.

Salmagard and Deilani had been set upon. Without decent weapons, they'd never had a chance down here in these tight corridors. Deilani had the fuel; Salmagard had tried to play hero and stall, giving the lieutenant time to get away and escape with me and Nils.

I supposed, from the perspective of the Service, that was the right and proper thing to do.

But it was naive for her to think that dying was all it would take to put her problems to rest. It was never that easy.

Salmagard hadn't been gone long.

This was why the Empress had given us stasis technology; there was very little that Evagardian medicine couldn't repair. As long as most of her brain was intact, if I could get her back to the satellite in the next few minutes, the Empire could put her back together at their leisure.

No, I wasn't a real admiral, but that didn't make it okay for people to die on my watch.

I tried to pick her up, but couldn't. I was shaking like a leaf. My luck had run out along with my strength, but I wasn't ready to quit. My arms weren't up to it, but maybe my back was. I put down the flare launcher and got her around my shoulders. She wasn't very big. Tiny, really. I struggled to my feet.

I couldn't go back the way I came. That part of the ship was infested, and I'd sealed it off regardless.

A few tendrils of green mist wafted around my ankles. Well, it was either that, or try to find my way through this labyrinth of a ship.

Besides, my last trip outside hadn't been so bad.

I doubled over, coughing, Salmagard's weight crushing me to the deck. When I opened my eyes, there was blood on the inside of my faceplate, and Salmagard's body was on the ground.

"Lieutenant," I choked, reactivating the com.

"Yes?" Deilani didn't sound good.

I got Salmagard back over my shoulder and set off, following the mist.

"I need a way in from the outside. To the silo. A fast way."

There was a tear in the hull ahead. I made for it, feeling like I was forgetting something.

The starlight seemed bright compared to the inside of the sealed-off portion of the ship. Blinding. The walls of the valley didn't block the view. There was this world's green sun, and beyond it I thought

I could see the bright blues and pinks of the Demenis system. I stumbled on the tear, and we tumbled down to a lower walkway.

"Lieutenant?" I groaned, picking myself up and crawling to Salmagard.

"There's a hatch by the silo for maintenance."

"Isn't it buried?" I pulled the private over my shoulders yet again and heaved to my feet.

"You didn't uncover it?"

I staggered into the open, planting my foot on the sloping hull of the ship, and looking up at the valley wall.

"Oh," I said. That was what I'd forgotten: the timers I'd set on the explosives.

The blast sent up a wave of black dust and vapor, nearly knocking me off my feet. There were shapes in the cloud, which fanned out hundreds of meters above the ship.

The destruction ahead was vast, and perfectly silent. It looked slow and lethargic.

The colony ship shook, and sank several centimeters, taking me with it. The valley walls began to move and crumble.

As I started to make my way up the hull, everything began to tremble. There was a second explosion—but it wasn't an explosion.

The formation hadn't been a formation, and it hadn't been some kind of nest structure.

It was a portion of the leg of a xeno twice the size of the colony ship.

I thought I'd seen large xenos earlier, but this one made it clear how little we understood these things. The scale of it was staggering.

I didn't know if I was looking at the mother of all these xenos, or just the one with the biggest appetite.

And I'd just woken it up.

The leg rose, casting aside boulders the size of shuttles like they were grains of sand. Rocks and xenos rained down on the ship, some of them punching through the hull, others pulverized on it. There was a second geyser of black dust and green mist as another leg broke free of the surface half a kilometer away, sending millions of tons of the black rock cascading to the floor of the valley.

A xeno even bigger than the one I'd bombed only minutes before landed in front of me, scrambling to its feet only to be smashed by more falling rock.

With Salmagard growing heavier by the second, I concentrated on putting one foot in front of the other. The hull of the ship was like the black planet itself when we'd been crossing it.

Endless.

The ship itself was in a frenzy, its emergency systems trying to acknowledge all of this new damage. Sealant and coolant were being vented in towering columns all around. Now it was easy to see the mist for what it was: there were green streaks and highlights in the sky, forming elaborate patterns against the stars as the swarms reacted to the chaos.

I couldn't see through my bloody faceplate to find the hatch, and even if I could I wouldn't have seen the rock that hit me. I fell to the hull, losing track of Salmagard's body. My suit was compromised, and I felt icy cold on my back as I rolled over.

The gigantic leg of the behemoth crashed down on the ship, tearing through it like it wasn't even there. The colony ship rocked and tilted, threatening to send me back to the valley floor.

Rocks, wreckage, and flailing xenos tumbled past. I lost control, sliding down the rising slope.

I caught a bloody glimpse of a white figure. I grabbed Salmagard's wrist and held on, putting a charge in my other hand and planting it, though it felt as if my arm was being pulled from its socket. Deilani was saying something, but I couldn't hear her. I pulled Salmagard to me and tried to crawl, but we weren't actually going anywhere. I couldn't move myself, much less the both of us.

Rubble exploded on the hull, opening up more tears in my suit.

I caught another glimpse of white, and looked up. A hatch had opened, and a figure that could only be Deilani was climbing out. She ran for us, dodging falling rock. She tried to pull me up, but I wouldn't let go of Salmagard. Making noises of undisguised frustration, she dragged both of us.

I didn't climb into the hatch as much as fall through. I hit the floor hard, blacking out for a moment.

Deilani came down the ladder with Salmagard.

She had to drag us into the satellite, where she unceremoniously dumped us both on the deck. I didn't see Nils—no, he was already in stasis. Deilani picked up the terminal and poked at it. There was a shudder, and we were all slammed to the deck.

The terminal bounced past me, its screen showing the enormous mother xeno shrinking away below us as it emerged from the surface, and the colony ship vanishing into the blackness of the planet, swallowed just like Captain Tremma's freighter.

21

THE *carbon shielding shattered like glass.*

The massive cruiser punched through the armored plates as if they weren't even there. The impact was deafening, even from so far away. The forty-five-hundred-meter vessel was out of control, smashing effortlessly through the city. Buildings and towers were brushed aside like kilometer-high blades of grass, breaking apart and toppling in the distance. Glittering structures disintegrated by the dozen. Flyers veered, little more than points of light trying to avoid the destruction.

The ship crashed through tier after tier of raised highways and elevated train routes, sending it all spiraling away, pulled toward the breach.

Blue and green flames flashed around the cruiser's hull as coolant was burned off. The station was depressurizing, and the

people and debris were like fine dust caught in the wind. Klaxons
tried and failed to wail over the din. The ship reached the super-
structure, crashing through and folding in on itself. The entire
station shook violently, and the deck rushed up to greet me.

"They're getting pushy."

"What do you expect from imperials? Where do they want to
take him? Their embassy?"

"I assume."

"Are they from the ship? The big one?"

"I'm not sure. I think so."

"Don't you think they're acting strange? Why'd they take the
other ones right away, but leave this one? Why the delay? Did they
say anything?"

"Look, is he cleared to leave or not?"

"He'll be fine. Will the imperials pay?"

"They already have. Why do *you* want to hang on to this guy?"

"Because there's something funny going on here."

"You know better than to try to understand these people."

"It has to mean something that they'd refuse to take him, then
come back banging on the door."

"Yes—exactly. They're banging on the door. We're talking
about the people that went to war with the Commonwealth and
won. We are *not* going to be divas here."

"Yes, we are. Call station security, find out where we stand
legally. We can buy time by negotiating."

"It doesn't *matter*. Imperials are asking us for a favor, and we
don't want to try to negotiate with them. That never ends well."

"I want to help them out. I just want to know what's going on
first, that's all."

It sounded like their backs were to me. I opened my eyes. This was a private medical room, common galactic design. From what I'd just heard, I was probably on Payne Station, and by the sound of things, at the Free Trade embassy's infirmary.

There was nothing restricting my movement, nothing binding me to the bed. I wasn't at my best, but compared to my most recent memories, I felt pretty good. I could move without shaking, but my body was covered in bruises. We hadn't been strapped in, or secured at all when the satellite launched. I was lucky to have survived it.

I looked at the two men, who were still arguing.

I had questions, but there was no time for them. One of the men stalked out of the room, and the door hissed shut behind him. I wouldn't get a better chance.

I slipped out of bed, ignoring my light-headedness, and locked an arm around the man's neck. He barely struggled at all. I lowered his unconscious body to the floor, and got him out of his medical coveralls.

Once dressed, I slipped into the corridor.

Compared to a Ganraen colony ship, a Free Trade embassy couldn't be difficult to navigate. Good, solid gravity. Clean tile floor. Art on the walls. Very nice.

I straightened up, checking myself for visible injuries. Nothing too attention-grabbing. They'd taken good care of me.

No one looked at me twice as I passed. Maybe I could credit that to my increasingly impressive stubble.

I emerged on a second-level walkway overlooking the domed lobby. Outside, I could see other domes, and the wheels and cylinders of the station.

People milled about below, but my gaze fell on the six masked figures in white.

Evagardians; here for me. Their leader was in a heated argument with an embassy representative. I looked at their uniforms. A colonel, probably a representative from the *Julian*. And there were both Evagardian Intelligence and Imperial Security markings on display.

I hadn't woken up a moment too soon.

I stepped into a lift, giving the imperials a wide berth, and left the embassy as an alarm went up behind me. That had been quick.

I walked through the plaza, taking every turn that presented itself, and tried to figure out where I was in relation to the harbor.

Despite it all, I found myself appreciating civilization. After a dead planet and empty ships, the close quarters, bright lights, and crowded spaces of Payne Station were more than welcome.

That surprised me. It was a testament to just how much I hadn't liked that strange black planet—because it wasn't so long ago that I'd thought that I could live a long and not especially happy life if I never set foot on another station.

I passed a towering memorial to the Ganraen capital station. They'd sure thrown that together quickly. There were people laying wreaths at it. I set my jaw and walked past it, shutting it out. I didn't have time to be sentimental.

I was in a bad situation, and I had to think.

We must have been picked up, and to end up at the Free Trade embassy for ransom, it could've been anyone from pirates to explorers. Merchants, traders. Anybody.

The embassy would gladly buy us so that they could ransom us in turn to Evagard. It sounded as if the Empire had immediately reclaimed the three trainees and, after working out who I was, come back for me. I hoped they'd gotten to the trainees in time to save Nils and Salmagard, but I'd probably never know.

It was a small miracle that they hadn't recognized me—but why would they? No one was looking for a man who everyone thought was dead.

The satellite plan had worked. I shook my head in wonder at that. Even dying, Nils had been able to—using Deilani's hands, no less—engineer a solution that kept us alive. Say what you want about Evagard—imperials deliver. But I'd already known that, long before I ever met Ensign Nils.

I kept walking, but I couldn't fail to see the people staring at the monument. It was a scale representation of the Ganraen royal residence, an elaborate tower that had stood at the center of the Ganraen capital station dome. I knew it well.

The fact that they hadn't ransomed me from the beginning meant that it was simply inconceivable to certain people that I might still be alive.

And I was alive only because of Deilani.

Not only had she not left without us, but she'd come back for the private and me despite her dislike, and at considerable personal risk. If she'd survived the stasis, she had a very bright future ahead of her.

Payne Station was relatively unfamiliar to me, but I didn't want to stop moving long enough to consult a map. Imperial Security and Evagardian Intelligence would both be on the lookout for that.

Leaving the monument behind, I made my way through a high-ceilinged plaza to a wide corridor with trendy cafés on one side, and a breathtaking view of open space on the other. I paused and leaned on the railing, enjoying the bright lights and the view. It was refreshingly warm. It was good to hear all these human voices.

I couldn't look at a map, but I could look out the window without attracting attention. Even people who lived on stations sometimes took a moment to admire things this way.

I was just a medical tech taking a break.

There was the *Julian*. It was nearly the size of the colony ship. I'd never seen such a magnificent vessel in my life, and I had a feeling I never would again. The Empress' flagship was worthy of the name, less a ship than a small battle station that could go wherever it liked.

That was the main Evagardian portion of the station; the commercial harbor would be at the other end. I needed to go down a few decks and find a speed lift—but they'd be watching those.

So I'd have to take down a maintenance worker and use his mobile to navigate to the docks. Those would be watched too, but I'd think of something.

This wasn't my first time.

I sighed. The events on the surface of the planet felt light-years and ages away, but the memories were only minutes old. The Free Trade people had kept me asleep while they treated me. I felt rested, and I was probably well on my way to being cured, too—but I was still exhausted.

This was all just one long, long day. I closed my eyes to one crisis and opened them to a new one. It wouldn't be over when I got off this station. My work wasn't finished.

A masked figure in white leaned on the railing beside me, and I tensed. It was a tall female imperial officer. The mask was angled toward me. I saw the rank insignias, and my heart sank.

"Good to see you up and about, Lieutenant."

"And you, Admiral."

Had Deilani anticipated this, and staked out the embassy? Of course she had. Her officer's sidearm was pointed at me discreetly.

"How are the others?"

"Full recoveries expected. They'll recuperate aboard the *Julian*. The ensign needs repairs to his nervous system, and the private is no longer dead. She'll need some new skin."

"It's never a bad thing to have an excuse to get a little personal augmentation on the Empire's tab."

"Her skin was good to begin with. I think they make sure of that. People like her aren't supposed to have any artificial improvements. She'll be devastated. The poor lamb."

"You're all heart. I imagine they'll both be all right. I'm sure everyone's very impressed with the three of you."

"Of course they are. We've been commended for our management of the crisis and daring escape, which apparently showed true Evagardian spirit and fortitude."

"Blowing everything up?"

"That, or our complete disregard for the preservation of Ganraen colonial property."

I smiled. Deilani was doing the same on the other side of her mask.

"I didn't figure it out completely until after I'd been debriefed," she said, sounding faintly annoyed. "So Tremma really was a spy. Running some kind of false-flag op. What was he going to do?" she asked. "Drop the cargo on some regulated station to make it look like someone was trading with the wrong people?"

"Probably. Then the armada would have an excuse to step in. It's a good way to get footholds in Free Trade space."

"That's illegal," she said darkly.

"That's intelligence," I told her frankly. "The Ganraens don't even pretend to try to make it look legit. That's how all this started. But I don't know what Tremma's orders were. He could've been selling that stuff to help war refugees for all we know."

"I should've figured you out sooner."

"The private did. Though she thought I was really Prince Dalton, not a double." I snorted. "She thought I was defecting."

"I'd even read about the Rothschild Mark they gave you. If only I'd recognized you. You don't expect a Ganraen prince to come out of one of our sleepers. Especially not one that was supposed to have died on the capital."

"Without the hair and the makeup, I almost don't recognize myself," I admitted. "I'm not as fabulous as Prince Dalton."

The corridor was crowded and buzzing, but all that fell away. Deilani and I were the only two people for light-years around. I kept my eyes on the stars.

"How long ago did you replace him?" she asked.

"A while," I replied.

She shook her head. "You never did *deny* that you were a spy. I just never thought you might be one of ours."

"It's dangerous for you to know. I couldn't tell you. No point lying, either. And I'm not exactly a spy."

"I'm not sure there's a word for what you are," Deilani said.

I didn't argue.

"I should have figured it out. So you were a double for the prince. How did they switch you? Is he dead?" she asked.

"Yes," I said simply.

"And the other royals that got assassinated? Was that you?"

"Does it matter?"

"And the capital?"

I thought about the royal cruiser smashing through the dome and barreling into the center of the capital station.

It was easy for the right person in the right place to make big things happen.

I didn't say anything.

"Then it really was you. You destroyed their capital, crippled their government—forced the surrender. You won the war, got us the cease-fire."

"You could also say I killed twenty million people," I replied.

"But you saved Evagardian lives. It was your mission."

"Was it? My orders didn't come from the Empress, Lieutenant. That's why Evagard needs me to die. This was someone else's plan. Some committee of admirals and tetrarchs willing to do something extreme to end the war. For the greater good, as they saw it. If they haven't been executed yet, they will be. It's best if no one ever knows it was an Evagardian operation. Or at the very least the Empress has to be kept clear of it. She would never order that kind of attack, not at that cost for civilians."

Deilani looked shaken, but she didn't say anything.

"But it doesn't matter. It *was* an Evagardian plan. At the end of the day." I shrugged.

"After Cohengard, who can say what she'd order? Then the sabotage . . ."

"It's not public knowledge, but at this point the people who matter in the Commonwealth know the truth. I had to break character at the end. I think the sabotage to Tremma's freighter was Ganrae's work. They messed up the computers and sent us off course. The sabotage to my sleeper was Evagardian. The shuttle could've been either one, and it was targeting Tremma and his pilot officer, not us. The possibility existed that they could learn the truth about me, and that made them loose ends to someone."

"But they still tried to reward you. They gave you the Rothschild Mark and made you an admiral."

"I *told* you it was an honorary title. Whoever heard of an admiral my age? Even an honorary one?" I smiled. "It only works if it's posthumous."

"Yes, but it never occurred to me you might be telling the truth."

"Salmagard should've tipped you off. She never hesitated to follow my orders."

"I thought she was just being . . . Earth born."

"She's not like that."

"I see that now. That's why she was so determined to protect you—she couldn't have anything happen to the hero of the Empire on her watch. Or to the defecting prince, if that was what she thought. And I suppose she recognized you because she keeps important company. She knew Prince Dalton's face when she saw it. She put it all together pretty fast." Deilani looked annoyed. We both gazed at the *Julian*.

The ship was beautiful; it was intimidatingly large, but also elegant. I'd heard about how the Empress had taken it into battle to save a ship in trouble in the Demenis system, even before the *Julian*'s weapons and defenses were fully operational. That had been only a few short weeks ago.

It was a shame I'd never get to see it from the inside.

"So they heap these honors on you, then try to kill you."

"Awkward, right?"

"Was it Tremma?"

"That sabotaged my sleeper? I don't know. He was a spy. It would've been perfectly plausible for him to get the order to switch me off. Maybe even likely. But the Empire's got plenty of people out there. It could've been anyone, anywhere. It's been a long road."

"But you think it was him. That's why it didn't bother you when we found his body," she said, staring at me.

"I didn't know him very well," I replied. "He gave me a lift once. A long time ago."

"You do think he did it."

"I'll never know. It doesn't matter. It wasn't personal."

"We can't admit to you—we can't admit to what you did. We can't admit to running ships like that freighter."

"There are a lot of things they don't teach you," I said.

"If you knew they were going to kill you, why come back at all? Why not run when you had the chance?"

"I was going to be awarded my honors by the Empress herself," I said. "Aboard the *Julian*. It's not easy getting into a room with the Empress. How many people can say they've done that?"

"You had to know something wasn't right."

I shrugged. "It seemed like a good idea at the time. Are you going to try to take me in?"

"Take you in? Admiral, I'm just a young officer on station leave. I'm required not to show my face to these common galactics, and to conduct myself by imperial standards. Not to go hunting for my own government's embarrassments." She holstered her sidearm.

"Risky," I said. "Being seen with me. You may regret this."

"I'll take my chances. I told her you saved her life."

"That was thoughtful. Can you pass something else on for me?"

She cocked her head. "What?"

"Ask her if she wants to get dinner sometime."

Deilani's mask stared at me. "Are you being funny?"

"What?"

"Half the galaxy is trying to kill you."

"Is that weird?"

Deilani just sighed. I went back to admiring the view.

"Or do you think she's too good for a guy from Cohengard?" I asked.

"What?"

"You really couldn't tell? I've got Cohengard written all over me. Binsey Surleau, Sustenance Block Delta. Two sections from White Square. I'm getting homesick just thinking about it."

The silence conveyed her surprise perfectly well; I didn't need to see past the mask. I knew what was on the other side.

"What's your real name?"

"What difference would it make?"

"None, I guess." Deilani stepped back and straightened. "Honor and glory to the Eternal Empress."

"Always may she reign," I replied dutifully, stepping back from the viewport.

For the first time since we met, she saluted me. I didn't return it.

"Have a good career, Lieutenant."

"Better than yours," she replied.

I grinned, then turned and melted into the crowd.